Tortilla Moon and Other Tales of Love

Tortilla Moon and Other Tales of Love

G. Davies Jandrey

Tortilla Moon was published by Blue Mesa Review. *The Hunchback of Barrio Anita,* published by Bilingual Review, won an honorable mention in the Lorian Hemingway Short Story Competition. *The Secret of Rain* was published by Main Street Rag in an anthology, Aftermath, 2012. The partial collection was a finalist in the James Jones First Novel Fellowship.

ISBN: 0971548412
ISBN 13: 9780971548411

Library of Congress Control Number: 2018900407
Cascabel Press, Tucson, AZ

Other novels by G. Davies Jandrey

A Garden of Aloes

Journey through an Arid Land

A Small Saving Grace

For Teresa Moreno,

whose beautiful voice inhabits these pages

FORWARD

———

WHEN I HAD FINISHED MY fourth short story set in Tucson's Barrio Anita, laced with Spanglish and populated by Lety and her friends and relatives, I realized I had a problem, three problems actually. First, it was becoming clear to me that these first stories were not discrete short stories or the beginning of a novel, but some sort of evolving hybrid. What would that hybrid be called? My second problem was that I was well acquainted with the concept of "cultural appropriation" and was sympathetic to the idea that people "owned" their own cultures and that those outside those cultures should not exploit them. Though I've worked on it for years, my Spanish is terrible, only one member of my family is Hispanic and he's not Mexican, and before my hair turned mostly white, it was mostly blond. As a gringa, what right did I have to be telling these stories in the first place? The third and most vexing problem was that Lety was not finished with me yet and would simply not shut up!

That said, I enlisted the help of my friend, Rosemary Solarez. Born of Mexican-Lebanese parents, Rosemary is the consummate chola. She attended Catholic schools for twelve years, where among other things, she told me, she learned the fear of hell. She received her bachelor's degree at the University of

Arizona, then as a single mom of two boys began volunteering at a local soup kitchen, where she became politically awakened. A born-again Buddhist, Rosemary has spent a lifetime in social services. One of her favorite tattoos reads: *One people, one planet, one future.*

Rosemary kindly read the first four stories of *Tortilla Moon.* When we met to discuss them she asked, "How do you know this stuff?" I went on to say that it was my habit to eavesdrop on the Spanish-laced conversations of my students, most of whom were either Mexican American or Mexican nationals. I counseled them informally during my lunch hour and spoke to their parents, but mostly I just listened. Rosemary's response? "Well, you're a good listener, then."

So it was with Rosemary's encouragement that I finished this, whatever it is. I will always be grateful to her for that permission, if it can be called that, because it wasn't until the last word of the last line of the last story was written that Lety finally stopped bending my ear.

So I am guilty of cultural appropriation. I am also guilty of loving a culture that was not mine by birth as well as loving the lyricism of the Spanish language and the people who speak it.

"La vida es commo una canción de amor,
agridulce. A veses te hace querer bailar.
A veses te hace querer llorar."

Life is like a love song, bittersweet. Sometimes it makes you want to dance. Sometimes it makes you want to cry.

– Leticia Esperanza Mendoza

Table of Contents

Tortilla Moon

———

Volver, Volver
(Fernando Maldonado)

...volver, volver, volver a tus brazos otra vez,
llegaré hasta donde estés yo se perder, yo se
perder, quiero volver, volver, volver...

This song is about someone who has lost his love and wants to return to her arms. Frankly, I think he cheated on her and now regrets it. Whatever, I love this song. It makes me cry every time I hear it.

– Lety

LETY OPENED THE DOOR. OCTOBER nights in Nogales, Arizona, were already getting cool and the air was hazy from the cooking fires in las colonias on the other side. Hugging her shoulders, she inhaled the tang of burning mesquite, as her friend crossed the threshold. The two girls appraised each other.

"Is that what you're going to wear?" Alma asked.

Lety looked down, craning her neck to see past her own bosom. "What's wrong with it?"

"Nada, Lety. It's perfect. Let's go."

But Lety turned abruptly, leaving her friend standing in the doorway. Without missing a stride, she stepped out of the skirt, catching it with her big toe and kicking it into the air as she entered her bedroom. With practiced agility, she snatched it up before it hit the ground and flung it on the bed where it landed atop a small pile of rejected clothing.

Though Alma was una flaca sin nalgas, she had a real sense of style, knew what would work and what wouldn't, and Lety understood by the tone of her friend's voice that her outfit had been all wrong. She flung open her closet door and stood before it panting. Nothing. There was nothing left to try.

"Come on Lety. ¡Apúrate! It's getting late."

"But I don't have nothing to wear. Look at this," she said pointing to the pile on the bed. "I wouldn't dress my dog in this mierda."

"You don't even have a dog, pues," Alma said, sifting through the pile of clothing. From the bottom she pulled out a pair of Levi's and a fluffy, magenta sweater. "Wear these. The guys will look at your ass and your chichis, and the rest won't matter."

Lety saw the logic in her friend's statement, saw the resignation on her face and knew she was telling the truth.

"Just hurry. We're missing everything."

Lety started to put on the jeans, then thought of Chuy's hands on her bare legs and tossed them back on the pile. "I'll wear the skirt."

"But you don't have any stockings."

Lety shrugged. What did she care? She didn't need stockings. She didn't need any of that.

Trying not to kick dust onto their legs, the two girls picked their way down a dimly lit back street. At the end of the street they saw a familiar outline.

"¡Chingado! Es mi madre," Lety whispered with disgust. "Now we'll be late for sure."

"Hola, mijas. ¡Ay! Damn! Why can't they pave this street?" The woman paused to empty some pebbles from her shoes as the girls approached.

Lety kissed her mother's cheek and steadied her as she balanced on one leg. "Gracias mija. ¡Estas chingaderitas!" She said, dumping several pebbles from her shoes. "So, you going to the dance?"

"Sí, pues, mamá. We're on our way. Why are you home so early?"

"Oh, el Greco," she said, smiling wearily. "He saw I was so tired and told me go home."

Lety understood what that meant. Later, that fat Greek would come by the house with a bottle of cheap red wine. "We gotta get going, Mamá. We're already late."

"Dame un beso, pues, and have a good time."

Lety kissed her mother again, but she didn't mean it. She hated the Greek, hated that her mother not only did not hate him, but seemed to think that she was lucky to get one of his big greasy fucks every so often.

"Hey, and mija, get a ride home with your cousin, Jonny. He'll be there now that the fat cabrona he married is pregnant again. I don't want you walking home so late."

"Chuy can bring us home."

"Chuy? Better you should ride home with the devil than that cabrón."

"¡Mamá! You hardly even know him."

"I know that he'll be drunk. How much better do I need to know him? Just promise me that you'll get a ride with Jonny. I already told him. Jonny may have trouble keeping his fly closed, but at least he isn't a borracho. Now promise."

"¡Ay, Mamá! I promise, all right?" Lety grabbed Alma by the elbow. "Vámonos."

As soon as her mother was out of earshot, Lety whispered, "Sometimes I just hate her. I mean, she doesn't even know Chuy." Lety hooked elbows with her friend, and the two girls hurried down the street.

The band was playing a cumbia as they entered the dimly lit ballroom, a cinder block single-story building the size of a gymnasium. Each paid a dollar and had her hand stamped with "La Estrella de Noche" in purple. As one, they moved toward the bathroom.

Lety stood before the sink and applied another layer of Black Cherry to her lips. "Dame papel, también," she said into the mirror.

Alma left the stall with a length of coarse, aqua toilet paper wrapped around and around her fist. She tore off a long piece and handed it to her friend, then dipped her own paper under the faucet and began wiping off her shoes. "¡Ay! Look how dirty," she howled. As she snapped at her nylons, little puffs of dust were released into the air.

Lety simply lifted her foot, shoe and all, up into the sink. "Get more paper, Alma."

"You take all day," Alma complained, plucking a glob of mascara from her eyelashes.

Lety lifted her second foot into the sink. "Dame más papel, Alma, so we can go, pues."

Alma handed the paper to her friend. "I guess we'd better find Jonny, eh Lety?"

"Jonny can go to hell," she said patting her ankles and shoes with the toilet paper.

"But your mother said."

"My mother don't know nothing. Do what you want; I'm going to find Chuy." Lety looked into the mirror again, straightening her skirt and smoothing her sweater over her breasts. "You coming, well?"

Lety and Alma circled the dance floor counterclockwise, pretending to be totally centered on their conversation, which they punctuated with an occasional laugh, shrill enough to make heads turn.

"Did you see him?" Lety whispered.

"See who?"

"Jonny. No! Don't look now," Lety hissed. "Just keep walking. I said, don't look!" She jerked Alma's elbow for emphasis.

"What's he doing?"

"The Lambada with Maria Herrera. Bending her over backwards like they were novios. Ay, I feel sorry for Maricela. She's got so fat with this one, she can hardly move, and here is Jonny, grinding his hips into that puta. Well, you missed it. But they'll be around again, just don't look, I mean, pretend you don't see nothing. I'm going to tell my mother we didn't see him. Chuy can take us home."

But Lety could not take her mind away from Jonny. She was personally insulted by his faithless behavior. Not more than six months ago he had pressed himself against her backside as she was at the sink washing dishes. When she turned, he pinned her there with his hips and kissed her. She struggled against him as the women on the telenovelas always did. Then, just as she was about to melt against him, as the women on television also always did, he drew back and laughed at her. Called her a baby. Well, she wasn't a baby no more.

On their third tour around the dance floor, Lety felt a tug at her elbow, and Chuy took his place between the two girls. She could smell the liquor on his breath, but Lety didn't care. After all, that was Chuy.

There was a pounding on the side of the truck and then it began to shake.

Chuy raised himself on one elbow. "¿Qué pasa?"

"What is it?" Lety whispered, pulling her sweater down over her breasts."

"I can't see. The windows are too foggy."

"Get off of me, well." Lety gave him a shove and felt around the floor with her bare foot for her underpants.

Again the pounding. "Hey, anybody home?"

"Ay. It's just your crazy cousin, Jonny." Chuy opened the door and jumped out of the truck, staggering a bit when his feet hit the ground.

"Eh, Vato." Chuy smiled and extended his hand. "Eh, ese, you got you a beer?"

Jonny handed him his half-finished bottle, and looked into the truck. He watched, as Lety tilted the rearview mirror and reached into her purse for a comb.

"Ven, Lety. It's time to go. Your mother said I should drive you home."

"Chuy's taking me home," she said without turning away from the mirror.

"Like hell, Chuy's taking you home. I said let's go."

Lety continued to comb her hair until she felt his hand on her ankle. "Let go of me, chingón. You don't own me," she screamed and stabbed at him with her comb. He continued to pull her by the ankle until she had no choice but to get out of the car on her legs or fall out on her ass. "¡Pinche cabrón!" she spat. She hit him once in the chest with her purse before allowing him to lead her to his car.

Alma was already sitting in the front seat. Lety shot her an angry look as she climbed in beside her, but was really furious when she realized Jonny intended to take her home first instead of Alma. When he pulled up to her house, Lety got out of the car without a word and slammed the door.

"De nada," Jonny shouted after her as she ran up the walk.

Her mother had left the kitchen light on for her. The empty wine bottle was on the table, and Lety could hear her mother snoring softly. She slipped into the bedroom they shared, not wanting to wake her mother before she had a chance to wash herself.

Lety put the plug into the bottom of the tub and turned on the taps, making adjustments until the water was as hot as she could stand. Quickly she stripped off her clothing, hanging her skirt and sweater on the back of the door so the steam could smooth out the wrinkles. She threw her bra into the hamper, but her underpants were still damp, so she hid them under the bath mat. Her mother would be up early and off to work. Tomorrow Lety'd do the laundry as always. Until then, her mother wouldn't find them.

In the little mirror above the sink, she examined her puffy lips, the smudges of blue mascara beneath each eye. She licked her lips and gave her hair a shake, turning away from the image only after the mirror clouded over with steam.

Lety was sleeping soundly on the sofa bed in the living room when mother shook her shoulder roughly. "Ay, Mamá, let me sleep, can't you?"

"What are these?" Her mother sniffed the underpants and threw them in the girl's face."

"My underwears, so what?"

"¡Puta!" her mother screamed. "You think I don't know what you've been up to? You don't think I can smell the spit and cum on you when you sneak in at night." The woman began to slap at her daughter randomly. Then she ripped the blankets from the bed so her hand could land with greater effect.

Lety curled into a ball in the middle of the bed and tried to deflect her mother's blows, but the woman was too fast. Like an angry wasp, her hand stung here and there, everywhere.

"You think I'm stupid? You think I don't notice the absence of your regla?"

These last words struck Lety with more force than her mother's blows. "What are you talking about?" she cried and rolled away from her mother's falling fist.

"Ay, I should have sent you to school with the nuns," the woman screamed, still trying to land a solid blow.

"What are you talking about?"

"You think I'm too stupid to notice?"

"Notice what?"

"Notice what? She says." Grabbing her daughter by the arm, she pulled her off the bed. "Notice what? When was the last time you had your period?"

Lety didn't know exactly, though she had been trying to ignore its absence for several weeks. Left without an answer, she returned the assault.

"You call me a whore, but what about you? You fuck that fat Greek."

The fist landed solidly this time. Lety's head snapped back against the nightstand with such force that the lamp rocked and fell to the floor.

"My lamp! Now you break my lamp!"

"You're the whore, Mamá. At least I love Chuy. And Chuy's young. You're just jealous because I'm young and you're not, and all you can get is some old man."

"Old? Well, he may be old, but he's a man, not some skinny assed borracho, with five hairs on his chin."

"At least Chuy loves me."

"Chuy loves me," she mocked. "Don't make me sick. He loves your ass."

Lety lept out of bed. From the dresser she shared with her mother, she pulled out a drawer and dumped it on the bed.

"What are you doing?"

"Getting out of here."

"Oh yes? And just where will you go?"

"To Chuy's."

"To Chuy's? You're going to Chuy's. Bueno. You go to Chuy's and live with all them borrachos chingados. See if I care. Here," she said reaching for the plastic shopping bag that hung on the doorknob. "I'll help you pack."

Lety batted at her mother's hand. "Get away from me. I don't want your help."

Lety looked up from her cell phone as a trio of grubby children ran into the Circle K. "What do you mean you can't right now?" She flicked at a tear and glared at the telephone. "The truck? What's that got to do with it? You got to come get me now! I'm going to start walking, well. If you love me, you'll come."

It was still early and though the sun bounced through the yellowing chinaberry trees, it was cold. A brisk, dry wind stirred up the grit that accumulated along the walls of the buildings and sent it swirling up Lety's skirt. She squinted her eyes, squeezing tears out the corners, and pulled her sweater closed.

She was uncertain how long she'd been walking, but it had been long enough and fast enough to get warm, and longer, she was sure, than it should have taken Chuy to reach her. By the time he finally pulled alongside her, Lety was angry beyond tears. Eyes straight ahead, she kept walking when he leaned over and opened the door for her.

"Get in Lety. It's cold out there."

Lety knew that she had nowhere else to go, knew she would give in, but continued walking until she was certain she had made her point. "It took you long enough, pues!" she said and climbed in.

Without a word, Chuy reached out and pulled her next to him, forcing her head against his chest. He held her tight there, stroking her hair, until she relaxed against him, In silence, they drove out of town.

The sky was smoky-purple, and the evening's first stars shined in the eastern sky as the truck pulled in front of her house. Chuy swung lightly from the cab, then went around to Lety's side and helped her out. The two embraced. He pulled her bag out of the back of the truck, then kissed her once again. Lety watched him get back into the truck, watched the truck slowly pull away from the curb and disappear around the corner. Come back! She wanted to shout. But it was too late.

Long after the truck had gone, Lety stood there, half expecting him to change his mind and return. Dry-eyed now, she was too tired to shed even one more tear for him. Finally, she turned and walked toward the dark house.

When she got to the door, Lety was surprised to see it ajar. She pushed it open and turned on the light.

"¡Mamá! What are you doing home?"

"What am I doing home, she asks. How could I go to work with this heartache?

I've cried so much I'm nearly blind, and she asks me why I'm not at work."

Lety studied her mother's face. The eyes were red and puffy. Dark trails of mascara stained her cheeks, and for the first time her mother seemed worn, old.

"Lo siento, Mamá," she whispered. "Can I get you some tea?"

"I don't want tea. I want my baby to come sit by me."

Lety closed the door and went to join her mother on the couch. "I'm sorry about the lamp."

"The lamp? Who gives a shit about the lamp? All I care about is you, here and safe, mijita. I don't care about no lamp." She was kissing Lety's hair now, her eyes, the corner of her mouth. "My little girl."

"I thought you hated me."

"Mi vida, I love you so much, sometimes I despise you. That's the problem. I can't explain it even to myself." She continued petting Lety's hair.

"But I don't understand. When Javier got caught with Luz you never hit him even once."

"Ay, mi amor. That's because it was her mother's problem, not mine. ¿Qué no? I'm going to beat my son because of Luz?"

"But it's not fair, Mamá. I always get hit for nothing."

"Having a baby isn't nothing, mija."

"Still I get hit and yelled at, and Javier can do no wrong. It doesn't make sense."

"It makes perfect sense. A son is different. It's not like looking into a mirror and being reminded every day of your own mistakes like it is with a daughter. Oh, I don't know what I'm trying to say. I'd die for you, Leticia. Is that enough?"

"Someday, Leticia, you'll have a daughter of your own, which I pray to God that you do so you'll understand what you put me through. Then you'll be sorry you didn't listen better. I know this myself. My own mother is dead, but if she were here now, I'd kiss her feet. If it would bring her back, I'd wash her feet in my tears and dry them with my own hair."

Lety thought about this. Her mother's hair was short and permed and she couldn't quite picture it. But she listened with respect because of the suffering plainly written on her face.

"If my mother was here today... if I could tell her just once how sorry I am for not listening to her when I was your age... but now it's too late for listening."

Lety could not remember anything her mother had told her that might have prevented her present situation, even if she had listened. But she did not say so.

"Do you remember nana back in Imuris? Sure you do. Remember what she used to tell you about the moon? It's hard to see the moon rise here, with the houses so close, but back in Imuris, when you were little, we used to watch the moon like it was TV. You were such a doll. ¡Qué chula! ¡Qué viva! Remember nana used tell you that the moon was a big tortilla rising up to heaven to feed God. And every night, nana used to say, God takes a bite until it's all gone. Then the earth sends him another. That was the same story she told me when I was a little girl, and I believed her, just like you did. ¿Recuerdas mijita?"

Lety didn't remember, but she nodded her head as if she did.

"Leticia," the woman continued, taking Lety's hand. "I want to tell my own grandkids about the tortilla moon, but I still feel like a kid myself. Inside I do. I'm not ready to be a grandmother. And you're still a baby. Didn't you learn nothing watching me struggle to raise you up all these years? I thought you'd be smarter than me." She took her daughter's hand and sighed. "My poor little baby didn't learn nothing."

"I'll get you some tea, Mamá," Lety said and started to get up.

"No. Sit still another minute." Gently she tugged on Lety's arm until the girl sat back against her mother.

"When was the last time we sat and watched the moon come out of the hill? When was the last time we saw the moon, big and round and so thin it was like you could see your hand right through it, just like one of nana's big tortillas, right down to the dark spots?"

"We're going to get married, Mamá." Lety waited for a response. When there was none, she went on. "But first he's going to California. Chuy says he can make a lot of money out in L.A. Then he'll come back, and after I have the baby, we'll get married."

"After you have the baby, you'll give him a little snapshot and he'll put it in his wallet. Once in a while he'll pull it out to brag to his friends, 'Mire, soy hombre. I have a baby.' And the girls will look at the picture and say, 'Oh, qué querida, qué cute' and hang on his arm."

Lety felt a little shock of recognition. Many times she had said exactly the same thing herself, Qué cute. Still, Lety knew things would be different for her and Chuy. "He loves me."

"He'd be a fool if he didn't," her mother whispered into her hair. "But men are fools, mija."

"Chuy's different, Mamá." She had to say it, even though she didn't really believe it.

Lety ran her hand over her belly. It was still flat, but she felt a fullness deep inside and a warmth. When Chuy returned from California, they would choose a girl's name and a boy's name, though Lety was sure this first child would be a boy. It's always best when the first is a boy, que no? She nestled her head against her mother's soft shoulder and the woman put her arm around her with a contented sigh.

Closing her eyes, Lety thought about what he would be like, her son, lips moist and rosy, holding his little arms out only to her.

Exhausted by emotion Lety fell asleep wrapped in her mother's arms. Some hours later, she woke, stiff and needing to pee. For a moment she sat there, wondering what could she possibly learn from her mother, whose life, as far as she could tell, was a wreck. Well, for her, things would be different. Lety would make sure of that. And tomorrow she'd light a candle to la Virgen de Guadalupe. What more could she do?

In fact, Lety would come to learn many things from her mother's example, but it would take years. Now she tried to extricate herself from her mother's embrace, but found she could not. That would take many years as well.

———

una flaca sin nalges skinny woman, without a butt
mierda shit well, then, so
pues then, well, so
hola hello
mija/mijo daughter/son, often used by an elder to address a younger person
mijita/mijito little daughter/son, an endearment
chingado/chingaditos fucker, little fuckers
cabrón general form of an insult
borracho drunk, a drunk
lo siento I'm sorry

IN THE HOUSE
OF TÍA SOFÍA

———

Un Viejo Amor
(traditional)

*... no se olvida ni se deja que un viejo amor de nuestra
alma si se aleja pero nunca dice adiós un viejo amor...*

This is a song about how you never forget an old love.
Maybe, maybe not. I'm working on it.

– Lety

LETY HESITATED OUTSIDE THE HOUSE, one of the little adobes in Tucson's
Barrio Anita. This one stood behind a fence made of old tires that
had been painted white. The muscles in Lety's arms burned from
carrying her daughter the twelve blocks from the bus station down-
town. She set the baby down. The toddler wobbled a moment, before balancing herself with the help of her mother's knee.

"Look at the pretty flowers, Araceli." Lety said pointing to
the hollyhocks, purple, blue and white and as tall as a man's head

that leaned against the bright pink plaster walls of the house. There were red petunias spilling over the sides of terracotta pots and snapdragons along the fence.

She thought about Chuy and the little house he had promised. There was to be a garden. She would have gotten her GED, then a nice job, maybe a bilingual secretary. On her glass-topped desk, she would have placed flowers from her own garden. But Chuy had died somewhere in California. She didn't know how or why, but she was sure only death could keep him away. Now there would be no house, no garden, no GED. Just Araceli and me and little what's-its-name, she thought, rubbing her belly.

Picking up her daughter and the plastic shopping bags with their clothes, she stepped onto the cement path leading to the screen door. "Tía Sofía," she called, suddenly afraid. It had not occurred to her until this moment that the old woman might turn her away. Smoothing the front of her blouse over her belly, she knocked on the frame of the screen door.

Tía Sofía's daughter, Regina, appeared at the door, hands dangling, still and limp as two dead doves. She smiled and licked the saliva from where it pooled in a cleft on her bottom lip. She turned and called, "Mamá, Leticia está aquí."

"Open the door, mija." Tía Sofía called from the back of the house, and in a moment she was at Regina's side, drying her hands on a towel pinned to the front of her housedress.

"Come in, mija," she said, taking the baby from her arms. "What have you done now to bring you all this way?"

Tía Sofía slowly poured a glass of water over the geraniums and begonias sprouting in coffee cans on the windowsill above the sink while she considered. Though this girl's sin was obvious, and double, it was not the fault of the unborn child, whose soul

G. Davies Jandrey

was pure. Besides, there was the question of Araceli. The child had already fallen into an exhausted sleep on the couch beneath the portrait of Christ's hands in prayer. Where would the girl and this child go if she did not take her in? Certainly, they could not go home to her mother, a worse whore than the daughter; that was clear. And Sofía knew too well what could happen to a girl, even one who was embarazada, who had no home to go to.

"You can put your things in Regina's room," tía Sofía said to Lety, who was sitting at the kitchen table sipping coffee with Regina. "We can borrow a crib, I guess, for Araceli. Regina, help your cousin with her bag."

"It won't be for long, tía. I promise."

"It doesn't matter, mija," she said, reaching out to touch the girl's cheek. "Stay as long as you like. Does your mother know you're here?"

"She doesn't care where I am."

"She's your mother, pues." She said this with the slightest shrug of her narrow shoulders. "She cares."

Sofía pulled up a fistful of small green blades. "Ay, they grow faster than the hairs on my chin," she said, tossing the weeds into a plastic bucket.

The soil was cool. Early morning light gilded the leaves of her roses, turning even the soil to gold. With effort, she got up from her knees and surveyed the buds with pleasure. Sofía had one dozen bushes in her rose garden. Each morning, as long as they were in bloom, she would pick thirteen of the most promising buds, twelve to set before la Virgen de Guadalupe over at Saint Margaret's, and one to set amid the dusty clutter of santos, curling photos, flickering candles, milagros and mildew that filled the corner of her living room where she placed her own statue of la Virgen, the one that had been blessed by Father Tom.

Filled with lush roses, towering hollyhocks, quince and lime trees, a dozen different annuals and herbs, the garden was Sofía's only passion, that is if you did not consider the passion she still felt for her husband. Even in confession, she never mentioned that he still came to her bed and lifted the hem of her nightdress when only the light from the candles might reveal the pleasure she took from his touch. Father Tom would think she was a crazy old woman if she told him how they still made love as in their youth, Eduardo not minding her pale nipples and flaccid breasts. He was still handsome, Eduardo. The dead don't age, she thought, looking at the spots on the back of her gnarled brown hands. Sofía smiled as she snipped the last rose and placed it gently beside the others in the large Tupperware container of water.

Lety could hear her aunt in the kitchen. I should get up and help with breakfast, she thought, cocking one eye toward her daughter, who was still soundly asleep on the make-do crib they had devised by pushing two chairs against the wall. Feeling weighed down, Lety closed her eye. The pervasive smell of warm candle wax was temporarily displaced by that of frying chorizo. The smell, combined with the lack of air and light in the room, made Lety's stomach roil with something midway between hunger and nausea.

She had not slept well. All night, Regina shook the bed with her tossing, while Tía Sofía moaned and snorted in the next room. Now she felt the bed bounce as Regina rose. Reluctantly, Lety opened her eyes.

"Buenos días, Leticia. How did you sleep?"

Groaning, Lety pulled herself to a sitting position. "What were you dreaming last night? You tossed and kicked, and once you even cried in your sleep."

"Last night I was being martyred for the sake of our Lord Jesus," she answered, eyes and bottom lip shining.

"What do you mean?"

Regina got up and retrieved the religious cards that were tucked into the mirror on her dresser. She handed Lety a card. "That's Santa Barbara. Her father locked her up in a tower and then cut off her head when she wouldn't renounce her faith. That couldn't happen to me, though. My father is dead."

Regina passed Lety another card. "Santa Regina, mi patrona. She had her head cut off too, and this one is Santa Lucy." Regina placed the card in Lety's palm. "She tore out her own eyes and I can't remember what else. And this is the best one, Santa Agnes." She gave Lety the last card.

Lety studied the picture. A radiant young woman seemed to be offering two small loaves of bread on a golden tray. "Why the bread?" Lety asked, fanning the cards as if she were about to play a game of Fish.

"That's not bread," Regina said, taking the cards from Lety's hand. "A man fell in love with her, but he wasn't a Catholic. When she refused to marry him because of her faith, he got mad and cut off her chichis, then rolled her in hot coals and broken glass," she said pointing to the tray.

"Those are her chichis?

Regina nodded.

"No wonder you have bad dreams."

"They aren't bad dreams. Mamá told me that God chooses only the pure and innocent to shed blood for Him. She says my dreams are signs of my pure heart and my faith in the Lord and the Church, so I shouldn't be afraid."

Lety knew that Regina had to be old, maybe even forty, but at that moment, in the yellow light, with her cap of short, black hair and slim body, she looked almost like a child, that is, if you could ignore the heavy breasts swaying beneath her cotton nightgown. Lety used to feel sorry for Regina, who had a tendency to drool and was so mensa she could not care for herself. But as she watched Regina take her rosary in hand and kneel on the dark wood floor to recite "Our Father," she could see that the woman was happy in her own way, happier than Lety was herself. It was amazing, but true.

A wave of hopelessness passed over her then, and Lety slumped back onto the bed. She wondered about her decision to come to Tucson. Was living in this house with these two half-crazy women who did nothing but jerk and moan and pray and clean and cook and garden, women who went nowhere but church and knew nothing but the lives of saints, better than listening to the screaming fits of her mother? She really did not know.

Lety selected the Black Cherry, her favorite, and began to outline her lips with care.

"Listen to me, Leticia," tía Sofía was saying as she poured water over the avocado seed rooting in a mayonnaise jar on the bathroom windowsill. "There's a life out there beyond your lips and you need to prepare for it." Tía Sofía grasped the wrist that held the lipstick, her fingers locking like the jaws of a coyote trap. "We can't change it and we can't refuse it, Leticia. All we can do is put one foot in front of the next and pray for the best. Así es la vida, mija."

Lety shrugged, twisting her wrist ever so slightly in hopes her aunt might let go. "So?"

"So, have you been to a doctor? You have to prepare, Leticia," she said releasing the girl's wrist at last.

"There's plenty of time."

"That's what I said the day before I gave birth to Jonny right on the bathroom floor. It's a good thing I had mopped that morning," she said waving her hand around like a flyswatter. "You need to be prepared. How far along are you? Do you even know?"

"Four months, maybe five."

Tía Sofía looked at her critically. "Six months a lo menos, maybe seven. I tell you, Leticia, it's no fun having a baby on the bathroom floor."

The nurse practitioner was different from the one she had seen last week. Lety climbed up on the examining table, and the nurse handed her the sonogram. She could see there was a baby, but it wasn't what she had expected. What she expected was a Polaroid. This was more like bad reception on the television. The nurse pointed out each limb, the little fists, the head and finally the testicles. Lety thought she had wanted a boy the first time – a boy would have brought Chuy back to Nogales, and then he wouldn't have gone out and gotten himself killed so bad — but this time she hadn't given it much thought. As she stared at the baby, floating in a pool of static, she smiled. A boy would make her mother sorry about the way she had treated her. She tightened her grip on the picture. Her mother had been so crazy that day.

"Jonny!" she had yelled. "I can't believe it! He's your cousin, for God's sake!"

"He's not my cousin. You told me he was the nephew of your father's first wife"

Her mother had to take a moment to think. "Is that what I told you?" Pues, what difference does it make? He's tía Sofía's son. But that's not the point."

"What is the point?" It wasn't that Lety was trying to be a smart-ass. She was just trying to understand her mother's fury.

"The point is, how could you be so stupid twice! First that pendejo Chuy."

"Don't call him a pendejo, Mamá. He's dead."

"So you say." She covered her face and started to cry.

Lety reached out and patted her mother's shoulder. "Calmate, Mamá. It'll be all right."

"It won't be all right," she screamed, batting Lety's hand away. "Jonny! I can't believe you're having his baby!"

Then, just like that, her mother picked up *People* magazine and started to hit her with it. She hit her on the head and the arms and the legs and across her belly and buttocks. It wasn't that it hurt, but the notion of it stung. Lety, herself a mother and a grown woman, was tired of her mother always hitting her.

"It's impossible to give you an exact due date," the nurse was saying. "But you're more or less in the 28th week. Full term is approximately 38 weeks, so figure another 10 weeks or so, and you've got your little boy. Do you understand? ¿Comprendes?" She said with her stiff, gringa tongue.

Lety nodded.

The nurse smiled and put the stethoscope to Lety's belly. "Want to hear his heartbeat?"

Lety put the stethoscope in her ears and listened. With a mixture of terror and awe, it became suddenly clear to her. This baby was more than a fuzzy picture. Tears pooled beneath her eyelids, but she squeezed them back. Two babies now.

"Are you planning to breastfeed?"

Lety shook her head.

"No? Why not? Here, let me give you some literature, and a number to call if you have any questions."

A number? The only number that mattered was two. Two babies, she thought. How am I going to take care of two babies? The nurse handed her a pamphlet. Lety put it in her purse without looking at it. Maybe for a boy, Jonny would leave his wife. But Jonny already had two boys. Stupid, stupid, stupid, Lety repeated silently. Her mother had been right.

Sitting in the half-light, Regina watched as Lety got ready for bed. "Does it hurt?" she asked, pointing to Lety's navel, which had turned nearly inside out.

"No. What hurts, sort of, is when he kicks me. And my back. My back hurts all the time now. But this?" she said rubbing the knob that was her navel. "Nah. It just looks ugly." Lety took off her bra, conscious of Regina's eyes upon her. It made Lety feel superior, this body that Regina would never have.

"Are you going to put those in his mouth?"

"You mean breastfeed? I haven't decided yet." When Araceli was born, Lety thought breastfeeding seemed nasty, something only a woman who could not afford formula would do, but they were trying to change her mind about it at the clinic, and now she was reconsidering. After all, she'd grown up since Araceli. Still feeling womanly and superior, Lety asked, "You know where babies come from, don't you?"

Regina pointed to the place where her legs terminated in a modest V. "A man touches you there and you get a baby. Mamá said never to let a man touch me below the neck of my dress or above the hem of my skirt."

Lety considered that advice. She wondered if she should tell her about el pene and the part it played, but figured Regina had all the information she really needed under the circumstances.

"I'm never going to have a baby because I'm not married, and it's a sin to let a man touch you unless you are. When's your husband coming to get you, Leticia?"

"Pretty soon, I guess." Lying was a sin too, Lety supposed, but it always seemed a little too late or a little too soon to be thinking about sin.

As Sofia lay on the bed, she willed Eduardo to make an appearance. Passion was a funny thing, she thought. She never expected to be bothered by it after her husband's death. After all, she had spent many years with no knowledge of it. It wasn't until she had been married some months and pregnant with her first child, that she had felt that first stab of pleasure. Sofia could still remember her fear. Ashamed, she never told Eduardo or the priest. But Eduardo seemed to sense her desire and even tried to inflame it – that's the kind of man he was. After her first son was stillborn, Sofía struggled against her passion, believing it had strangled the baby in her womb. But Sofía was not always able to hold out against the delicacy of Eduardo's caresses.

Eventually, Sofía realized that she was not the only one who could not resist Eduardo's caresses, but that was so many years ago, pues, she could hardly recall the intensity of the pain her love for him had caused her.

Poor Regina, she thought. She would never know about passion, but it was for the best. Once, when Regina was little, she had caught the girl with her hands in her underpants. At that moment, Sofía made a decision. To allow passion to be awakened in a girl such as Regina, who could never be wife or mother, would only increase her vulnerability. It was difficult enough that she was so trusting. Sofía was determined to spare her daughter not only the pain of penetration and childbirth, but more, the pain of loss and sin. So she had gone directly to the kitchen and made a mixture of red chili and lard. This she rubbed into the cleft of her daughter's naked pubis, not with anger, but with the same gentle efficiency she used when applying tea leaves to the girl's hands to cool the burn from a morning of peeling roasted poblanos.

Shortly after her husband's death, Sofía had applied the same remedy upon herself when to her shock and grief, she felt the familiar throbbing in the presence of Hortencia Lopez's no good husband when he tried to run his hand over her nalgas. Unfortunately, the knife of her own passion, honed so well by her husband, was already too keen to blunt. It had been her burden for years, until Eduardo's return.

Where was he? She thought, as she took her beads from the bedpost and began to recite the rosary. Closing her eyes, she breathed deeply, as her fingers passed over each bead, again and again, until she smelled his familiar scent of warm candle wax and crushed marigolds. Yes, Sofía could even feel the bed give way under his weight. "Eduardo," she murmured. But her husband only smiled. Eduardo never spoke.

Sofía saw her coming up the walk, took note of the tight skirt accentuating her full hips and slender waist, the flowered blouse. Even from the door, she could see a gap across the woman's bosom that revealed a purple brassier. Purple!

Sofía opened the door. "Come in out of the heat, Zulema," she said then pointed to the car where a heavyset man with bristling white hair sat behind the steering wheel. "What about him?"

"El Greco?" she said, waving her hand. "You know him. He likes to mind his own business. "Is Leticia here? I've come to take her home."

Sofía stepped aside so the woman could enter. "Leticia's lying down. I'll go get her," she said, then started down the hall.

"Leticia, levántate, tu madre esta aquí," she whispered, not wanting to wake Araceli who was napping beside her mother. "Get up." Sofía waited until the girl rose heavily from the bed, waited as she hesitated before the mirror, then followed her into the living room.

"Mijita," Zulema cried, opening her arms to embrace her daughter. Lety remained rigid, and the woman's arms retracted.

"Do you want some iced tea, Zulema? I've got some already in the fridge."

"Gracias, no, tía."

"No? In that case. Do you mind? I've got to water my roses before it gets too hot," she said, tugging lightly at the towel pinned to her dress.

"Not at all, tía. Go tend to your roses." Zulema was silent until she heard the back door open then close. She sat on the couch and patted a spot next to her. "Siéntate, mija."

Lety sat on the arm of the recliner across from her mother.

"So you're still mad at me?" She blotted a film of sweat from her brow with the back of her hand. "Ay, que hace calor. How can you stand this heat and you so big."

Lety said nothing.

"You won't even talk to me. Is that it, Leticia? Well, you don't have to talk. Just listen. Okay? You have to forgive me."

"Why should I?"

"Because I'm your mother. Because I love you and you love me no matter what. You know it's true." Zulema rose from the couch and stepped over to her daughter, taking the girl's face in her hands. "Please, mija. I miss you. I miss Araceli," she said, then pouted. "I can't stand it when you're mad at me."

Lety brushed her mother's hands from her face. "You can't keep hitting me, Mamá. I'm not a little girl anymore."

"Oh yes, that's right. At seventeen you're a big grownup lady," she said and tossed the hair back from her face. "I talked to Jonny, by the way."

"And?"

"He says it's not his."

"And of course you believe him."

Zulema shrugged. "What I believe is that you should come home with me. Come on. El Greco is outside waiting. He'll take us all out for a nice lunch and then we can go back home to Nogales."

"I'm not going with you. I'm having the baby here; then I'm going to get my own place."

"With what? You got some money? That borracho Chuy left you a nice little life insurance policy you never told me about? You're still a baby, Leticia, an ignorant child, if you think you can get a job with no education and make enough money to support two babies. You don't know nothing, mija."

"And you know everything?"

Zulema picked up her purse. "Have it your way, Leticia. Come home when you've had enough …," she flicked her hand around the room, "of this." The woman started for the door, then turned. "It's no fun being on your own. I guess you don't remember how it was when we lived in Colonia del Sol, dust so thick it should have been called Colonia del Polvo and you sick all the time and how I worked and scraped to keep you alive." She slammed the screen door behind her, and hurried for the parked car, but halfway down the walk Zulema hesitated. "Please, mija," she said rushing back into the house. "Come home with me."

Lety saw the tears in her mother's eyes. If she could take it all back, Lety would, every last, brave word. She was not brave. In fact, she felt like the child her mother had accused her of being. But wasn't that why she had left home to begin with? If her mother had her way, Lety would remain a child forever. At least here, in tía Sofía's house, she was allowed to grow up.

"Leticia, please. Un beso por lo menos."

Her mother was crying now, but Lety could not go to her. To kiss her mother's cheek would be too great a risk. Without saying a word, Lety turned and walked down the dark hallway to the bedroom where Araceli was napping.

Quietly, she lay down on the narrow bed, closing her eyes as she waited for the release of tears. When they did not come, Lety tried to will them with thoughts of her first love, the lost Chuy, whose gentle touch she would never know again on this earth. But no matter how hard she tried to pull Chuy's face out of the clouds filling her head, it was Jonny's face that emerged floating just above her own.

"Leave me alone, can't you?" she begged, but smiled when she felt a slight pressure on the arch of her foot. Lety opened her eyes to the golden candlelight bouncing on the ceiling. It created pictures – a rose there, a fox face over there, and there the flickering silhouette of a man. He leaned close. The warm pressure traveled slowly up her ankle, lingered over her calf, then skated in circles over the inside of her thigh, barely grazing her pubic hair. Lety, lips parted now, and eyes closed, let the warmth dip inside her. His lips were at her nipple, then, licking and tugging, fingers pinching lightly, slipping over her flesh, down and into her.

"Ay, Jonny, even in your mother's house, I'm not safe from you," she whispered, parting her legs, raising her hips against the air.

Lety set Araceli on the floor while tía Sofía stood at the sink rolling masa into bolitas, each the exact same size and shape as a golf ball. Without saying a word, the woman handed a bit of the masa to Araceli and watched as the child patted the dough.

"That's good, mami," Lety crooned as she sat down to the café con leche tía Sofía had set out for her. "Make Mamá a tortilla,"

"You look pale, Leticia. Didn't you have a good nap?

Lety shook her head and thought of Jonny. Just the thought caused her chest to contract. She breathed deeply to dispel the sensation. "Tía," she paused unsure how to proceed. "How many babies did you have?"

"I had five. Jesús died before he was born, María, I lost when she was three, and Teddy, well, you know. Teddy was killed in that war, or whatever they called it, and Regina and Jonny. Of course there were some babies that left me before I hardly knew they were there."

"How sad you lost so many," Lety said, though it wasn't her aunt's losses she wanted to discuss at the moment.

"Yes, mija, but what is it you wanted to know?"

"While I was napping, I had a dream." Lety had no intention of telling her that it was her son, Jonny, who had come to her while she slept. "In my dream, someone was kissing me. It seemed so real."

Tía Sofía stopped rolling out the masa. "Go on."

"Well, I was just wondering," Lety could not continue. How could she ask this old woman, who had so long been a widow that she was probably a virgin again, the question on her mind. But such a strong passion so late in her pregnancy, what might that do to her baby?

Sofía turned back to her masa. "This kissing was just a dream, mija, right? Only a dream?"

"Yes, just a dream."

"Did this dream have green eyes, maybe, and thick, wavy hair and a handsome face?

Lety was shocked into silence. Her aunt had somehow guessed about her and Jonny. He would be furious if he found out that his mother knew the truth.

"Don't worry about it. Dreams aren't sins."

"But what about my baby?"

"Dreams can't hurt your baby either," tía Sofía said, rinsing the masa from her hands. "Isn't it time for Araceli's bath? I can't work with her under my feet."

Lety took the masa from her daughter's hands, noting the sudden edge in tía Sofía's voice, and led the child from the room. Now everyone was mad at her.

Sofía filled a glass with water and went to her bedroom, closing the door behind her. She poured the water over a philodendron that was rooting in a canning jar on her window ledge, its green tendrils reaching for the dim light along the casement. She picked up the jar and watched the roots undulate in the water like so many pale arms waving goodbye. If I don't plant this soon it's going to die, she thought, and returned the jar to the windowsill.

On her dresser, amid a candle for Santo Niño de Atocha, the talcum powder, the china jar of hairpins, were six photographs. She looked at each one, her husband, Eduardo, a daughter who would forever remain in her heart a precious, rosy-lipped child,

Teddy killed in a place she had never heard of before or since, poor Regina, eyes and lips always shining, and Jonny. She picked up the photo of Jonny and that of her husband, studying first one, then the other. So much alike, these two, with their green eyes and beautiful, dark faces. Neither one was able to keep his pantalones abotonados.

They had been novios since childhood, she and Eduardo. When he took fast girls down to the river at night or to dances, he promised her with kisses that it was because he was saving her for marriage. At the time she believed him. And why not? On Sundays, it was she whom Eduardo escorted to church. And when she turned seventeen, he married her just as he'd always promised. As long as she ignored the rumors, their marriage was a happy one.

But when Regina was born after an arduous pregnancy and difficult birth, things changed. From the beginning the baby had been so placid, so gentle, Sofia had thought she had given birth to one destined for the church. But at six months her daughter still slumped like a cloth doll. When by her first birthday, she could barely stand or even gurgle ma ma ma ma, Sofia knew the child would never grow up in the usual sense of the word. How frightened she had been at the thought of another pregnancy. Was she too old to have healthy babies? At thirty-eight she didn't feel old, was certainly not ready to give up the pleasures de la cama matrimonial. What was she to do? She consulted the priest about her fears and she was given two choices: abstinence or risk another like Regina. So lovemaking became a rare occasion. Though Eduardo protested, he remained his usual kind and charming self, but the rumors became harder to ignore. Even after Jonny was born, healthy and robust, quelling Sofia's fears and firing her desire, the rumors persisted.

Tía Sofía continued to stare at the photos for several moments then placed Jonny's back on the dresser. Eduardo's she threw in the trash.

Suddenly, Sofía was so tired she could hardly lift her arms to remove her hairpins. As she lay on the bed, she watched the candlelight lapping upon the ceiling. Usually she found this soothing, but this evening, nothing could soothe her. She knew the truth about her husband, had turned it over in her mind many times like the dark soil in her garden. Eduardo, she thought, you couldn't be faithful to me even in death.

Of course, she could simply send Leticia back to her mother. But such a selfish act would certainly be a sin no matter if you believed in ghosts or not. And this late in life, Sofía needed to be concerned with sin.

No, it was Eduardo, not Leticia, who had to go. Like a foxtail, he had dug himself into the secret garden of her heart and now, once and for all, she would have to do some weeding. The thought of it burned her heart. Closing her eyes, Sofía said her prayers and waited for them to be answered.

Regina was being martyred again. Lety could feel her jerk and toss. The baby pressed into her spine. Will I ever sleep again, she wondered. She tried to rearrange her bulk, but no position could relieve the pressure and the thickness of the air. It was as though she had to compete with every candle and rooting plant for breath. Living with her tía and Regina was like being buried alive, every movement encumbered by the absence of air and light and the weight of things growing silently in the dark.

How much longer could she stand it? Lety didn't know, but what choice did she have? At this moment, it seemed she had never acted in a manner of her own, exact choosing. If she had the choice, she would not have this candlelight and this earth inside her weighing her down.

Lety got up, crept across the wood floor, spongy with age, and down the dim hall. She could hear soft snoring as she passed by tía Sofía's open door. Silently, she made her way through the dark kitchen to the back door and stepped into the freedom of night air. Gripping the cool dirt with her toes, she thought about the choices left to her.

As a way to repay tía Sofía's kindness, Lety would choose to name her son Eduardo. She would choose to stop behaving like a child. Would make this baby her last, and when she was able, she would find a job, any job. Then she would leave this house of virgins and martyrs and suffocating absence of light.

A warm breeze circled her bare legs, carrying upon it the perfume of damp roses. She inhaled deeply. "Nunca más," she whispered. "Never again."

————————

pues then; well; well then; so
embarazada pregnant
mensa/o dim-witted
así es la vida that's life
chichis teats/tits
pendejo stupid
mami, mommy, but also an endearment used with a little girl

LA ALMA'S SWEET
REVENGE

———

No Sabes Comprender
(Juan D. Montes)

*...mi suerte es fatal, pues la persigue el
mal, el hombre es promotor de el.
Para ella no hay perdón, ni menos compasión...*

In this song, a woman complains that men can basically
do whatever they want, but for women there is no for-
giveness or compassion. True, but from experience, I've
learned that if you don't want somebody to walk all over
you, don't lie down like a rug.

– Lety

WHEN HER FATHER'S FATHER DIED, it was only natural that Alma's parents would send her to Tucson to provide care and company for
her elderly, and sometimes cantankerous, grandmother. After
all, Alma was the only daughter out of eight who was unmarried.

In fact, both mother and father agreed it was unlikely that their youngest would ever find a husband, given her attitude toward all things domestic. There was that, plus the fact that at seventeen she was still without most of the womanly attributes that would cause a man to stop, turn his head, and cry, "Ay, mamacita."

She and her belongings were packed up with care and many tears, not Alma's, of course. She was glad to be leaving the stuffy little town of Nogales where there was nothing for her to do after high school but work in a shop or a restaurant until some distant cousin or family friend noticed that the youngest daughter of Abelardo and Concha Aguilar was still single and not getting any younger, pues, and maybe a likely match for their loser pendejo of a son, brother or uncle. Besides, Alma had big ideas about going to the university and a career in medicine or law or something, anything that would require her to wear nice clothing, drive a fine car and eat many meals in fancy restaurants.

So when their pickup, a late model Ford Lariat, pulled into Barrio Anita, stopped in front of the slightly crumbling adobe duplex with its chinaberry trees and large, cyclone-fenced yard, Alma was filled with a sense of happy anticipation. At eighteen, what could she know of life? Casi nada.

"Bienvenidos, mijitos," said la abuelita, a short, plump woman with breasts that rested on her panza like twin loaves of pan de huevo. She once had beautiful red hair and so was called nana Rosadita. Now her hair was a rather startling magenta, thanks to the administrations of su comadre, Sra. Campos, who touched up the white roots with henna every Friday night while they watched the telenovelas and drank little glasses of a special elixir for their reumatismo.

"Ay, mijita," nana Rosadita chimed. "Thank you for coming. I've been so lonely since" She paused to pull a paper towel from her cleavage and dab her eyes. To her son, a thickset man with brown eyes nesting beneath bushy, black brows, she tossed an expression of disdain.

"What can I get you to eat? She asked. "A little coffee. Or maybe some frijoles con arroz? I could heat up some carnitas and ..."

"Nada, Mamá," he said, setting down the first of three large boxes. "We got us some chilidogs at Pat's."

"You stopped for chilidogs? You feed your daughter ese junk? No wonder she's so skinny," she said, pinching with her pointed fingernails the centimeter of extra flesh above Alma's tightly cinched waist.

"Ouch, nana! That hurts!" Alma complained.

"Hurt? You know nothing of hurt, mijita. Try 43 hours of labor," she said, tipping her head toward her only son. "And this one eats chilidogs, feeds them to my granddaughter, pues, qué sinvergüenza. You come to my house and deny me the pleasure of feeding you?" Again she patted her eyes with the paper towel.

So Alma and her father sat at the table while nana Rosadita, who could move with astonishing speed and agility despite the arthritis that swelled her knuckles to the size of pigeon eggs, served the comida. Only after the frijoles, tortillas, papas, carnitas, as well as the calabacitas and rice pudding left over from the covered dish she had prepared for a neighbor with a stomach condition – in other words, only after practically the entire contents of her refrigerator was on that table – did Nana Rosadita sit and rest her throbbing varicose veins, and inquire, "I could make some buñelos, or how about an empanada de calabaza?"

Both Alma and her father shook their heads dully.

"Fresh this morning from el Rio Bakery?" she said, starting to rise from her chair. "No? Okay. I'll just send them along, mijo, for the trip home."

After the table was cleared – and it was "No mijita, you must sit and let your food digest" – and the dishes washed after the same admonition, Alma's father rose to leave.

He embraced his mother then turned to Alma, saying only, "Ay, flaca," for on his tongue, flaca was a tender endearment. Of his eight daughters, Alma, with her ambition and head for numbers, was the most like him and therefore the closest to his heart. He opened his arms and embraced his daughter, certain that he was the only man who would ever love her.

After Abelardo Aguilar had left and the shades were drawn one by one in the windows of Barrio Anita, nana Rosadita and Alma sat before a large color TV, last year's Christmas gift from Abelardo. Both women were engrossed by the scene: A darkly handsome man with slim mustaches and distinguished wings of gray at each temple was leading a darkly beautiful girl with tear-splashed eyes and heaving bosoms through the bedroom door. The camera panned to an open window where filmy curtains billowed in the breeze.

"Ay," nana Rosadita sighed and pressed the mute button on the remote. "And to think he was once married to that girl's madrina. Well, they'll never stay together. Not those two. He doesn't know it yet, but she's pregnant. And she used to be such a nice girl. Pues, she's ruined. He'll never marry her now that he's gotten what he wants. It's a fact of life, yo te digo. It's always the woman who pays."

Alma rolled her eyes toward the ceiling.

"Go ahead. Make faces at your nana, but I tell you, mi mamá me dijo y voy a decírtelo, porque es la verdad: What makes him the man, makes a woman the puta."

Alma only nodded her head. These were things she already knew. Lety, formerly her best friend in the whole world, was already the mother of two, an infant and little girl still in pañales two years old. Alma didn't know who fathered the baby, but the father of the girl? Pues, Lety was convinced he had met his death in California, for only death could keep him from returning to her. But certain chismosas had been saying that the boyfriend, ese borracho, had been seen by this or that primo in some bar in El Centro. Sometimes it was Yuma or Bakersfield, but always he was alive and well. Whatever the truth was, Alma never mentioned these rumors to Lety, for what good is a friend, pues, if she doesn't believe the lies told to keep the heart from breaking.

When the telenovela was finally over, Nana Rosadita got down two small glasses wreathed with gracefully etched flowers. "These are the last of a dozen I was given as a bride nearly 54 years ago. Fifty-four years! You can't imagine how quickly that 54 years flew." She shook her head sadly and handed a glass to Alma. Into each she poured a pale gold liquid from a matching cut-glass decanter. "For my reumatismo," she said. "Every year, Sra. Campos goes to Elfrida and picks the peaches herself to make este remedio. Sometimes I rub it on my joints, but usually I just drink it."

Alma sniffed at the contents of her glass and her eyes watered. "What else is in it besides peaches?"

"Creosote leaves."

Alma took a sip and the burn spread from her throat to her chest. She coughed. "What else besides creosote leaves?"

"Chiltepines, azúcar, canela, I think, and maybe just a touch of vodka," she said, pouring another glass for herself. "It's good for the heart too. You know Sra. Campo is also a widow. Su marido was shipped off to Korea the day after their wedding. Three months later, he was dead. So many years ago and she has remained faithful to his memory." Nana Rosadita took a sip of her remedio and a sidelong glance at her granddaughter. "Of course she replaced her husband's kisses with buñuelos, not to mention the sopapillas she prepares for others, but eats herself. I suppose no man would have her, she got to be such a gorda. But what a good heart, a heart as big as her nalgas."

"Nana!"

"What? It's a fact of life, mija. Men don't like their women tan gordas o tan delgadas."

Alma considered this. Which was worse, to be too fat or too thin? People were always pressing her to eat tortillas, rolled, buttered and warm from el microonda, fat burros stuffed with carne seca y chile verde, saucers of flan made from cans of sweet condensed milk. It seemed the more they tried to make her eat, the less food appealed to her. Her mother, her nana, she supposed even her father, assumed that she was too skinny to attract a man, but she would show them. Next week she would register for classes at the college and there she would find him – the boy who would desire her narrow hips, slender waist and small but perfectly matched breasts. He would be tall, clean-shaven, with a lean, muscular, build. Alma didn't care if he was Mexican or white, but the man who would win her heart must be an educated man, muy inteligente, articulado y suave. And most important, when he looked into her eyes, which she had always been told were her best feature, it would be with love and respect.

"Señora Campo's son lives in San Diego," nana Rosadita was saying.

"I thought you said Sra. Campo's husband went to Korea the day after they were married."

"It's true. They married, and boom he was gone the next day, never to return. But such is the power of two virgins joined in matrimony by the holy church, she became pregnant on their wedding night. You see," she said, tapping the coffee table for emphasis. "When the vital force has not been squandered before marriage it is very powerful. Her son came three months early, but gracias a Dios, he was born healthy. Un milagro."

"Do you believe that?"

Nana Rosadita shrugged her shoulders. "God is very powerful, mija. Who am I to say?" she said, a smile barely lifting the corners of her mouth. "Sra. Campo has always been very pious."

Even to Alma, who had no firsthand experience with matters surrounding the making of a baby, the delivery of a healthy infant after such an abbreviated pregnancy seemed less a miracle than a consequence of squandered vital force, though, out of respect to her nana, she didn't say so.

"Anyway, every July," nana Rosadita continued. "He buys her a round trip airplane ticket and she spends the entire month with him and his family in San Diego. It's nice there in the summer, Sra. Campo says. Maybe this July we should take us a trip to San Diego, go to Seaworld, walk on the beach."

"That would be nice," Alma said, picturing lacy waves breaking gently over white sand and the endless sparkling azure of the Pacific. But instead of strolling arm and arm with nana Rosadita, she was holding hands with a well-muscled surfer whose golden skin turned white along the edge of his chones. Silently she vowed, this year she would have a novio.

It happened the first Friday before the campus had settled into serious study. The morning had been so hot the lip balm melted in the bottom of Alma's book bag, turning several pages of her English syllabus transparent and impervious to ink. But by the end of day, the humid late August air was a relief after frigid classrooms. Alma welcomed it like a damp kiss.

A boy from biology lab was standing in the narrow shade of a palm tree. He had a ruddy, wind-burned complexion, and his white-blond hair was buzzed so close to his head, at first she thought he was bald. "Hola," he offered, as she passed.

She turned and smiled. "Hola. ¿Habla Español?"

"Not much more than hola," he said, and fell in step alongside her as she crossed into the parking lot. "You're Alma, from biology lab, right?"

She nodded, impressed that he knew her name. "I'm sorry but..."

"I'm Jason," he said.

Alma searched for words to fill the silence that followed, but soon he was pulling out his car keys. Again she was impressed when she found they unlocked the door of a '67, baby blue Corvette. So impressed, in fact, that when he told her about the kegger a friend was throwing that night, Alma agreed to meet him there.

He slid behind the wheel and wrote an address on a page of his biology text. "Here," he said, tearing off the corner. "See you about eight, then."

As he pulled out of the parking lot, Alma smiled and waved, feeling that perhaps her real life was about to begin.

Alma had given great consideration to her appearance. To make her hips look broader she had chosen a short skirt with a large flowered pattern. The turquoise sleeveless blouse she wore showed off her smooth, copper skin to its best advantage. She followed the sounds of music and high-pitched laughter through the gate. Though no one's head turned when she entered the backyard, her eyes shone beneath slim, symmetrical brows, and her brightly painted lips curved up ever so slightly, hopeful.

The yard was a blur of boys in baggy shorts and shirts that flapped open, exposing beer-arched bellies. Singly and in pairs, girls in low-riding cutoffs and tank tops bobbed to the heavy metal that blistered the air, and everyone seemed to know each other, at least there was considerable shouting between the clots of bodies. Suddenly shy, Alma was about to leave when she heard her name. Jason and his buddies were standing by the keg. He waved. Relieved, she edged her way through the dancers to his side,

"Hola," he said, offering a plastic glass of beer. Though Alma really didn't care much for beer, she took a sip, whisking the foam away from her upper lip with her tongue. Feeling a bead of sweat trickle down her side, she quickly drained the glass to get past the nerves she imagined cutting dark half-moons beneath her armpits. He took the glass from her hand and poured her a second.

Since Alma had refused the plate of garlic and jalapeño spiked machaca her nana had prepared for dinner, she now filled her empty stomach with beer, the second tasting less acrid than the first. The third had practically no taste at all, as she bobbed her head and tipped her pelvis to the bass that thrummed the warm night air.

Though her head throbbed against the pillow, Alma refused to open her eyes. When the sun fell across her face, she merely pulled the sheet over her head, hoping the snatches of memory that flooded her mind would be displaced by the dream she was clinging to, something about chopping juniper into kindling with her father. It was chile season and there were many gunnysacks full, waiting to be roasted on the old woodstove under the ramada. If she could get back to that place – the pleasure of hefting the ax, its own weight pulling it through the soft, dry wood, the scent of resin released into the October air, Alma would not have to acknowledge the image of her pretty flowered skirt pushed up around her hips or the blood and slick washed away by the hottest water she could stand. She moaned, not from the pain that hammered her skull, but from the memory that refused to be dispelled.

Alma's first impulse had been to run home to Nogales, but what would she say to her parents? Could she say that she'd gotten drunk at a party and passed out? Did the word *rape* apply? Could she even say the word? No. She could never say such a thing to the ones who loved her most on earth.

Instead, each morning she left for school so everything would appear normal. Alma didn't go to her classes, however, but sat on the floor in the deepest recesses of the library. With her back resting against the stacks, she allowed her mind to go slack. She did this for days.

Then one evening halfway through the chuletas con nopales y papas, Nana Rosadita said, "You're so quiet, mija. And you've hardly touched your food. ¿Qué pasa?"

"Nada, nana."

"Don't nada nana me. I know you too well. For a week, all you've done is go to school, and shut yourself up in your room with your books. It's too much, mija, all this study. It's not healthy. You need to get out more. Tonight it's bingo at the VFW. Come with me, pues, and give your mind a little rest."

It was not a request and Alma didn't have the will to argue.

She parked her nana's Buick sedan in the dirt lot surrounding the VFW, a squat, concrete block building constructed by veterans of the Korean War. Alma helped the old lady get out of the car and offered an arm to steady her.

Once inside, nana Rosadita cast off Alma's helping hand. Quickly, she scanned the room, waving to this viejita or that. Finally, she approached one of the long, institutional tables. Before dropping into a metal folding chair, she kissed the women nearest her and waved to those out of reach. "Mi nieta," she announced proudly, pulling Alma down into the chair next to her.

Alma obliged with a smile and took her place just below the cloud that hung in the air. On bingo nights, the VFW was filled with two kinds of people, grandmothers and smokers. The only person under 50, Alma was surrounded by las nanas who were exchanging remedios for clearing los bronquios which were already beginning to seize up in the smoke-filled hall.

Nana Rosadita had bought them each three bingo cards. In the mind-numbing search for A7 or B3, Alma felt an easing in her throat, as if the bone that seemed lodged there since that night was beginning to dissolve. Each time Alma located a number, she slashed it with her red magic marker and felt a little easier in her skin. She imagined a future, night after night calmly scanning her cards and occasionally shouting, *bingo!* as a second-hand-smoke-induced cancer slowly ate away at her lungs. Life could be worse, she supposed. Certainly, returning to class seemed far worse than bingo night at the VFW.

The next morning, when Alma awoke, the bone was once again lodged in her throat. No longer could she stand it. She would call Lety. Recently, her mother had kicked her out of the house. Now she was staying only a few blocks away with an aunt. Alma had intended to let their friendship lapse – after all, Lety was an unwed mother going nowhere, whereas Alma was a college student going somewhere, or at least she had been before her world ended up in la basura. If anyone could understand and not judge, it would be Lety.

"Technically it doesn't count," Lety proclaimed, stroking her enormous belly. "In your heart, you're still a virgin."

Not count? She'd lost something important, something she'd been saving for special, something that could never be recovered. How could it not count? It didn't matter that before the white-blond boy, no one seemed much interested in what she might have to offer. It was hers to offer, not for someone to take. She hated the white-blond boy, but she hated herself as well. For sure, she felt wounded, shamed, angry, confused and unclean, but worse, for the first time in her life, Alma felt stupid. It was as though along with her virginity, that boy had stolen her brains.

"So what did you do the next time you saw him in class?" Lety wanted to know.

"I didn't see him," Alma said, plucking at the chenille bedspread. "I stopped going to class so I wouldn't have to."

"You stopped going? Ay, how could you give in to him like that? I would have walked into class and slapped his ugly white face."

"His face is more red than white."

"I would have slapped his ugly, red face, pues. You should have gone to the cops."

"What would I have told them? When I passed out I was a virgin, but when I woke up in the back seat of somebody's car, I don't even know whose, I wasn't?"

"Pues ... It's not right that he should get away with it."

"Pues," Alma shrugged.

"Don't worry," Lety said, taking Alma's hand. "Any man who really loves you, if he's worth having, won't care if you're a virgin or not. Believe me."

Alma considered this. Lety, now a mother of two, was getting to be an expert at love, it seemed. So maybe she was right.

"Wait. Does this guy have a car?"

Alma nodded. "A vintage Corvette."

"¡Perfecto! I say at least we pour sugar into his gas tank."

Alma thought of the baby blue sports car and for the first time in a week, she smiled.

It didn't take long to spot that shiny baby blue on a sea of black asphalt full of practical, sun-deflecting whites, tans and grays. Alma pulled into the row behind the Corvette, which was parked diagonally across two spaces.

"What a pendejo!" Lety observed, as she struggled to get out of the car. She glanced into the back seat where Araceli was sleeping soundly in the car seat tía Sofía had bought for her secondhand.

Alma took the sack of sugar from her backpack. "You do it," she said, pushing the sack towards her friend.

"Ni modo, girl. This you got to do it yourself. Believe me, when it's done, you'll feel better. Verás."

As she unscrewed the gas cap, Alma's hands shook. They shook as she poured the sugar, pure and clean as rain, into the tank. And they were still shaking moments later when she put the key into the ignition of her nana's sedan and drove slowly out of the parking lot, careful to come to a complete stop at each sign.

"Pues?" Lety asked.

Alma sighed. "Maybe tomorrow I'll go back to class. Maybe I'll look him straight in the eye and smile so he'll know it was me."

"¡Perfecto!" Lety said clapping her hands, "Eso seria perfecto."

"Si, perfecto."

When Alma got home that evening, nana Rosadita was watching television as usual. "Sit down, mija, she whispered, patting her freshly hennaed hair. Sra. Campos had just left, and the two little floral wreathed glasses with their skim of sugary elixir were still on the coffee table.

"Ay, can you believe it?"

"¿Qué esta pasando?" Alma asked, sinking down on the couch beside her nana.

"Shush," nana Rosadita whispered, pointing to the television with her chin.

Lety watched as a darkly beautiful girl with tear-splashed eyes and heaving bosoms pointed a gun at a darkly handsome man with slim mustaches and distinguished wings of gray at each temple.

"She'll never pull the trigger," nana Rosadita whispered.

Silently Alma watched as the woman hesitated, hand trembling. Only in her mind did she cry out, *házlo mujer!* Do it! It's not always just the woman who pays. The fact is, sometimes the man has to pay too.

———◆———

abuelita little grandmother
madrina godmother
chismosos gossips
primo/a cousin
chones underpants
novio/a boyfriend/girlfriend
viejita little old woman
nieta granddaughter
basura garbage
varás you'll see

You Can't Call God Usted

———

Bésame Mucho
(Consuelo Velazquez)

Bésame, bésame mucho
Como si fuera esta noche la última vez.
Bésame, bésame mucho
Que tengo miedo perderte, perderte después

This is a song about a woman (it has to be a woman, right?) who's going to go to bed with a guy for the first time. Well, the song only goes on about kissing, but we know she's going to sleep with him and she's afraid she'll lose him once he's gotten what he wants.

– Lety

THE TWO WOMEN SAT ON the couch while their stair-step children, a baby barely walking, a toddler still in diapers and girl of three, sprawled on the floor in front of the television where Casper floated across the screen in search of a friend.

"That pendejo, Chuy," Lety was saying, shaking her head. "If he hadn't gone and got himself killed, my life would be so different."

"You don't love him anymore?"

Lety shrugged. How could she explain? It might be cold and disloyal to his memory, but these days she loved Chuy only in her dreams. In the light of day, she could hardly remember what he looked like. "Of course I still love him," she said, not wanting to sound heartless. "It's just that he's dead and ... pues, I'm not."

Though Alma nodded, Lety could tell by the way her friend's eyes slipped up to the ceiling that she was not convinced, but what did it matter now? Chuy was dead and there was another child to take care of. That Chuy was not the father of the second was water under the bridge and not worth thinking about. After all, if he hadn't got himself killed, Chuy would have been this baby's father too, ¿qué no?

"Come here, mijito," Alma whisked the smallest child off the floor. "Let me wipe your nose." The baby tilted his face up towards his mother. "Blow. Blow hard," she said smoothing her hand over the boy's back where the spine began to twist.

"What did the doctor say about his back? You going to put him in a brace?"

Alma shook her head. "He said it wouldn't do any good."

"You should take him to New Mexico to el Santuario de Chimayo. Rub some of that sacred dirt on it. Mi tía knows a lady who had pains all up and down her legs so bad couldn't even walk. She went and got her some dirt from there, rubbed it all up and down her legs. Anyways, mi tía says, pretty soon this lady was making a pilgrimage to Magdalena. Walked all the way from Nogales to give thanks to St. Francis. Maybe you should try it."

"Your tía's a superstitous old bat, Lety, if you'll excuse me for saying so. She's just like mi suegra, always telling us to take Billy to Chimayó. Chimayó this and Chimayó that. I get sick of it. Now if it were Lourdes that would be different. I've always wanted to go to France. Maybe after Rudy and I get our new house, I'll start saving up for Lourdes," she said on her way into the kitchen.

"So what about el Güero? Alma called, as she opened the refrigerator. "I'm going to have me some chips and salsa. Quieres?"

Lety shook her head. Alma's idea of good salsa was a jar of Pace extra chunky. "I'm watching my weight. I don't know how you stay so skinny."

"I'm on the heartbreak diet," she said as she placed the chips and salsa on the coffee table.

"That's a good one," Lety said, laughing. "When I went on that diet I gained fifteen pounds." She took a single chip from the bag and nibbled it along the edges. "So what do you have to be all brokenhearted about?"

"Just the usual. Rudy's still complaining about my cooking and running back to his mamá every time he gets a yen for una albóndiga."

Lety only nodded. Though she would never say so, she felt some sympathy for Alma's husband. Alma was a terrible cook and anybody could tell by looking that Rudy liked his chimichangas.

"So? Are you still seeing him?" Alma asked.

"¿El Güero?" Her friend knew perfectly well that she was still seeing him. Didn't they live right next door to each other? Didn't she just three days ago watch the kids for her? "He gave me twenty dollars for groceries last time, did I tell you?" Lety said looking casually at her chipped nails.

"No! Twenty dollars? I would have thrown it in his face."

"Are you kidding? I need that money. We barely get by on what I make at Bingos and I can't get that pinche, Jimmy, to give me more hours."

Lety took another chip and dipped it delicately in the salsa. "Oh, oh, oh! Did I tell you that he gave Anita, who's only been working there like two weeks, the seven to two shift? That's breakfast, lunch and 7 hours! When I asked him why her, and not me, he just shrugged. 'She's a hard worker,' he says. I'm pretty sure *hard worker* is English for ella chúpame el pito."

"Mentiras," Alma said, laughing so hard she had to cover her mouth with a paper towel so she wouldn't spew Pace Salsa.

"It's the truth, I swear," Lety insisted, but it was true in part only. The full truth Lety was ashamed to tell. She sighed deeply. "Anyway, I need every dollar I can get. I'm trying to put some aside so I can to go back to school. Going to get my GED, I can do that for free when I get the time. Then maybe go to Pima College so I can get me a good job like you. I'm not going to wait on tables and clean up other peoples shit for the rest of my life. A bilingual secretary or a para-something, that's what I want to be. Work someplace nice and clean, someplace where my hair don't smell like French fries when I come home."

Alma scooped up some salsa with a tortilla chip. "Might be a job opening up at Crazy Casey's. One of the girls says she's getting married and moving to San Diego. Personally, I doubt it, but you never know."

Lety didn't want to work at Crazy Casey's either. But Alma was her best friend through thick and thin. She didn't want her to think she was too good to work in a place that sold RVs. "For you that's fine. You're the bookkeeper and you got Rudy. But me? What would I do? Clean toilets for minimum wage? I need to make more than minimum." Lety looked longingly at the chips. She took a broken one and held it in her mouth until it dissolved. "Besides, I don't think my novio would like it."

"So it's novio now."

Lety smiled and raised her eyebrows. "Sure, why not? When a guy gives you twenty dollars for groceries, that means something, ¿qué no? That's more than my kids' fathers ever did for them."

"Jonny gives you money for Eddie once in a while, doesn't he? What does he say about your boyfriend?"

Lety turned off the television set and clapped her hands. "Hey you little rug rats. Enough television. Araceli, take Eddie out back to play."

"Mamá," the child complained, but Lety was already pulling her son to his feet and herding the two of them toward the door.

"Go play in the sandbox, but don't let him eat any. Be good, mija, and maybe later we can get us a Dairy Queen."

Lety closed the door and turned her attention back to her friend. "What can he say? Besides, Jonny likes to help out when Jonny likes to help out. Amor de lejos, amor de pendejos. I can't count on him for nothing. When I needed money for the abortion, he was all, 'Have it querida. I'll take care of you and the baby.' But he doesn't take care of his son now, so I knew he was just bullshitting me, and how am I going to take care of three when I'm just barely making it for the two I already got?"

"Well, Jonny's always been a pretty good Catholic. What did you expect?"

"Sure. He's a good Catholic in the way only a man can be. After all, they don't have their little pecados, hanging on their knees, wiping their snotty noses on their pant legs. No, it's you I have to thank for helping me out of that one."

"You paid me back."

"I can never pay you back enough," Lety said, looking out the kitchen window. You took part of your nana's life insurance to help me out. We just went to the bank and got the money. But Jonny? You know he never said another word about it. Never asked about how was I doing or nothing. Pretended the baby went away all by itself, or maybe he just forgot. Men are like that, I swear."

Alma brought out a quart bottle of Diet Pepsi from the refrigerator and set it and two glasses on the coffee table. "How's your mother?"

Wanting to be sure she had her friend's complete attention, Lety waited until Alma had poured them each a tall glass of soda. "Didn't I tell you? The Greek had a stroke. The whole half side of his face, my mother says, is like melted. Melted just like candle wax, she says."

"No! You're lying."

"I'm not lying. And you know she's all terrified that he's going to die and she's going to lose her job. If he dies, his wife will fire her ass for sure."

"Fire her?"

"Si pues, wouldn't you?"

"I don't know, I guess. So what's your mother going to do?"

"What can she do? Just wait. I mean, I'm not all that crazy about the Greek, but I don't want to see her out of a job. She's my mother, pues."

Lety went to the kitchen window. "Araceli," she shouted. "Don't let your brother eat that dirt." Turning back to her friend, she said, "I swear, Eddie would eat caca if I let him. So how's it going with Rudy?"

Alma frowned and shrugged. "Like I said, he's still running back to his mother whenever."

"That man's crazy."

Alma shrugged and drew a heart in the water that had rolled off the Pepsi bottle and pooled on the laminated surface of the table.

"I mean you're a real pretty woman when you fix yourself up, and your figure, well, I wish I had a waist like yours. I mean, for reals. It's tiny just like in the underwear ads."

"That's not it."

"Then what is it?"

"It's because..."

"Because he's a cabrón," Lety interrupted. "They're all cabrones, even Rudy. Let me tell you something. Men have been treating me like a whore since my first regla. Since I was barely twelve, they been treating me like that, and I never even did it for the first time till I was fifteen! You want to know what I think? I think they do that because of my big chichis. It's true, I swear. You should be happy yours are small. I mean, is it my fault that I got big tits? See, that's another reason I want to become a bilingual secretary. I want to work someplace nice, where people will look at my face when they talk to me. Even Jonny, who's probably seen my chichis more than just about anyone, still has trouble looking me in the eye."

Alma poured a little more Pepsi into her friend's glass. "But you still love him, right?"

"Who, Jonny? Ay. I wish I didn't. I wish I loved my güero like I love Jonny." Lety sighed and went to the refrigerator. She opened the door and searched around until she found a jar of jalapeños. "It's true, Alma. If I loved Jonny like I love El Güero, and loved El Güero like I love Jonny, I'd be a happy girl."

"Do it one more time," Lety commanded, grinning big.

"Again?"

"Come on, Güero. Please?"

The young man grabbed the foot that had been resting in his bare lap and pinched the big toe. "This little piggy went to market," he said, wiggling the toe back and forth. Then pinching the second, "This little piggy stayed home." He smiled and pinched the third toe. "This little piggy had roast beef. And this little piggy had none. And this little piggy went wee wee wee all the way home."

"That's the cutest thing I ever heard. I'm going to have to try it on Eddie. It's going to crack him up for reals," Lety said, laughing and pulling her foot away. "Lie down now and let me rub your pretty shoulders. I swear, Güero, you got the prettiest shoulders, so white. Just like milk."

He did as he was told, stretching his long frame diagonally across the bed. "Speak to me in Spanish. I want to practice."

"What do you want me to say?"

"Say anything."

"¿Cómo estás?" she said rubbing his shoulders.

"Muy bien, y usted?"

"You don't use usted with someone you're lying in bed with, Güero. It don't sound right."

"What do you mean, it doesn't sound right? That's exactly what my phrase book says. '¿Cómo esta usted? Muy bien y usted?'"

"Yeah, but that's for people you don't know so good. With me you got to use tú."

"Oh," he said, adjusting the pillow under his chest. "So how do you know when to use tú and when to use usted?"

Lety shrugged her shoulders. "You just know. It comes naturally."

"Nothing about Spanish come naturally to me. So tell me exactly who you use tú with."

"Well, I use it with my kids and my mother and my aunt and cousins and friends and my brother and his wife and their kids and you, because we're sleeping together, and God, when I say my prayers."

"You use tú with God? Isn't that a little, I don't know, arrogant, or something?"

"I don't know if it's arrogant or whatevers, you just use tú. I mean, you can't call God usted."

"But why not? It's respectful."

"You just can't. Look, it's like this. God's known me since I was a little girl, before that even, see? It wouldn't be right for me to call Him usted. It's hard to explain. Let me think." Lety paused for a moment. "Okay, okay. It's like, He'd be hurt. Like I was saying that we're not on friendly terms, or that we're strangers or something. I don't know. You just can't do it. Now do you want me to speak Spanish, or what?"

"Yeah. Say something else."

"Yo amo tus pecas," she said slowly, making each syllable distinct.

"My what?"

"Tus pecas, freckles."

"Oh, I thought you said pecker."

"Well, don't get all disappointed." Lety laughed. "Pecas, pecas. They're so cute, these ones on your shoulders. I think I'm going to do me a little dot to dot," she said and rolled off the bed.

"Where are you going?"

"To find a pen. I got one by the phone."

"I don't know if I want you drawing on me."

"Just shut up and lie still." She straddled his waist and studied his shoulders, looking for a pattern. "Ah ha. I see a cross," she said tracing it with her fingernail. "And over here, I think a little dog."

Lety smiled. This guy must be crazy about me, she was thinking as she connected five freckles to form the outline of a house.

Lety was standing at the stove when there was a knock at the front door. She tossed another small hamburger into the spattering grease. "See who's at the door, mijita," she called to her daughter, who was watching television. "But don't open unless you know who it is."

The little girl crawled up on the couch and drew back the curtain. "It's a man, Mamá, but I don't know who."

"Okay, just a minute." Lety turned off the heat under the hamburgers and went to the front window. In the failing light, she examined the young man who stood on the top step studying his fingernails. She opened the door a crack. "Yes?"

"Ah. I'm a friend of Ralph's from the university. You know, Ralph. Güero?"

"Yes, I know who Ralph is." Lety opened the door wider and looked beyond the young man to see if El Güero was there or perhaps out in the car that was parked in her drive. "Where is Ralph? I haven't seen him for a while."

"That's why I'm here. Ralph wanted me to come by and tell you. May I come in?"

Lety stepped aside. She went to the television and snapped it off.

"¡Mamá! I was watching."

"So now you're not. Take your brother into the bedroom for a minute, will you, mijita? Play in there for a little bit while mamá talks to the man."

The child tugged her brother up by one arm and led him into the other room.

"Meata. That's an unusual name," the young man said, following the girl with his eyes. "Cute kids."

"Her name's Araceli. Mi-ji-ta. It means my little daughter. So what did you want to tell me?"

"I've got some kinda bad news. It seems that when Ralph was home on Christmas break, well, I guess he got his girlfriend pregnant, and well, he wanted to tell you himself, but he had to get home fast, because I guess everybody back there is pretty much in an uproar, and the girl was threatening to just about commit suicide or something. Anyway Ralph went back there to marry her. "

"Marry her?"

"Yeah, I guess by now they've already done it. He wanted you to know. Told me to come by and tell you myself." He paused and chewed on his lip. "You know, Ralph told me all about you. He told me you were pretty, but I didn't realize that you were this pretty," he said looking at her chest.

Lety picked up the phone and dialed. "Alma. This is Lety. Can I send my kids over?"

"So your Güero finally show?"

"No."

"Jonny?"

"No."

"Then who?"

"Look. I'll tell you about it later. Can you take care of the kids?"

"Well, I was just about to go out."

"Come on, Alma," Lety whispered. "This will only take a minute, believe me."

"Hey, you're getting to be a puta for reals."

"Si pues. So they tell me. So can you watch them for a minute? I'll give you three dollars."

"Keep your three dollars. Send them over. Just don't take all night, well."

Lety hung up the phone. "So what did you say your name was?"

"My name's Andrew."

"You studying Spanish too, Andrew?"

"No. I'm from Maine, so I'm taking French. We're close to Quebec, you know, so French is the best second language to have for up there."

"Yeah, French. Makes sense. So you got a rubber, Andrew? I don't want to end up like Ralph's girlfriend."

Frank pulled out his wallet and extracted a condom along with a twenty-dollar bill, which he placed on the dresser. His hand was clearly shaking.

Lety was nervous too, but her nerves were all on the inside. It was her stomach, not her hands that trembled as she took the condom from the boy and unwrapped it.

"You ever done it before, Andrew?"

"Yes, I have. I mean, I think I have. I'm not sure. See, I was pretty drunk at the time, so I'm not quite certain."

"Well, this time you'll know for sure, eh, Güero?"

"Güero? I thought that was what you called Frank."

"Güero?" She laughed, but her eyes were hard. "No. Güero is just what we...

You know the word puta, Güero?

"Yeah, I've heard of it."

"Yeah, well. It's just what we putas call you guys, you know? Be sure you tell Ralph. Okay? I wouldn't want him to get the wrong meaning, since he wants to learn how to speak Spanish so bad, and all."

She closed the door behind him, then leaned her forehead against the warm, sticky wood, her hand still on the knob. Lety wanted to cry just as she had the first time she had sex. She cried so hard that night, Chuy got scared. "¿Qué tienes, Lety? Did I hurt you?"

Lety had said no, but in truth, that act had changed her, pierced deep inside her heart, and she knew she would never again be the same.

It was like that now. Never again would she be the same person she had been just moments before that boy had knocked on her door, that stranger.

"¿Diós, tú sabes y comprendes, no? God understands," she sighed, "Sólo tú." Using the belt on her terry robe she wiped her eyes and nose, then reconsidered. How could she expect God to understand her now. God understood love, she was sure. But what she'd just done had nothing to do with that.

"Sólo usted," Lety said softly, experimenting with the word *usted* to see how it felt. "Usted sabe. Usted comprende. Usted. Uuuuu-sted," she repeated.

No, the word was totally wrong, felt totally foreign as it fell from her tongue.

Smiling with relief, she whispered, "Tú comprendes. Sólo tú. Sólo tú, tú, tú, tú, tú, tú."

———◆———

suegra mother-in-law
guero/a a fair-haired person
amor lejos, amor de pendejos love at a distance is love for fools

LOVE IN A LATIN LANGUAGE

———

La Tumba Será el Final
(Traditional)

*...La tumba sera el final allí será la separación y
hasta en la tumba te sigo amando si quiere Dios...
Solamente a mi madre la quería más que a ti.*

This one's an oldie but moldie. The guy swears that he'll
love his woman forever and nothing but the grave will
separate them. So far so good, but then he tells her that
the only woman he ever loved more than her was his
mother. Really, he should have quit while he was ahead.
Just ask Alma.

– Lety

RUDY DIDN'T SPEAK MUCH SPANISH. When he was still waddling
around in loaded diapers, Al, his half-gringo stepfather, moved
the family up from Palomas to Las Cruces where he had a good

job in construction. Right from the beginning, Al insisted that Rudy's mother speak only English to the toddler and later to the boy's half-brothers and sisters. "I don't want kids to sound "like a bunch of ignorant wetbacks," he had said. Of course, it's possible the real reason behind his mandate was that Al didn't speak much Spanish himself (his mother was the gringa) and didn't want to be left out of a conversation, or worse, have his wife and kids talk about him in a language he couldn't comprehend. They say such paranoia is common among white people, even half-white people.

Even so, from his father, who was basically good natured, but occasionally intemperate, Rudy learned the many rich and satisfying swears and insults in Spanish: cabrón, puta, the many nuanced meanings of chingar and all the hijos y madres — rowdy, even joyous words, and especially useful if you were a Mexican who doesn't speak much Spanish.

From his Mexican mother, Rudy learned a completely different vocabulary. Words of celebration were synonymous with albóndigas, birria, barbacoa, costillas and carne asada. Ordinary fare included tortillas, made fresh daily on the comal, tamales de elote or carne con chile colorado, empanadas, pozole. To stretch a dollar she made tripas de leche, burros filled with carne de cabeza and, of course, frijoles. What real Mexican woman does not start each day by putting a pot of beans on the stove? During Lent, there were tacos de pescado y papas, enchiladas de queso, quesadillas and caldo de queso. When someone was sick, either physically or spiritually, there was sopa de arroz con pollo. For congestion in the chest, his mother brewed hojas de tomatillo con limón, miel y canela and served it in a little blue mug that exactly fit a child's hand. And when he was older, after a night of drinking with his buddies, his mother heated up the menudo — even at 3 a.m. In fact, Rudy's familiarity with the language of the Mexican kitchen and his notion of home, that is to say, love, satisfaction, well-being, health maintenance and the proper occupation of women, were casi lo mismo.

Imagine Rudy's dismay when the first meal his young wife, Alma, served him after their return to Tucson from a romantic honeymoon in San Diego, was a lasagna from Costco. At first he wasn't worried. Alma worked hard, sometimes six days a week, keeping books and answering the phone for Crazy Casey's Campers and Recreational Vehicles. But after several weeks of hotdogs served on Wonder Bread, macaroni out of a box, take-out Chinese and the occasional Lean Cuisine, he began to wonder. It wasn't until they celebrated their six-month anniversary with a plate of Rosarita refried beans, melted Velveta and corn chips preflavored with ranch dressing, that he got seriously concerned, and, to be honest, un poco barracho y enojado.

"What's this?" he said, taking a swig from his third Bud.

"Nachos. What did you think?"

Rudy nudged the plate as if it were roadkill. "Looks like pile of caca."

"Well it's nachos, and don't talk to me like that. I'm not your mother."

This major understatement was one he wisely chose to ignore. Comparisons with his mother, however well-meaning, never led to a happy ending. "But where are the chiles, the queso, the homemade refritos?" He pronounced chiles, queso, refritos with the perfect, pure vowels he had learned in his mother's kitchen. "¡Chingado! You call this cheese?" He said, forking up a rubbery strand with a suspect plastic sheen.

Alma looked at him flatly. "So I don't like to cook. Actually, I don't even know how."

"You can't cook and you call yourself a Mexican?"

"You can't cook and you call yourself a Mexican," she countered. "At least I speak Spanish. ¡Al menos, soy una Mexicana que puede hablar como una Mexicana y no soy un pinche cabrón que no puede decir nada que palabras feas, un chillón que se queja cuando no tiene frijoles y arroz todos los dias como un indio!"

Of course, from Alma's rapid stream of Spanish, Rudy could grasp only the words — lousy, bastard, Indian, beans and rice, but they were the ones necessary to follow the gist of the conversation. In response, he gulped down the last of his Bud and grabbed a fourth for the road.

Normally it was a four-hour drive from Tucson to Las Cruces, but Rudy made it in a little more than three. It was Friday night, and he could already taste his mother's menudo, steamy and fragrant with cilantro.

Heating a tortilla on a cast iron griddle, his mother said, "What did you expect from a girl who's skinny like a palo de escoba."

"A what?"

"Broomstick, Rudy. A girl who don't like to eat, don't like to cook, pues."

Rudy thought about this as he squeezed limón over his menudo. Sure she was unlike his mother who had to spread a dishtowel across her vast chichis when she cooked to keep from ruining her blouse as the tasting spoon dripped from pot to mouth. But he didn't mind that Alma was skinny. It was her eyes, dark and lustrous, that drew him, and her enthusiastic participation in lovemaking that kept his interest. And they shared a vision of the future. They would move out of the crumbling duplex left to Alma's care by her late nana Rosadita and into a brand-new custom four-bedroom house with a late model Ford truck in the carport on an acre of land in the foothills where they would raise exactly two children. It was this shared vision, and the pleasant fact that the flatness of Alma's belly complemented the round-ness of his own, that sealed their love.

"She likes to eat okay," Rudy responded at last. "She's just not much for cooking."

His mother put the hot tortilla with several others between the folds of a cotton dishtowel, which she set before him. "Well, you should have known better, is all I'm saying. Now you're stuck."

But Rudy didn't feel stuck. With the steam from the menudo clearing his head, he didn't even feel angry anymore. "The subject just never came up."

"Bring her over here. She's still young. I could teach even esa burra to cook."

"What?"

"¡Madre de Dios! Burra, burra. Donkey, mijo, stubborn donkey."

"Oh. Well, maybe next weekend, Ma," he said, tossing a hand-ful of chopped green onion over the menudo.

Despite the lateness of the hour and his mother's promises of chorizo and eggs for breakfast, Rudy drove back to Tucson that very night with a full belly and renewed hope. By the time he slid into bed beside Alma, dawn was blushing her cheek.

"Híjole, Rudy!" she said, rolling away from him when he tried to kiss her. "What have you been eating? Menudo?"

But in spite of their cross words and the lingering redolence of tripas and garlic, when he slipped his hand underneath her nightie, she received him with her usual ardor. So what if she can't cook, he was thinking as he smoothed his palm along her skinny haunch.

"Give me some mantequilla," he murmured, and she did, con mucho gusto.

But a man can only satisfy one appetite at a time, ¿que no? So it's not surprising that the next morning Rudy's appetite was of a different nature. As he poured the 1 percent Alma insisted he use on his cornflakes, he longed for the chorizo, the frijoles, the huevos con queso and slivers of jalapeño his mother would have laid before him had he stayed the night in Las Cruces. When Alma came into the kitchen still sweetly disheveled from their lovemaking, his hunger prompted him to suggest she take his mother up on her offer.

"Go to Las Cruces on the weekends so your mother can teach me to make tamales or whatevers? I don't think so, mi amor. On my days off, I need to rest. Besides, your mother doesn't like me."

"She likes you."

"Rudy…"

"She likes you. She told me so. Mama said you're so smart, she could teach you to cook in no time."

"Mentiroso."

"What?"

"¡Hijole, Rudy! Mentiroso, mentiroso. Big fat liar." She put his dish in the sink. "Hey, I got an idea. Why doesn't your mother teach you how to cook? Then we'd all be happy."

Rudy was incredulous. Could Alma really believe that such a thing would be possible, that his mother, of all mothers, would allow something so unnatural? Besides no man on earth could ever learn how to make a tortilla. (Little did Rudy know that in years to come his mother would teach his very own son this exacting skill, ignoring Rudy's concerns that she was turning his son into a maricón.)

"Well?" Alma prompted.

"But Alma, mi chuleta, I know you could do it. It would be so easy for you."

"Easy? Even my own mother, who loves me and has the patience of a saint, couldn't teach me. Many times when I was a little girl she tried to show me how to make tortillas, but no matter how many bolitas I patted out, they always looked like somebody's old chones." She paused and looked at her husband. "Underpants, Rudy. All my tortillas looked like somebody's old underpants. Nobody wants to eat that. Finally she gave up, gracias a Dios. And as you know, my mother's not one to give up easily, which is why there are eight of us girls in the family. Eight girls, each a chance for a boy, pues. No, cariño. If you love me, you're just going to have to live with it. I don't cook. ¡Ni ahora, ni nunca!"

Rudy was confused by her obstinacy. It was incomprehensible to him that the woman he'd chosen to spend the rest of his life with was the only girl, in a family full of girls, who never learned to cook. No matter that she knew how to keep books, fix the cooler and change the oil in the truck. But Rudy was not one to give up easily either, so he tickled, caressed and cajoled until Alma agreed to give it a try just so she could get some rest.

"You won't regret it, my little sopapilla," he said, biting her neck. "You're going to love my mother. She's going to love you. And I love you both so much." Rudy could hardly wait to see what Alma would learn to cook first.

"Beans?" Alma said as she watched her mother-in-law pour three pounds of pintos into the hug pot.

"Sí pues," said la suegra, tucking a dishtowel into the collar of her blouse and over her chest. "Frijoles are at the heart of every Mexican meal, breakfast, lunch and dinner. "Here. Rinse these carefully, make sure there are no little rocks." she said, while crushing dried epazote between palm and thumb.

"What's that?"

"Epazote, of course," proclaimed la suegra. She always tempered her beans with this herb to rid the bean of the fart inherent within.

"Epazote," Alma repeated, thinking she should probably write it down. That was the last real thought she had until eight hours later (her mother-in-law berating her all the while with rolled eyes and sighs and tsks and shaking head) the beans – plain and refried, cheesed, crisped, in burros, on tostadas, con carne, a feast of beans – were on the table.

"You're not eating, Alma," la suegra said, her tone more accusation than observation, as she dished up a plate of seconds for Al and Rudy who had set about the task of beans with determination and zeal. "Aren't you hungry?"

Overwhelmed by fatigue, irritation and beans, Alma could only sigh as she watched the food that had taken hours to prepare, rapidly disappear, and wondered if divorce would be less painful than learning to cook.

But Rudy and Alma did not divorce, and even though Alma refused any more cooking lessons, things went along smoothly enough. Pues, they were young and in love, and when you're young and in love, all longings seem possible to satisfy, and all hurts are healed by besos y abrazos. So if Rudy sometimes secretly, sometimes defiantly, returned alone to Las Cruces for chilaquiles perhaps, a cazuela or machaca, Alma simply bought him pants with larger waistbands and said nothing. For her part, Alma continued to work long hours enjoying the boss' praise and often repeated claim that he could not function without her.

And every two weeks, she put all her paycheck in savings for the dream house in the foothills.

Of course with all their lovemaking it wasn't long before there was a slip-up. It was Alma who was upset. Rudy accepted the unplanned pregnancy with his usual equanimity. After the sonogram, she announced their first would be a boy.

"Chingado, for reals?" he said happily.

"Si, mi amor," she whispered, warming to the idea. Then they celebrated the event in the same manner they celebrated every event, happy or sad, by making love. But this time Rudy executed the act with a delicate and gentle solicitude that penetrated her more deeply than his firmest ardor.

So it was surprising that it was the very birth of this baby, and not Alma's disinterest in the kitchen, that ultimately led to the separation of the young maridos.

Even in infancy, Billy was homely, with a pointed, fox face and a spine twisting into a hump above his left shoulder, but so sweet and affectionate, so happy and inteligente, that he was loved without prejudice by Alma and Rudy, his nanas and tatas, tíos, padrinos and primos. This was not the problem. The problem was that Billy was her mother-in-law's suegra's first grandchild. It was Billy who at the age of thirteen months gurgled, "fufi, fufi, fufi," holding his thin little arms out to his grandmother, who became from that very day and ever more, nana Fufi. Her own mother was simply nana. Since she was already a grandmother to many she felt disinclined to fight Rudy's mother for primary nanaship. In fact, Alma's mother encouraged her to allow nana Fufi as much access to Billy as "la pobre mujer" craved.

It soon became apparent to Alma that, even as an infant, her son was attracted to the comfort of his nana's ample flesh. Oh, there was no doubt in her mind that the baby loved her too, but Alma couldn't help feeling she was in competition, not only for the affections of her husband, but for those of her son as well. To make matters worse, they all accused Alma of being selfish and unreasonable.

"Move here," said la suegra on one of the increasingly rare occasions Alma conceded to accompany her husband and son to Las Cruces. "Papi and me ain't getting any younger, you know. We need to spend more time with the baby."

"What would I do in Las Cruces?" asked Rudy.

"Take over the business," said Al. "Frankly, son, I'm worn out; ready to retire."

"What about Floyd or Ernie?" Alma asked, thinking that with five other kids, they could find somebody, anybody besides her Rudy, to take over the business.

La suegra batted her hand in the air as if shooing a fly. "Rudy's the only one could take over the business. Right, Papi? You two should move here, Alma. You could find you a job and I could take care of the baby," she said, eyes shiny with hope.

"I can't quit my job just like that," Alma said, snapping her fingers.

"Why not?" la suegra wanted to know.

"Because I just can't," Alma said, examining the reasons why she had trouble breathing at the mere thought of moving to Las Cruces. Was it her mother-in-law? The fact that she'd have to leave friends and family behind? Sure, that was part of it, but at the heart of her discomfort was the little adobe duplex her nana Rosadita had left only to her. She owned it free and clear. Without it, she would feel like she was at the mercy of…Rudy? ¿La suegra? Not exactly that, but at the mercy of everybody's idea of what a Mexicana was supposed to be. Of course, she could not use this as an excuse. It was selfish, not at all the way a Mexican woman with a husband and a son should be thinking, which was exactly what made her feel short of breath. "I get good pay where I work now, and we're saving money for the new house."

"Move to Las Cruces. Papi and Rudy will build you a new house right down the street – as many bedrooms as you can fill."

"I can't just quit my job."

"So keep your damn job if you think it's so damn important. You come down here on the weekends, and I'll take care of the baby in between. No need for that woman to take care of him while you're at work, when he's got his nana Fufi who loves him."

Alma tossed a glance at Rudy. That woman was Lety, who rented the other half of the duplex from her for $150 a month, plus free babysitting. Sure, Lety was getting a reputation for having too many boyfriends, a fact Rudy had obviously shared with his mother, but she was a warm and caring person, Alma's best friend. She would trust Lety with her life.

"Billy loves Lety, loves her kids. Besides, she's right next door and I don't even have to pack up his pañales or put him in the car seat."

"Hey, Pop, is that big lot down the street still for sale?" Rudy asked.

"And cheap. You can't find a lot that size in Tucson so cheap."

Sensing conspiracy, Alma told them all in no uncertain terms: She was not giving up her job, or her son, (or her duplex), and she was definitely not moving to Las Cruces. "Thank you very much. ¡Ni ahora, ni nunca!"

Though no one spoke to her again of moving to Las Cruces, Alma began bringing home takeout every Friday night from Tanya's, el Minuto, Mi Nidito, el Charro, Rosa's — the best Mexican restaurants in a town full of great Mexican restaurants – in hopes of keeping Rudy from straying.

They say a mother's cooking is the standard by which all cooking is judged and found wanting, ¿qué no? So invariably Rudy would sample the refried beans and say, "These beans are good, but I don't know..."

On one such Friday night, Rudy mixed beans, rice and a little salsa together for baby Billy, who sat between his mother and father in a high chair, mouth opening like a little bird for his father's every offering and shutting like a zipper when his mother tried to pop in carrots and peas, the occasional piece of Vienna sausage. When Rudy asked for seconds of the inferior beans and everything that went with them, Alma looked at the rejected peas and carrots and her husband's stomach, which now brushed the edge of the table, and observed, "El pez muere por la boca."

"What?" Rudy asked, mopping up the remnants of his dinner with a tortilla.

"The fish is killed by his mouth."

"What's that supposed to mean?"

"Putting too much food in your mouth will kill you."

With the rolled tortilla, he pointed to the untouched food on Alma's plate, "Not as fast as putting nothing in your mouth."

And it was true. As Rudy's panza grew, Alma's shrank, as if in silent opposition. How long could they go on this way? A long time, pues, because the panza she scorned at the dinner table, she caressed between the sheets.

One night after their lovemaking, Alma's thoughts wandered back to that first year in Tucson. Though she had come up from Nogales to attend college, she dropped out only weeks into the first quarter, taking the bookkeeping job at Crazy's. Her heart really wasn't in her job, but at the time, it seemed a better alternative to school or going home to Mexico to face her parents' silent inquisition. She had promised herself that she would return to school the following year, but then she met Rudy.

It had been on a Saturday, the first warm day after the last snap of cold in April, and nana Rosadita had arranged for the coolers on the roof of each side of the duplex to be readied for the hot weather to come. Alma was painting her toenails on the couch when she heard a strangled cry and the crash of the aluminum ladder. Without even removing the cotton from between her toes, she rushed out into the yard where she found him sprawled beneath his ladder.

"¿Qué pasó?" she said lifting the ladder aside.

"I fell on my head."

"Are you alright?"

As the veil of shock lifted, his gaze focused on hers. "Yeah, I'm okay. I said I fell on my head, didn't I?" He smiled at her then and his eyes... his eyes were nearly amber in color and as warm as sun on adobe. Reflected in those eyes, Alma saw humor and light and something else so unexpected that she experienced a mad fluttering in her ribcage, as if a moth, no, a butterfly, were pinned beneath her breastbone. Gradually, inch by inch, he began to take over the rest of her body, until finally on their wedding night, she was ready to give him full possession.

Alma was abruptly cast back into the present by the burr of a fart. She pulled the pillow over her face, as her husband snored, oblivious, by her side. No question she loved him with all her heart – except for her son, she had never loved anyone more than Rudy – but clearly the romance was not what it had once been. Though her sisters and girlfriends all said this was normal and to be expected, she felt a pang of disappointment and loneliness that was entirely new.

When their son was three years old, Rudy convinced Alma to leave Billy with nana Fufi while they relived their honeymoon in a condo on the beach in San Diego. And it was glorious, ocean sparkly and blue as a sapphire, nights cool and damp with spume. For five days, like novios, they walked hand and hand on the white sand. On the sixth, they returned to Las Cruces.

The baby was sitting in the middle of the living room rug surrounded by toy trucks, Legos, a Wiffle ball and plastic bat, a plush panda bear, scattered books and a half dozen diminutive army guys in camouflage.

Alma picked up her son and hugged him to her. "Ay mi corazón. Did you miss mamá?" she said, her hand gently stroking his twisted spine and hump. It was with a certain satisfaction that she noticed his back was covered with a dull powder as if he'd been rolling in the dust. "¡Qué sucio! Didn't your nana give you a bath this morning?"

"I certainly did not," said la suegra, wiping masa trigo from her hands. "That's the holy dirt from Chimayo. Papi and me took Billy up there last weekend and dug us up some. I've been rubbing it on his back every day after his bath. You never know. With the grace of the Holy Mother of God, it might cure his spine."

"What are you saying, cure his spine? My son's spine is not some sickness that needs to be cured. He's healthy, perfect. Never in his life has he been sick." Alma said wetting a washcloth. "Come here, mijito, let mamá wipe this old dirt off your back."

"Let it be, Alma," said Rudy. "A little dirt can't hurt him."

"That's not ordinary dirt," said la suegra, her voice rising. "It's blessed dirt from the sacred shrine at Chimayo."

"Whatever. I don't want my son growing up thinking his back makes him some kind of freak that needs to be cured by dirt, sagrado o no!"

"I didn't say he was a freak."

"It sure sounds to me like you think his back is some sort of freak disease, if it needs to be cured, pues. Recuerda Dios le dió este espinanzo."

Both the women leapt into Spanish then, the only language that could give the full range of expression to the anger and jealousy that had been building between them since the day they met. Al and Rudy exchanged looks. Together they scooped Billy up and carried the laughing child between them out to the back-yard, where a small turkey was slowly roasting on the Webber — tomorrow's leftovers would be bathed in the rich mole that was simmering at that very moment on the stove.

Ignoring the incomprehensible noise from the house, the men retrieved a couple of cold ones from the ice chest and settled onto lawn chairs. They drank their beers in companionable silence, while eddies of smoky scent rose from the grill, and the barefoot boy tripped across the soft, mown grass after a soccer ball. For some, life can be as good and simple as this, ¿qué no?

Though Alma now refused to go to Las Cruces, and often refused to allow Billy to accompany Rudy when he did, the marriage somehow prevailed. Then one day, la suegra was suddenly yelling and crying on the telephone.

"Slow down, Ma. Speak English, for Christ sake." But his mother, in a state of crisis, only yelled louder in Spanish. In desperation, Rudy handed the phone to Alma.

"Oh, Rudy, it's Papá Al." Alma whispered, hand pressed over the receiver. "It was his heart."

Immediately Rudy, Alma and Billy made the sad trip to Las Cruces. A week later, Alma and Billy returned to Tucson alone, leaving Rudy to see to his father's business. At first, it was to be a temporary arrangement, Rudy staying with his mother during the week and coming home on weekends. Over time, the weekend visits became twice monthly, monthly, then once every so often.

It was a relatively painless process, the unraveling of this marriage. In fact, it wasn't until Billy was in kindergarten, that it became necessary to make arrangements for visitation because Rudy missed his son, and the boy, Alma had to concede, needed his father. Long vacations at Christmas and Easter, the occasional weekend and chunks of summer belonged to Rudy, but even more, to nana Fufi, since Rudy worked seven days a week, as his father had before him.

At first Alma was resentful, making up a bed for Rudy on the couch when he came to Tucson to pick up his son. But eventually she softened, (who was she punishing?) and their marriage would resume for one night every so often.

How long could they go on like this? A long time, years even. Though there was a man from time to time who took notice, Alma never considered any permanent arrangement. She had her son's feelings to consider, ¿qué no? Besides, no one suited her better than Rudy.

As for Rudy, if there were other women in Las Cruces, he had the sense not to mention them. And Billy, when he returned from this or that visit with his father, seemed truly puzzled when Alma asked, "So, mijito, did your papá take you to meet any of his lady friends over there in Las Cruces?"

If Alma's new life was imperfect, it was not without its satisfactions — she had even put on a little weight. Since Rudy sent her money each month, and she was no longer saving for a house in the foothills, she could afford to cut back her hours at work so she could go back to school and follow her lifelong dream of becoming a medical technician of some sort, any kind that wore a crisp white coat would do, or maybe even a doctor. ¿Cómo no? At first, she started taking courses required to enter premed at the university. She passed algebra and geometry, calculus, biology, chemistry, physics, but Alma was concerned that with both school and work, she was neglecting her son, whose basic sweet nature was becoming more and more obscured by his growing need to be exactly like every other twelve-year-old boy – in other words, a little pendejo. To a mother's eye, this unattainable desire left him as vulnerable as a baby bird. Reluctantly, Alma short-circuited her dream, training to become an x-ray technician so she would have more time to worry about her son every moment he was out of her sight.

And as Billy got older, Alma noted with satisfaction, he was no longer quite so willing to leave his friends in Tucson to run off to his father and nana Fufi in Las Cruces, though, Alma did have to give la suegra her due. Somehow, she had managed to teach Billy to cook – not just frijoles either, but anything else he might want to go with them, including slightly misshapen, but perfectly delicious tortillas, which he made by the dozens, swearing his mother to secrecy. And la suegra had taught the boy to iron, a most useful skill, since Billy now insisted that every article of clothing he wore, over and under, be pressed to a knife's edge.

So if she missed Rudy, missed his caresses, the warm belly that fit so snugly against her back, the erect penis bumping against her spine, awakening her in the middle of the night,

Alma was too busy with her new job and her son's emerging adolescence, to dwell on it. Los hombres vienen y salen, aún mueren, pues, pero los hijos se quedan para siempre, ¿verdad?

As for Rudy, he had to hire someone to oversee half of the construction sites, business was so good. So much work, he didn't have time to be lonely, though he thought of Alma often, her beautiful eyes, her lusty appetite. But even as he missed his wife, he found solace, as he had from his earliest years, in his mother's kitchen. After all, women come and go, even singular ones like Alma, but a man has only one mother, que no? And if your mother needs you...? Well, what choice does a man have.

quisás who knows
casi lo mismo almost the same
enojado angry
híjole jeez
pobre mujer poor woman
maricón homosexual
mi chulita my little porkchop
cariño dearest
ni ahora, ni nunca not now, not ever
sopapilla fried dough covered with honey
besos y abrazos kisses and hugs
sagrado or no sacred or not
recuerda dios le dio este spinanzo remember God gave him that spine
los humbres vienen y salen, aún mueron, pero los hijos se quedan para siempre, men come and go, even die, but sons are forever

El Milagro de la Rosa

Por un Amor
(Gilberto Para)

Por un amor he llorado gotitas de sangre del corazón
Me has dejado con el alma herida sin compasión

She's singing about how he broke her heart so bad her
heart cried tears of blood, blah, blah, blah. This women
is such a chillona, except I know exactly how she feels.

Lety

LETY LAY CROSSWISE ON THE bed, stomach down. She reached for
her iPod, which was on the wicker basket she used as a nightstand. The little stretch hurt every muscle and she grimaced as
she popped in the little earbuds. For the fourth time this morning, Lola Beltran begged her lover to return.

"Volver," Lola pleaded.

"Volver, volver, volver," Lety sang, but she was too sore
and tired to match the anguish and emotion required by the

words of the song. She adjusted the earbuds then let her head fall onto the pillow. Her back was aching from lying on her stomach for so long, but she had no choice. The burns she had gotten on her backside when the metal rivets on the pocket of her skin-tight jeans had melted, prevented her from lying any other way.

I should be grateful to be alive, she thought. But it was hard to be grateful under the circumstances.

Everybody was saying it was a miracle. But Lety thought miracles were supposed to bring good. She didn't see anything good about being struck by lightning. And why only her? She hadn't been the only one standing under the chinaberry tree. Alma had been right next to her and felt nothing more than the hair raise on her scalp. And there had been no warning, no rain, and the sky above them was clear, except for that one little black cloud. It seemed to Lety that she had spent most of her life standing under that little black cloud.

Some miracle. It was more like a punishment. It reminded her of school. She had always been the one singled out, the one sent to the office for talking, the one given detention for ditching, the one suspended for having a pint of Jose Cuervo in her locker. She hadn't been the only one talking, the only one ditching. That tequila hadn't even been hers; it had belonged to her boyfriend, Chuy. Of course, she couldn't tell on Chuy. She had been in love with Chuy, so she took the blame, even though she had taken only a single sip from the bottle.

Some miracle! Miracles are rare, but punishments are as common as chinaberries. Lety could not deny she probably deserved to be punished; everybody in Barrio Anita knew her sin. But she was not the only one guilty of that particular pecado.

Even Alma had done that one. A sin is a sin, ¿qué no? And whether or not you get paid for doing it shouldn't make a difference, pues.

Lety closed her eyes for what seemed like seconds and was startled awake by the banging of the screen door.

"Leticia?" The old woman stood at the door to the bedroom, hands hanging loosely in front of her as if bits of masa from this morning's tortillas still clung to them. "Are you awake?"

Groaning, Lety pulled the plugs from her ears. "Ay, tía, I am now."

"Sorry, mija. I just wanted to see how you are before I go to church. Put a clean bandage on your poor nalga, rub some salve on your feet. Have you been to the toilet?"

"Por Dios, yes."

"Don't be mad. I'm just asking."

"Lo siento, tía. Thank you for coming. Ven. Dame un beso."

The old woman came around the bed and pressed her dry lips to Lety's cheek while Lety kissed the air. Her aunt smelled faintly of Johnson and Johnson's foot powder, roasted chiles and urine. The familiar odor brought Lety a small degree of comfort.

"I brought you tortillas y frijoles. Are you hungry? The tortillas are still warm. Want I should heat up the frijoles now?"

"Gracias tía, but not now. My arms are like Señora Cruz' buñuelos, too heavy to lift to my mouth, besides, beans give me gas, and it even hurts to fart. I'll eat them maybe later."

"I'll just put your medicine, pues." Lety caught a glimpse of her aunt's flowered housedress. The dress, she knew, was protected by a cotton towel pinned to her chest, which tía Sofía would only remove at the last possible moment before entering the church. She would stuff the towel into the woven plastic shopping bag she carried instead of a purse and put it right back on the moment she left the vestibule. Once a day Sofía would replace the towel with a clean one. Each week, seven towels, it never varied.

This woman was not really her aunt, but the second wife of her father's first cousin, or something like that. To Lety, who never knew either of her real grandmothers, she was like the nana she never had, though she called her tía, a title given out of love and respect. Everyone except her own son called the old woman tía.

Tía Sofía set the gauze patch on the bed and unscrewed the cap from a tube of smelly ointment she had purchased at Botanica Evita. Gently she lifted each foot and inspected the place where the lightning had entered Lety's body. "These ones on your feet are looking better today." She rubbed a little salve on each burn, then lifted the Lety's nightgown and gently peeled the old bandage off her rump.

"Ay, Madre de Dios," the old woman said crossing herself numerous times.

"What? What is it? What's wrong?"

"Madre de Dios, Leticia."

"What? ¿Por Dios, qué pasa, vieja?"

"Madre de Dios, Leticia. A rose."

"A rose?" Lety thought of the little metal rivets on her pocket of her jeans that formed the outline of a rose. "Let me see. Bring me the mirror."

"You see I was right, mija. Fué un milagro. Didn't I tell you? Now here is the sign, la rosa de la Virgen. Nuestra Señora de Guadalupe has put one of her roses on your nalga. Un milagro de seguro." The old woman crossed herself again three times for emphasis.

"Hold the mirror so I can see. Over to the left a little. Now up." With difficulty, Lety was able to turn her head just enough to get a view, and there, indeed, was the outline of a rose, still puffy and red, but clearly branded on her right cheek. The realization hit Lety almost as hard as the bolt of lightning.

"Goddamn," she whispered reverently.

Tía Sofía was pushing the mop around Lety's little kitchen floor. "You got to call your cousin Jonny. He can build you a shrine. It should go right under that chinaberry tree to mark the spot."

Jonny was not her cousin, but tía Sofía's youngest and only living son, and Lety did not want to call him. She did not want to go on and on about this miracle business. She did not want to bring all this attention to herself, and she did not want Jonny, in particular, to build a shrine to la Virgencita in her backyard.

"Jonny will be happy to come up and build you a shrine. It's the least you can do para la Virgen, after all she has done for you."

All the Virgin has done for me, Lety thought, remembering the terrible burning that charged through her body. She remembered looking up into her neighbors' dark, scowling faces, and trying to understand, trying to form the question: ¿Qué está pasando? Then she was drifting up into the chinaberry tree where she lit on a limb and watched the whole scene play out beneath her. Watched as Alma lightly slapped her face; watched as Alma's son dragged the hose across the ragged patch of grass and sprinkled water over her. She heard them call her name, saw the straining backs as they picked her up and carried her into the house. Then she jumped out of the tree and floated after them, hovering just above their heads. When the ambulance arrived, she climbed in after her own body. The memory scared the hell out of her.

All la Virgen did for me, Lety thought, was knock me on my ass and nearly kill me. But she didn't say this. Her aunt would be hurt by such disrespect. Instead she complained. "But it's long distance to call. Besides, Jonny doesn't have time to come up from Nogales; he's got a business to run." Jonny's business was salvage. He got paid on the U.S. side to haul off trash, which he then sold on the Mexican side. Bald tires were his specialty. He worked hard, six days a week, and rested on the seventh, which may or may not be a Sunday.

"Jonny will do it. He owes la Virgen a favor. He is not without sin either, mija," she said, patting the back of Lety's hand a bit too firmly.

How could Lety deny this woman's simple request? She would do it, not out of gratitude to la Virgen, but out of gratitude to her tía. It was her tía, not la Vírgen, who was always there in her time of need. It was the old lady who had taken her in when she first came to Tucson, pregnant with her second child. How well she remembered those endless months — the bed she had shared with tía Sofía's daughter, Regina, who was sweet, but so mensa, she drooled if she tried to do two things at once, the geraniums and avocados sprouting on every windowsill, the candles for twelve different saints burning day and night, the shadows waltzing on the ceiling, and everything, living and dead, competing with her for every breath of air.

Still, her tía had done everything in her power for Lety, and though it had not been within the old woman's power to do much, Lety appreciated her willingness to share what she had, for it's what's in the heart that matters. ¿Qué no? And if that had not been enough for a seventeen-year-old girl with one child clinging to her knees and another clinging to her by his navel, it was not the fault of her tía.

And tía Sofía was practically a saint. The woman had been a widow for more than twenty years. By virtue of her chastity and piety she had regained the respect one gives to a virgin while attaining the authority and deference of an old woman who is a mother to many. Such a woman was herself deserving of a shrine.

"Okay. I'll put a shrine, but not a great big one. A little shrine is all I can afford. My kids come first, you know."

Lety thought of the daughter and son she supported with the wages of her sin. She visited them every month without fail, and without fail she provided one hundred dollars to her mother in Nogales for their care. She never spent a penny of her earnings on herself until she had five twenty-dollar bills in the coin purse she kept in the refrigerator tucked inside a loaf of whole wheat bread. Lety bought a new loaf every month expressly for the purpose of hiding her coin purse there, knowing a loaf of whole wheat bread was the last thing anyone looking in her refrigerator would ever touch, even by accident, even if they were half-starving.

Twenty dollars. With her looks she could charge more, but the price kept her off the streets. Her clients were regulars, no bad surprises. Even the occasional new face was a friend of a friend. The worst that ever happened to her was somebody slapped her a couple of times and refused to pay because he was too drunk to get a hard on. Pendejos, they always blamed the women. Even her friend Alma, who never charged a single penny, had experienced worse from this or that one who swore he loved her, a black eye one time, and once her VCR was stolen right from under her snoring nose. Alma sure did snore.

No, twenty dollars kept things simple. And there was no overhead. Word of mouth was her pimp.

"So you going to call Jonny?"

"I'll call, but remember I can't afford much."

"You know I always keep a little money tucked away for just in case. Let me help. Helping others and my garden are all that are left for me to enjoy in my old age.

Lety took her aunt's hand. She knew the old woman's passion in life was to be of use, as clearly as she knew her own destiny was to be used.

"No tía, you keep your money. A little shrine I can afford."

Lety sat on her back stoop, arms dangling between her legs, as Jonny placed the last tire in the trench that encircled the little brick shrine he had built the week before. He held the tire upright with one hand and troweled dirt around it until it could stand by itself. Lety would have helped him, but she still had some weakness in her muscles, and her joints ached if she did too much work in the heat. It had gotten up to 102 degrees that day, hot for so late in September, so she just sat and watched. Even so she was sweating. If she hadn't drunk most of the quart of Budweiser she had bought for Jonny, her joints would probably be aching right now.

It was just lucky that Jonny, who could put away plenty of beers, had refused her offer. "I can't drink beer while performing an act of devotion," he had said. She knew from experience that Jonny had a pretty wild side to him, but he had a serious side too. It made him the successful businessman he was, and when he took religion, he took it from this serious side. Lety sipped her beer, grateful to be the beneficiary of his piety and sat back to watch the muscles in his back and arms play beneath his thin T-shirt. Jonny's body had thickened over the years, but that never bothered Lety. Strong, brown, solid and nearly hairless, it was still a beautiful thing to behold.

"Hey, Lety," he said, stripping off the T-shirt and using it to wipe his face. "Bring that can of spray paint from the bag by the door."

Lety took the can from the bag. Appliance White, the label said. It was the color of purity. She hauled herself off the stoop. Jonny was standing under the chinaberry tree, sweat running off his head, down through his sparse chest hairs and over his rounded belly. "There," he said, stamping the ground around the tires. "You can paint them, while I have me some beers."

"I thought you couldn't drink during this act of devotion."

"I'm finished with this act of devotion, so now I can have some beers."

Lety looked at the ground. "It's too hot to paint right now. I'm still weak in the muscles. You finish up, and then I'll get you a nice cold one, huh, Jonny?"

Jonny took another swipe at his head with the T-shirt then trailed it across his chest and under his arms. "Ay, hijo de puta, Lety. You drank the whole quart, didn't you?"

"Yes, but by the time you finish painting the tires, I can get some more." She patted his damp shoulder and went inside for her wallet, happy to get more beer. She could use another cold one herself.

Lety took two long necks from the carton and went out the back door. For a moment, she stood on the stoop to let the total effect sink in. The little red brick house was neat and sturdy. It looked like it could stand forever there in the sanctuary of shade beneath the chinaberry tree. The tire fence was now as white as the Immaculate Conception. All that was needed was la Virgencita and her roses.

She handed Jonny a beer and pulled two wire chairs into the shade. They had once been white too, but now the paint was chipped and rust bled through the cracks. "Looks good, Jonny, a perfect little house for a lady, with a perfect little white fence. I should get me a little white pit bull to put in her yard to keep the bandidos out, ¿qué no, Jonny?"

Jonny smiled and offered his bottle to click against hers in a toast. For a moment they sipped their beer, quietly appreciating the shrine, the shade and a breeze that cooled the afternoon.

"My mother tells me you've got a rose on your ass. Un milagro, she tells me. I'm a pretty good Catholic. I believe in miracles, but I've never seen one. Can I see yours?"

"¡Ay Cabrón! You can go to hell, is what you can do." Lety smiled and licked the top of her beer bottle.

The screen door slammed and tía Sofía appeared on the stoop, the thick elastic stockings she wore to ease the veins in her legs wrinkling at her skinny ankles. She waited for her sun-blinded eyes to penetrate the purple shade beneath the tree. "Mijitos, are you out there?"

"Aquí, Mamá," Jonny called and handed his beer to Lety. "Out by the shrine." He pulled on his shirt. "Come out and see." He got up and made his way to assist his mother to a chair.

"Ay, it's beautiful, mijo." She hugged his arm and sat in a chair.

"Can I get you a beer, tía?" Lety offered and rose from her own chair.

"No Leticia, just water. I'm on my way to church. I just wanted to see the beautiful shrine. I left tamales de elote on the table." she said, looking at Lety. "Are you drinking two beers at a time these days, Leticia, or does the extra one belong to my son?

Never mind. I'd have one myself, but in this heat it would make me *borracha*. Sit down, Leticia. Jonny will get me water."

The old woman drew a Kleenex from between the buttons of her housedress and patted her face. "So hot for September, but it's nice here in the shade, beautiful by the shrine and peaceful. Wait till we have la Virgen and her roses. It will be even more beautiful. ¿Qué no, mijos?"

Jonny had decided to escort his mother to church. Just as well, Lety thought, as she picked up a tamale. It was hardly bigger than her two fingers together, and still warm. She peeled off the cornhusks and ate it in two bites.

Lety rubbed the film of grease on her fingers into her palms and opened a drawer. From beneath a stack of bills she removed two photos, each a baby with the squinty expression of the newly born. From the back of the drawer she pulled two more. One, a school picture, showed a little boy, grinning widely despite the absence of one front tooth. The other was of a little girl in the white dress of her first Holy Communion. That little girl now had breasts. "Aye, the years are passing too quickly."

Lety rummaged through the drawer and found first a blue and then a pink plastic identification bracelet. She returned the pictures to the drawer and dropped the little bracelets into the pocket of her blouse. From the counter, she picked up a heavy serving spoon.

Though it was nearly dark, the glow from the white tire fence guided her to the shrine. There, within the shelter of the little brick house, she dug a hole with her kitchen spoon, just deep enough and wide enough to hold the little bracelets. She coiled each into the hole before covering them with dirt, then patted the surface smooth with her hand. As an afterthought, she drew a cross over the spot with her finger. Tomorrow she would encircle it with the little turquoise colored stones that outlined her flowerbed so she would always know their exact location.

Lety began to pour coffee into tía Sofía's cup.

"Only half, mija," tía Sofia said. "I have trouble enough sleeping as it is these days. Oh well. Pretty soon I'll be able to sleep forever."

"Don't talk that way," Lety said, pouring a full cup of coffee for herself. "I don't want to hear it."

"You may not want to hear it, but it's true. And I don't mind telling you it doesn't bother me a bit. I'm ready to go. Except for just one thing, I'd die in peace tomorrow, my heart so light it would float all the way to heaven like steam from la tetera."

Lety didn't have to ask what was preventing the old woman's peace of mind. It was not the first time her tía had tried to blackmail her by threatening to die with a heavy heart.

"Mija, listen to me. You had a miracle."

"Don't talk to me anymore about this miracle. I put the shrine. What more do you want from me? Besides, to me I don't think it was a miracle. I mean, miracles are supposed to be good. It makes no sense."

"Well, that's because you've got the wrong idea about miracles. Miracles aren't just loaves and fishes, Leticia. Some miracles hurt."

"Well, the shrine is all I can afford to do. It cost me almost fifty dollars already."

"Fifty? Jonny charged you?"

"Just for the materials. The labor, and of course the tires were free."

"Well, you need at least some candles, a picture of la Virgen. Otherwise it's just a nice little house for a dog, not a shrine."

"Ay, tía. So I'll get me some candles. I already got the picture."

"And you need your kids. And they need you, especially Araceli."

"They're both better off with my mother."

"Leticia, la Virgen has spoken to you. What else could she have had in mind but that you should bring your kids to live with you? You can't ignore the sign, Leticia. She left you that rose so you would remember you are a mother and to start acting like one."

Lety understood that to pretend ignorance of her profession was the only way tía Sofía could continue to hold her head up when she entered the church. This was the closest the two women had ever come to speaking of it, and she had to proceed with care. The old woman loved her like a daughter, but if it came to a choice between Lety and the church, her tía would choose the church for certain. No, she did not want to force the old woman to face the realities of her life.

"I send money, tía. I go see them every month."

"It's not enough, I guess. la Virgencita wants you to do more. She wants you to bring them up."

"I need money. I need a job to bring my kids up here. Who's going to watch over them if I to go to work? But this is stupid. Who will give me a job, anyway? I never even finished high school."

"Maybe you can work for some rich white lady. Do her ironing. Bring your kids over and I'll watch out for them when you go to work. I'm old, but I'm not useless."

"A job ironing? I can't raise two kids on ironing. They're not babies any more. Just their shoes alone... tía, you live in a dream world."

"Okay, so we'll make tamales on the side to sell at the grocery store. People do it all the time. They make good money, too. Those gringos pay sometimes ten, twelve dollars a dozen. We should make some green corn. The chiles are in from Hatch this week at Food City, and we can pick us up some seven-day candles too. The Costco's got them for a dollar nineteen."

"Ay madre," Lety sighed and she began to calculate. Ten dollars for a dozen tamales. Two dozen tamales equals one man. Ten dozen tamales to make a hundred bucks. How long would it take her to do ten dozen tamales? Certainly lots longer than it would take her to do five men.

Lety was sitting in front of the television with her hands soaking in a bowl of tea leaves when someone banged on the screen door.

"Who is it?" She shouted over the noise from the television.

"It's me, Jonny. I got my hands full. Let me in."

She put the bowl on the floor. Shaking her hands in the air, she went to unlatch the screen.

Jonny entered holding two quart bottles of Budweiser in his hands. A large paper wrapped package was tucked under one arm. "Take these," he said, handing her the beer. The package he set on the kitchen table.

"What you got there, Jonny?"

"For the shrine. Take off the paper and see."

Lety peeled the paper from around the Virgin of Guadalupe who was balancing serenely on her half moon. Around her head and shoulders was a blue cape studded with golden roses. "Ay, she's so beautiful, Jonny, but so big. Will she fit?"

"She'll fit. I measured, but leave her for now. I want one of them beers."

Lety could see by the way his eyes drooped that he'd had more than one beer already. So much the better, she thought, then said, "Go sit down. I'll bring it to you." Lety unscrewed the cap from one and put the other two in the refrigerator.

She took a swig from the bottle. Leaning over, she stuck her cold tongue in his ear. "Thanks, Jonny." Lety handed him the bottle and put her hands back in the bowl of tea leaves.

"What did you do to your hands?"

"La madre loca tuya. She wants me to help her make tamales to sell. We must have peeled five hundred chiles this morning, and my hands are burning like fire. Damn chiles."

"What does she need to sell tamales for? I send her plenty of money to get by. Jonny rose from the chair taking a long pull from the beer. "Here," he said, handing the bottle to Lety. "Put your hands around this. I'll get me another."

"So how's your miracle, woman?" he shouted from the kitchen. "You going to let me see it this time?"

"That depends."

Jonny returned with his beer and stood behind Lety's chair. "Depends on what?" he said and poured a little of his beer down the front of her blouse.

"¡Ay pinche cabrón!" she said laughing. "Get away from me."

Jonny pulled her hair into a knot around his fist and rolled his cold beer bottle along the nape of her neck. "Depends on what? I'd pay twenty bucks to see a miracle." He tucked his hand beneath her breast.

Lety brushed his hand away and stood to face him, her fingers curling around his belt. "Look Jonny. I need money. The reason your mother wants to sell tamales is because she thinks that'll bring in enough money so I can have my kids here. That and me doing ironing for some gringa."

"That's crazy. My mother's crazy."

"Not so crazy, Jonny. I could do it, but I need more than I can make with tamales and ironing. I thought maybe if you'd pay me some money each month, you know for Eddie."

"You mean like child support?"

"Si pues. A hundred dollars a month. I could make it, maybe get a part-time."

"I won't pay you fifty cents a month," he said, pushing her hands away. "Who says Eddie's my son? You? Los hijos de putas no tienen padres."

"He's your son. All you have to do is look at him to know it. But I don't want your money anyways. Just get the fuck out of my house. Take your money and pay your wife what you owe her. If she sleeps with you, she's a worse whore than me."

Jonny slapped her hard across the side of her head.

"Don't like the sound of the truth, Jonny?" Lety's ear was ringing so loudly her own voice sounded to her like was shouting through a pillow. "I know who the fathers of my kids are."

"Then get Chuy to pay.'"

"Chuy! Chuy's dead."

"So you say. And you'll get your hundred dollars from him before you see it coming from me."

"Cheap bastard. You know what, Jonny? You're a fucking liar, that's what. And you know what else? You're right. You're not my son's father, but I know who my son's father is. Can your wife say the same?"

He knocked her down so fast, Lety was unsure whether it was the impact of the blow or her head hitting the floor that caused bright lights to dance in front of her eyes. Before she could move, she felt his hand pulling at her jeans. He peeled them to her ankles with one hand, and grabbing her hair, he yanked her to her knees with the other.

"You been listening too hard to my mother, Lety. That ain't no rose on your nalga. It ain't nothing but an ugly scar." He pulled out his wallet, removed twenty dollars and dropped it on the floor by her knee. "The only thing I'll ever pay you for is a piece of your ass."

She heard the rumble of Jonny's truck as he peeled away, heard his tires squeal when he rounded the corner. The ringing in her ear had stopped and she was no longer dizzy, but she did not move.

So, it's come to this, she thought. How simple-minded love is. Once I lived for him. For a little while, my love for him was my glory. For a long time it was my burden, and now? Lety could actually feel the burden of love lifting. She was free of it at last. But freedom felt more like a congestion in her chest, not all lighthearted, not good at all. It hurt. "Must be another goddamn miracle," she said, rubbing the knot that was rising on the side of her forehead.

And what about the rose? She had seen it herself. Maybe it had faded. Miracles fade, she guessed.

She rolled over and pulled her feet free from the jeans. With effort, she got up and made her way into the bedroom for the hand mirror. Angling it to her backside, she inspected the burn. Jonny was right. There was no rose, only a big, ugly scar.

She put the mirror down on the dresser and picked up the candle she had bought at the grocery. The Virgin of Guadalupe was on the front. Turning the candle in her hand, she traced the golden edge of her mantle with her fingernail. Maybe she should fill her house with seven-day candles and geraniums like her tía. Maybe start acting like a widow. Her first man was dead, at least that's what she'd always told herself. And now her second was just as good as dead, so cold he lay in her heart.

Lety took up the mirror again and spoke to her reflection. "Maybe you could charge twenty bucks for a look at your big milagro." She laughed hoarsely, her eyes burning.

Some miracle. It would take a miracle to support herself and her kids on tamales. Jonny had been right about that too. Lety considered her options. She could just let things stay as they were. Her children were safe. They were clothed, schooled, fed, que no? But she was alive when she should be dead, pues. La Virgen must have intervened.

Maybe she could go back to school, get training as a bilingual secretary like she always wanted. She could see herself sitting behind a glass-topped desk with a rose in a bud vase, pictures of her kids in heart-shaped frames and a telephone to answer. She would wear dresses and high heels. Get her hair and nails done once a week. Meet men who would take her out for a steak dinner, men who liked to dance and have a little fun before they expected you to get in bed with them.

Maybe she would do that. Go back to school. She'd have to put aside a little nest egg first. And she couldn't do that if the kids were living with her, could she? No. So the kids would continue to stay with their nana for a while longer. Tía Sofía and la Virgencita would just have to wait. That's all. They couldn't expect a miracle overnight. Even the Virgin needed nine months to give birth.

Again she studied her backside, holding the mirror at different distances, playing with the angles. Through the window, the late afternoon sun streamed, dust motes twirling in its mellow light. She tried reflecting this light on her rump. Finally, she closed one eye, squinting the other just a little. Gradually, almost petal by petal, it began to take shape, a single, nearly perfect rose.

———◆———

chillona crybaby
fué un milagro it was a miracle
los hijos de putas no tienen padres the children
of whores don't have father

LOS SACRAMENTOS SECRETOS

———

Plegaria
(traditional)

...Traigo estas flores de mi jardín
A tu santuario con devoción
Vengo buscando consuelo a mis males,
El amparo de tu protección...

A woman – who else – is bringing flowers to the Virgin
and asks for her advice and protection.

– Lety

LETY HAD JUST PUT HER purse in the oven when she heard the car
door slam. She pulled the curtain back. Tía Sofía and her daughter, Regina, were coming up the walk. "Damn," she whispered,
and wondered if she could hide in the backyard until the women
left. Before she could make it to the back door, her aunt was letting herself in the front.

"Oh, Leticia, you startled me. I didn't think you'd be home yet," tía Sofía, said looking around the living room.

"I just walked in the door. The house is a mess." Lety didn't want them to think she hadn't noticed the dust and the clutter that had been building up since school had started.

"Too busy to clean now with your new job," she observed, extracting from her bolsa a dozen tortillas and a mayonnaise jar of her homemade sopa de arroz con pollo. "Mijita," she said to Regina. "Put these in the kitchen." Then turning to Lety, "We need to talk."

"¿Qué pasa?"

"Tu mamá. It's back."

"What's back?"

"The cáncer, pues, what else?"

"Are you certain?"

"I can see it in her eyes."

Lety lowered her head into her hands.

"And her house is dirty," Regina added, as she passed through the living room on her way to the bathroom

"Dirty?"

"A rat's nest," tía Sofía confirmed. "This is not like your mother. Always so clean."

"I should go to her. Take care of her."

"No Mija. Not yet. She'll need you later, when it's closer to her time, and you got your job and your school. What's more important is that you start making a place for your kids. Tus pequeños compromisos, they're not so little anymore. ¿Requerdas tu manda? Pues, it's time to keep it."

Her vow, of course she had not forgotten. When her children became old enough to wonder about all the tíos, padrinos, primos y amigos de la familia who were coming nightly to visit her, she had taken them to Nogales to live with her mother. It was supposed to be temporary, but time had slipped by disguised as dreams and hopes. Her daughter, Araceli, was nearly sixteen now. Her son, Eddie, lately seemed older than his fourteen years, and well beyond the need for a mother. When they were little, they begged to come home with her each time she visited. But now? Lety was afraid she had lost any claim she once had on their love. Would they allow her to fulfill her promise to la Virgencita and bring them back to live with her?

Sofía touched her hand. "No longer children, but not old enough to take care of their dying nana."

"Dios, yo sé, tía, pero…"

"¿Pero?"

Regina poked her head into the living room. "The bathroom mirror is dirty, Lety. Where's the Windex?"

"You don't have to clean the mirror, Regina. Sit down and relax, querida."

"Let her clean. ¿Quires café, Leticia? I'll make us some."

There was nothing to do but let these women have their way. Neither would leave her alone until the bathroom was clean, the coffee gone and a plan made to bring her children home at last. "Gracias, tía. And Regina, querida," she said, putting her arm around the woman's slim shoulder and kissing her cheek. "Thank you. You are so good to me, both of you."

Lety and Regina stood side by side in front of the little shrine under the chinaberry tree. Lety placed a candle, the kind that last seven days, in front of la Virgen and crossed herself before saying the first novena on behalf of her mother. When she opened her eyes, Regina was peering at the ceiling where the smoke of countless candles had blackened the brick.

"What are you doing?" she asked.

"I hear that sometimes She will appear in the soot from las velas."

"Who?"

"La Virgen, pues. Who else?"

"Listen, querida, I don't need another miracle," she said, recalling the day she had nearly died right beneath this very tree.

"How did it feel, when the lightning hit you?"

Lety shook her head and whispered, "I was burning. My whole body. Then I went numb. That was when God lifted me up."

"Can I see your scar? Mamá says it was un milagro. La Virgen put a rose."

"I don't go around dropping my pants no more, pues." Regina looked hurt and she quickly added. "Besides, it's not a miracle, just an ugly old scar. The real miracle, you can't see."

Regina nodded her head. "My brother, Jonny, says the real miracle is that you ain't no puta no more."

Regina arranged the roses from her mother's garden in the large vase, replacing the ones she had put there the day before yesterday. Now yesterday's yellow ones and today's red ones flanked the statue of la Virgen balancing gracefully on her crescent moon. Of all the statues in the church, this was Regina's favorite. So beautiful la Virgen in her robe of blue, star spattered satin and creamy-white mantle, her face alight with grace. Only her beseeching eyes betrayed the depth of her loss and sorrow.

Regina, lips wet and soft, rearranged the roses. In the jewel-washed light of stained glass, she still looked very much like a young girl, slim hipped and raven haired, with a face unlined by worldly care. She loved this church, this light. Loved to inhale the warm perfume of the velas, dozens of them burning beneath the holy portraits and statues adorning the walls and niches. Within the quiet, she would dream the lives of saints.

This habit of dreaming had developed many years ago when she and her family still lived in Nogales. Briefly she had attended a school where she was to learn self-sufficiency by weaving colorful place mats from old rags. Though no one treated her unkindly, she found the other students frightening. Some could not talk plainly. Some could talk only with their hands. Others could not walk without lurching forward. There was one boy with a huge head, which bobbled when he laughed and he laughed at almost everything. The boy's laughter was more frightening to Regina than the size of his head, for she could not understand what he was laughing about. Was he laughing at her?

To calm herself, Regina would consider the lives of saints, especially the holy martyrs, whose deeds were summarized on the devotional cards she had been collecting since childhood. She tried to be like them – accepting, kind, brave and concerned only with God. Day after day she tried, but each day her fear grew until it was like torture. Every day she would cry and her mother would ask, "¿Qué haces?"

Everyday Regina would answer, "No sé."

Pues, how could she explain? Did she really belong among these mensos? The very notion made her cry and beg to stay home. At last her mother relented. Instead of going to school, she was allowed to help with the roses, the tortillas, the cleaning. What little formal schooling she had had was supplied by Sister Agrippina who taught catechism every Wednesday afternoon.

She was no longer afraid, but the sameness of her days that comprised years, 43 of them now, had created a longing for some extraordinary event that would transform her. This longing had become almost as torturous as the old fear.

Regina stepped back from the altar and began to recite the rosary. Soon she heard an even tread on the tiled floor, but didn't turn away from her prayers until the familiar hand touched her shoulder.

"Buenos días, mijita," said Father Tom. Though he was not a Mexican, he spoke flawless Spanish. Instead of priestly attire, today he wore a white guayabera, starched and expertly ironed by his housekeeper.

"Buenos días, Padre," Regina said, eyes shining. "I brought the roses."

"As always, but today you're early."

"Yes, we have to go to Nogales to deliver clothing to the poor and clean my cousin Zulema's filthy house because the rats are building nests there."

"Ah, yes. Your cousin Zulema. I remember your mother saying... but I might have missed you and that would have been a shame, for you are la Virgen's most perfect rose, Regina, sencilla y inmaculada."

Regina smiled at the priest. She loved the way he spoke to her, loved his voice, soft and deep close to her ear.

"Well then, mijita, do you have time to pray with me before you go?"

Regina nodded and followed him into the garden where he always took her to pray within an arbor bending beneath its burden of scarlet bougainvillea.

Jonny was already waiting by the window when his mother and sister pulled into the drive. As always he was in a hurry. He helped the old woman out of the car and kissed her cheek. "Buenos días, Mamá. How was the drive?" he said, trying to keep the impatience from his voice.

"Long and getting longer. ¿Cómo estas, mijo?"

"Bien, Mamá, bien." He opened the trunk and removed the large carton of used clothing his mother had collected. "Just busy is all."

"What else is new? And Mari, how is she, y los chamacos?"

"Everybody's fine. And you, mi gallinita, hola," he said, opening his arms for his sister's embrace.

"Ay, Jonny," Regina said smiling. "No soy una gallinita, soy una mujer."

"If you say so," he said. But to Jonny, she would always be his little chicken. Though he was the baby brother, from the time he could make a hard fist, he had watched over her, protecting her from the ones who might point a finger or take advantage. That's just the way things were. She would remain la gallinita and his burden until death took one of them.

Turning to his mother he asked, "You ready to go?"

"Coffee first, Jonny, then we have to take Regina over to Zulema's."

"I'm kind of in a hurry, and Zulema's is in the opposite direction. Next time she can go visit with Zulema."

"She needs to go today so she can clean Zulema's house. Since... tu sabes," she said, making a slicing gesture over her chest, "It seems like Zulema got no strength to do it for herself. Araceli, well she's got school, and she has to do all the cooking and shopping. And Eddie, pues. You know Eddie."

"Eddie? Why are you always picking on Eddie?"

"I'm not picking on anybody. Eddie is just Eddie. I'm sure he doesn't even see the dirt. In the meantime, Zulema's not getting any better and everybody's seems too much in a HURRY these days and too BUSY to help out."

"So where's Lety been?" He said, ignoring his mother's efforts to make him feel guilty. "I suppose she's too busy to come down and take care of her own mother?"

"Oh Jonny, didn't cousin Lety tell you?" Regina asked. "She's got a new job."

"Oh? And what kind of job would this be, I wonder?"

"A real job this time," said Sofía. "She's a campus monitor now."

"Sounds important," he said, sucking his teeth. "More important than cleaning her mother's house, I guess."

"I said this is a real job. She can't just take off work cuando quiere."

"Neither can I."

"Pues, Zulema needs our help today. She's very weak, mijo."

"She'll snap out of it."

"Almost six months, it's been."

"It takes time."

"Time, mijo? Face it. Zulema's time is running out."

"¿Qué estás diciendo?"

"She's dying, mijo."

"Dying?" It never occurred to Jonny that Zulema would die, ever. When had he last seen her? He tried to think. What was it two, three weeks ago, certainly not more than a month. Sure, she'd seemed tired, but dying? "Ni modo."

"She's dying. But then we're all dying. It's only the dead who are free of it. ¿Qué no?"

"But Zulema. She's still so…"

"When did you say you last saw her?"

"A couple of weeks, maybe."

"A couple of weeks maybe? If that's so, when you saw her last, you didn't really look. The cancer is back, I'm telling you."

"No disrespect, Mamá, but since when did you become a doctor?"

"Have it your way, mijo. The cancer's not back and Zulema's not dying. Now, do I get a cup of coffee o no?"

When Zulema opened the door her face was carefully made up, brows two thin black arches, lips full and red, cheeks a little too heavily rouged. Jonny could smell the rose water she always combed through her hair, which today she wore pulled back from her face with two silver combs. Still beautiful, but how thin she'd become since he'd last seen her.

"Well, tía Sofía and Regina," she said offering her cheek. "And who's this stranger?"

"Stranger?" said Jonny. "It hasn't been that long."

"Don't worry, Jonny. I know how busy you are. Work, work, work. Come in, pues. We can have a nice visit."

"I'll make coffee," said Sofía, already halfway to the kitchen. "Regina, why don't you start in the bathroom? Where do you keep the cleaning supplies, Zulema? Regina's going to do a little housework while she's here."

"Forget it, tía, I'm not so far gone I can't clean my own house, como alguna gringa rica. It's just that I've been feeling lazy lately."

"Let Regina do it. She loves to clean. Right, mija?"

¡"Simón! ¿Tienes Windex, Zulema?"

Jonny looked at his watch. Nearly ten o'clock already. He tried to sit back and relax, but there was that truckload of used tires he had promised to deliver before noon and after that, a dozen more promises to keep. Even as his eyes saw the truth in the sagging flesh on Zulema's once plump arms, he was impatient to leave. Perhaps it was this truth that made him impatient, made his throat thicken and his eyes sting. Zulema, his first woman, the only woman he had ever truly loved.

He remembered the first time he had seen her. She was living on the other side back then, in a shack in la Colonia del Sol. Didn't have ten pesos to put to her name, pero que guapa. ¡Y las chichis! They spilled out of her blouse every time she leaned over, and to his sixteen-year-old brain, it seemed she was leaning over all the time. How he longed from the first moment to place his hands on those soft mounds of velvet flesh, to bury his face between them and breathe in her scent of roses and beneath that her own fragrance of dark earth.

Even though those breasts were gone now, he would never forget the way she was that first day. He had always loved her, would have married her. But Zulema never wanted to marry him or any man as far as he knew. For so many years they had been lovers, their loving joyful and simple as breathing. From now on, loving her would merely be painful.

Suddenly he could sit in that room no longer. "I've got some business," he said already halfway to the door. "Mamá, you stay here and visit. I'll come back for you in a little while and will take the clothes to the church."

"Momentito, mijo," tía Sofía called. "Ay. He can never sit down for minute. Groaning, she got up and followed him out the door.

Regina spritzed the bathroom mirror with Windex. It was true. She liked to clean. In particular, she liked to clean windows and mirrors. Spritzing again, she inhaled the pure scent, which she loved better than the air after a summer rain. Regina gazed at her reflection as the liquid ran down the glass like aqua tears, her own. She considered these for a moment. Were aqua tears some sort of sign? Probably not, she thought, wiping them away.

For a long time now, she'd been looking for a sign from God that she was one of the chosen ones, like the saints on her holy cards. For weeks, she expected to sweat blood or sweet perfume. Daily she watched for la Virgen to appear with a message for the whole world that could only be delivered through Regina's lips. She looked for Her in candle wax, in the masa she prepared for the daily tortillas, in the scorch marks on the tortillas, in the bark of the chinaberry tree, in the roses she took to church and, of course, in the soot left by las velas.

Last week, she had been pricked by a thorn. She squeezed the tiny wound until a droplet formed, then blotted it with a sheet of white paper to see if a message was there for her. But all she could see was a smear of her own blood. Nothing miraculous there.

Ever since Father Tom had told her that what they did together in the arbor was like the Holy Communion, a special secret sacrament that only the purest of the pure performed, she had been expecting a miracle. Ever since he had touched her, there, in the place her mother had said should never be touched, she had been waiting. But so far, nothing. She was beginning to suspect that there would be no milagros, that the extraordinary, life altering event she'd been so long awaiting, would never occur.

Regina finished cleaning the bathroom, kitchen, dining room and bedroom. Still Jonny and her mother had not returned from delivering the clothing. Only the living room was left, but Zulema was asleep on the couch so Regina could not run the vacuum. She sprayed Endust on a terry rag and slid it across each surface, carefully moving photos aside, porcelain figurines, little glass dishes

that Zulema always filled with candy at Christmas. A small vase
rested on a doily crocheted by Regina's own mother. She picked it
up and wiped it with her cloth as fear uncoiled like a snake inside
her once pure belly. Instead of becoming a saint, she was certain
now that she would be doomed to hell. And her mother! What if
she found out about Father Tom and the things they did in the
arbor? Regina let the vase fall from her hand and started to cry.

Poking his head in the doorway, Jonny called out to his sister.
"Andale, Regina. Mamá is waiting for you in the car." His sister
was sitting on the couch next to Zulema. Both women looked
worn out, and for the first time, Jonny realized that his gallinita
was no longer young. Everybody he loved, it seemed, was growing old and falling apart.

"Ratito, Jonny. Don't be in such a damn hurry, pues!" Zulema
said, gripping Regina's shoulders. "Thank you for my beautiful,
clean house, querida." With a loud smack, she planted a kiss on
each of the woman's pale cheeks. "Everything will be okay. Verás.
Jonny will take care of it. Now, go on."

Regina tried to hurry past Jonny, but he caught her by the
arm. "No kiss for your brother?"

Regina hung her head and hurried out the door.

"Now what does Jonny have to take care of?" He said, turning
to Zulema who was shaking her head. "¿Qué está pasando?"

She sighed. "Go get the tequila, Jonny. We need to talk."

Reluctantly, Jonny shut the door. This day was de la chingada. He retrieved the bottle where it was hidden inside the box of
Bisquick and filled dos copitas. He belted one back, and refilled
it. "¿Qué está pasando?"

"Some Father Tom at your mother's church is putting it to
your sister."

Jonny's eyebrows shot up. "You mean? ¡Ni madre! I don't believe it."

"Believe it! He told her it was some secret sacrament."

"I don't believe it."

"Believe it, I'm telling you."

"¿Está embarazada?"

"No, not pregnant yet, gracias a Dios."

"¡Hijo de la chingada madre!"

"¡Exactamente!"

"How could she be so stupid?"

"Jonny. Your sister is kind of mensa, si! Pero no es estúpida. It's your mother's fault, keeping her at home all these years. And she never explained nothing to her. Don't look at me like that! I'm telling you, Regina hardly knew what's between a man's legs, pues, until ese Father Tom. And he's a priest, right? So Regina did what he told her to do, just like she's always been taught. Secret sacrament. That's what he called it! Somebody should secret sacrament his ass!"

"¡Pinche puto, cabrón!"

"¡Exactamente! So what are you going to do?"

"I don't know yet."

"Pues, whatever you do, don't tell your mother. Regina is afraid of two things. One is that she's going to go to hell when she dies. The other, is that your mother will find out and send her there directly."

Jonny dipped his finger into the bowl of holy water that was just inside the vestibule, then dabbing his forehead, heart, left and right shoulders, kissing the cross his thumb and index finger formed, he walked down the aisle. Normally, he went to confession only twice a year, just before Christmas and just before

Easter. For more confessions than that he saw no need. After all, he was too busy to sin much anymore, and he was healthy, so the chances of his dying unconfessed just weren't that great at the moment.

There were several women ahead of him. As he waited for all of them to finish their confessions, he considered his relation to God, who'd always been kind enough to leave him alone so he could take care of his obligations. From the time he was fifteen he'd seen to it that his mother and sister were well fed, with a good roof that didn't leak over their heads. His wife and kids, they never had to worry about being too cold in the winter or too hot in the summer. They had all the necessities and every reasonable comfort. For this ability to fulfill his compromisos, Jonny was proud, even grateful, though if you were to ask him, he'd say his family – mother, sister, wife, kids, the whole lot – were un dolor en el culo. To Jonny, doing what one thinks is a pain in the ass was better for the soul than confession, and he only hoped God would agree. In fact, though he'd never shared this conviction with anyone, Jonny was almost 100 percent certain that it was not God who invented confession anyway, but some priest who wanted to stick his nose into everybody's bed.

At last the church was empty. Jonny stepped up to the confessional but instead of entering the dark, curtained cubical, he went through the little door to the side, which opened into an adjoining room where a priest sat, seemingly dozing.

"Ay, perdona. ¿Padre Tom?"

"¿Si?" The man stood abruptly as if caught in an illicit act. He was tall, slender, younger than Jonny had imagined he would be.

"I'm the brother of Regina Guerrero."

"Ah, Regina..."

Jonny delivered one punch, a sharp upper cut to the gut, which was unexpectedly soft. The look on the priest's face, a pained surprise, was so totally satisfying that Jonny delivered another blow to his solar plexus. "Just think of this as a confession in reverse," he said, as he watched Father Tom's face turn from red to white. "Now, sin no more, you pinche cabrón, hijo de puta!"

As he walked out of the church, he silently prayed. "Dear God, it was you who gave me this family to take care of. ¿Que no? I'm just trying to do my job. If I'm doing it wrong, forgive me."

Before getting into his truck, he paused to look at the sky. It was the same solid blue it had been an hour ago, the air dry and clear. "Okay, pues," he said, climbing into the cab. He felt good, uplifted even, the way he had felt when he took his first Holy Communion, the body and blood of Christ sweet on his tongue. Like that, like he had just fulfilled a holy sacrament and was beloved in the eyes of God.

When Regina did not eat her supper, not so much as a bite of calabacitas or a nibble of the chile verde that was left over from the night before and especially good, Sofía had had to ask, "¿Qué tienes, mija? You got a bellyache?"

Regina nodded and took the cup of té de yerba buena her mother then offered and went off to bed. The sky was still light. That, coupled with her troubled heart, made sleep impossible. She tossed and rolled, grunted and sighed. Finally, she got up and gathered all of her devotional cards, her favorite ones that were tucked in the frame of her mirror, and stacked them neatly in the palm of her hand. On top was her patrona, St. Regina, whose head had been chopped off by her very own father when

she refused to marry a pagan. But their situations were totally different. Regina's own father was dead and she didn't even
know any pagans. She doubted St. Regina would understand.

Shuffling though the cards, she lay back down on the bed. Here
was St. Agnes who'd been sent to una casa de putas when she would
not give up her faith. But she was only eleven when she was martyred and miraculously still a virgin. Her age, and the fact that St.
Agnes had kept her purity whereas Regina had more or less willing-
ly given hers up, made it unlikely that Agnes could be of any help.
Lucy, Barbara, Catherine, Agatha, Apollonia, all martyrs for the
faith and pure until death. None could understand her pain, her
loss, her fear, she thought, tears beginning to fall. She should have
never confided in Zulema. By now she had probably told Jonny, who
would talk to Father Tom, who would be angry at her for telling the
secret and would surely tell her mother. Or would he? She did not
know. She knew nothing except that she needed someone right now
to talk to, but who could possibly understand?

"Madre de Dios, ayúdame," Regina cried. And she continued
to cry until she was worn out.

It was dark when she was awakened by the smell of Windex
drifting around her bed. Regina felt the mattress give way as if
beneath a heavy weight and the scent of Windex became stron-
ger. Suddenly there she was in all Her splendid glory, la Virgen
de Guadalupe, perched on the edge of Regina's bed.

"Ay, que cochina soy," la Virgen said, scratching at a spot,
dried enchilada sauce perhaps, on her beautiful robe.

"¡Madre de Dios!"

"Si."

"¡Madre de Dios!" Regina cried again, tumbling out of bed
and onto her knees before the holy apparition.

"Get up, comadre. You're embarrassing me, pues."

That voice. So familiar. Regina opened one eye and dared a peek. La Virgen looked uncharacteristically dark and plump. "Cousin Lety?"

"Lety, Madre de Dios, whatevers."

"Pues, what are you doing here?"

"Didn't you pray for somebody to talk to a little while ago?"

"Sí."

"I'm here to answer your prayers, pues."

"Ay Lety... I mean, Madre. What am I going to do? I've committed a mortal sin."

"Prima...hermana...amiga...mija, not a mortal sin. If you committed a sin at all, it's the kind that's way down on the bottom of a long list of sins. The sin of curiosity, the sin of loneliness, the sin of wanting to be someone other than the person you are. That's the nature of your sin. Just forget it, chica."

"But how am I to confess?"

"You already have, mija."

"What about Father Tom?"

"Father Tom? Believe me, his name is at the top of another long list. I saw it there myself."

Regina sighed, tears starting again.

"Mira mija, I know what's in your heart," la Virgen said, taking Regina's face between her two plump hands. "Don't you love God?"

"Sí, pues."

"Aren't you always kind to everyone you meet?"

"I try to be."

"And don't you love to clean?"

"Sí."

"To me, if you are kind, if you love God and love cleaning, you're perfect just the way you are. Believe it, almost a saint." She said, kissing Regina's cheek. "Now go back to sleep, 'cause I'm out of here. You're not the only one calling my name tonight."

Regina awoke as the first rays of sunlight slipped beneath the shade. She inhaled deeply, but the scent of Windex was gone. With her index finger she patted the spot where la Virgencita's lips touched her cheek and felt a slight tingling beneath the skin. "Un milagro," she whispered, and fell immediately back into happy slumber.

"Finally you're up, mija. I was beginning to worry," Sofía said, turning the heat on under the kettle. ¿Como estás?"

"Bien, Mamá, muy bien."

"You must be hungry then. I'll fix you un café con leche and I've been wanting me some huevos con chorizo. How about it?"

"Last night... last night, Mamá, la Virgen de Guadalupe came to me."

"You dreamed of la Virgencita? Que bonito," she said to the stove. "¿Huevos con chorizo, o no?"

"It wasn't a dream, Mamá. She sat on my bed. She kissed my cheek. See?" Regina said pointing to a spot on her cheek.

Wiping her hands on the towel pinned to the front of her dress, Sofía turned to her daughter then. "A mosquito bite. Maybe a little pimple."

"No Mamá, this is the exact spot where Her lips touched my cheek. It couldn't have been a dream."

"Mira, mija. You had a lovely dream. Not everyone gets to see la Virgen even in dreams. Be happy with that."

"But why would she come to me in a dream?"

Sofía took her daughter's face between her rough palms and smiled. "Because you're a good, sweet girl, mija. Of course, She loves you, just like everyone else."

———

pequeño compromisos little obligations
requerdas tu manda remember your vow
queirda dear
sincilla y inmaculada simple and pure
que haces what's the matter
no sé I don't know
gallinita little chicken
chamacos kids
simón of course
que chochina soy what a pig I am

THE LESSONS OF LOVE

Perfidia
(Alberto Domingues)

...si pudes tu con Dios hablar pregúntale
si yo alguna vez te he dejada de adorar y el
mar, espejo de mi corazón, las veces que me
ha visto llorar la perfidia de tu amor.

In this case, the woman has been betrayed big-time, but still loves whoever this person might be. Sometimes we just got to dig deep and forgive people, no matter how badly they've hurt us. Forgive yes, but forget? I don't think so.

– Lety

FROM A CHAIR BY HER mother's bed, Lety watched the woman's chest, flat as a table, rise and fall almost imperceptibly. Sucking her thumbnail, she listened as each breath, a sound, half sigh, half moan, escaped her mother's parted lips. The whispered human lowing shot through with air, filled the little bedroom, bouncing off the walls and piercing Lety's heart like a thorn. She put her face in her hands and sobbed loudly.

Her mother rolled over on her side. "Ya basta, Leticia," she croaked. "Don't you have nothing better to do than sit there and let your nose run onto the sheets?"

"You're awake?"

"How can I sleep with you crying and carrying on like this. Enough is enough."

"Lo siento, Mamá. Can I get you the morphine?"

"Morphine? No, mija, the kind of pain you give me won't be cured by morphine. Ven."

Lety slipped off her shoes and crawled onto the bed beside her mother. "I'm sorry, Mamá."

"Ay, Leticia. I love you with all my heart, you know that, but you make me tired."

Lety pressed her body against her mother's side, stroking the woman's worn face.

"Just promise me before I die. Promise me, Leticia, that you'll make a home for your kids. No more of this fucking strangers for a living."

Lety sat up, the tears suddenly gone. "¡Mamá! I told you already, ¿recuerdas? I got a job now. I'm a campus monitor and I'm going to school at night to become a bilingual secretary. Besides, they weren't strangers, most of them."

"There's a little money for you and the kids. The house goes to Javier, of course."

"Why of course?"

Her mother made a long hiss, like air escaping a tire. "Don't, Leticia."

"Don't? Don't what, Mamá?"

But her mother simply resumed her lowing. Lety lay her head beside the dozing woman, and tried to push down the hard feelings that were creeping up her throat. Damn it, Mamá, she thought. Why can't you just be nice for once so I can feel sad the way I want to? Lety pictured the funeral, she standing above the coffin gazing at her mother's ruined face. The vision restored her grief. She kissed her mother's dry brow, smoothed back the sparse and brittle hairs at her temples. Hardly more than a year ago, the hair had been a rich, lustrous black, like her own.

The woman absently brushed at her brow as if waving away a fly.

Lety rolled over on her back. "Okay, Mamá. Have it your way. I'll leave you alone." She closed her swollen eyes and inhaled the smell of burning candles and Vicks and beneath that, the sweet, rotting earth smell of her mother's dying.

Yesterday her brother, Javier, stopped by. He had presented their mother with a rosebud still in one of those little plastic things to keep it from falling apart until the moment after he walked out the door. The dullness in her mother's eyes had been replaced by the luster of tears as if that rose had been a dozen, and perfect. Not ten minutes he stayed, but Lety could see that those few minutes meant more to her mother than all the services she had so tenderly rendered over the past two weeks. Daily Lety pushed back the cuticles on every finger and scraped beneath each nail. Daily she helped her mother bathe, afterwards smoothing Johnson and Johnson's over her entire body. Daily she rubbed Vicks on her chest and inside her nostrils to ease her breathing. And every day she concocted soups, teas, bowls of jello in every flavor to tempt her appetite. Lety massaged her mother's back, her feet, her head whenever she asked, which was many times daily. All the things Lety had done with great gentleness and care meant nothing in the face of those ten minutes with Javier and that limp rose. But that's the way it had always been.

Lety rolled over and looked at the wall. It was yellow. Not a deliberate yellow, but yellow like the calluses on her mother's heels. She could not remember if the room had always been this color, or if it had happened gradually over the years, fifteen since Lety had run away to Tucson.

She awoke with his hand on her arm and listened for her mother's breathing.

"Leticia," he mumbled.

Lety turned toward the voice. The color had gone from the walls except for a golden oval above the seven-day Vírgin of Guadalupe candle burning on the dresser next to the drooping head of Javier's rose. Its light cast the man's bulky shadow across the bed.

"What time is it?" she asked.

The old Greek shook his lion's head, the slack side of his jaw, swinging loosely. "Levántese," he slurred tugging at her arm. His Spanish had always been garbled, but since his stroke, it had become nearly impossible to understand.

She could smell him, the garlic and the old-man sweat layered beneath the Aqua Velva. Perhaps it was his smell that had turned the walls yellow over the years, she thought as she rose from the bed.

Lety watched the Greek take his place next to her mother. "Ah, Zulema," he sighed, enfolding her slack hand between his own big mitts. He pressed it then over his heart and closed his eyes.

Lety turned away. In the past she had despised this man, but no longer. Over the years, he had given more comfort to her mother than any other. It was only right that he be the one to inhale her final breath. She looked at the two ruins in the bed, her mother a broken reed, the Greek the crumbled remains after a hurricane.

In the living room, Lety's son slept sprawled carelessly across the daybed in the corner. She kissed her fingertips and touched his hair. He wore it long and it fanned across the pillow, dark and thick. Lety went into the back bedroom, which she had been sharing with her daughter. For a moment she rested her head against the doorframe, observing the girl's sleeping form. Araceli lay on her side, knees tucked, one arm across her chest like a shield. Her slim body was all but lost in baggy sweats. How long, Lety wondered, had her daughter been so careful and protective of herself in sleep?

She missed her children. Not these two nearly grown ones, but the ones, hardly more than babies, she'd sent to her mother so long ago. She had meant to come for them years sooner. Now, at sixteen, Araceli was older than Lety had been when she gave birth to her. And Eddie, for years she had only been an occasional visitor in his life. It was probably too late to be more.

Lety slung an ancient afghan around her shoulders. Probably crocheted by Moctezuma's nana, she thought, sniffing at a corner as she settled into the big armchair. The cushions on the chair were sprung and yielded without resistance beneath her weight. What do I care for comfort, she thought, as she sank deeper into the dusty, flowered upholstery. While my mother is dying, there is no comfort.

Dying. She could not even think of the word without the painful pressure in her throat. All those years of ugliness and tears and hateful words between them were ground to powder in the face of it. Leticia had so many regrets, she could count them like sheep and hope sleep would come to her. A net of yellow light cast from the street fell over her head and shoulders. Lety tucked the afghan under her chin and tried to pretend that the next day would bring something better.

A strangled cry sliced though the thickness of sleep, and Lety sprang from the chair toward the candlelight flickering in the predawn gray.

"¡Mamá! ¿Qué pasa? ¡Mamá! Is it the pain? Do you need the morphine?"

"¡Ay, Leticia. Es mi Greco! Ay," she cried, tears streaming down her jaundiced face. "Está muerto, Leticia. He's gone."

"Dead? Are you sure?"

"Of course I'm sure. Look at him! Ay, Dios, how could you do this to me? It's not enough that you take my breasts, my hair? It's not enough that you take my life? You have to take el Greco from me too?" she wailed.

Leticia put her hands to her ears. She could not believe such a force could emanate from so frail a body. Her mother flung herself across her lover's immobile chest.

"Mamá, we've got to get him out of here. What will his wife say?"

Her mother sat up and made a spitting motion over her shoulder. "She had him in life. He chose me in death."

"But Mamá, it's not right."

"Who the hell are you to tell me what's not right!" The woman threw herself across the body once again. "Leave me alone."

Lety turned away. Her children were standing in the doorway. With eyes big and mouths forming imperfect O's, they looked younger than their years. "Ay mijitos, el Greco is dead. Call Cousin Jonny and tell him to come quick."

Lety stood in the kitchen, praying that Jonny could dissuade her mother from this tontería. It would surely kill her, not that she wasn't as good as dead already.

The street lamp blinked off as the weak winter sun peaked over the horizon, turning the haze banked against the hills on the other side of the border a watery sulfur. Serpentine columns of greasy smoke rose from the cooking fires in las colonias de Nogales, Sonora. As a child, they had lived in those hills in a tin and plywood shack.

She filled the kettle for coffee and set it on the burner then took out a carton of eggs from the refrigerator and set out the tortillas. It was early, and Jonny would want something to eat. She heard his heavy step on the stairs, heard the screen door creak, but she did not turn away from the stove.

"Go talk to her, Jonny. You've got to get him out of here!" This was all she said.

Though Lety stood by the door, she heard little other than an occasional wail. After an eternity, Jonny called to her, "Come get the feet." She did and the two half carried, half dragged the corpse out the bedroom door while her mother blew kisses.

"Cuidado, mijitos," her mother cried. "He was a good man, the best, so don't drop him."

Zulema slumped on the pink satin upholstered bench in front of her dressing table. A gift from the Greek, it had a large mirror and elaborately carved wood. She plucked the wig from its stand, and started to tug it in place. "You do it, Leticia, my arms are too heavy."

Lety adjusted the wig, a brutal black and tightly curled.

"What do you think?"

"No one will know it's not your own."

"You think?"

"Está perfecto, Mamá."

"Get me some panties from the drawer, six pairs should do it."

Lety handed her mother the underwear, which she stuffed into her empty bra. "Dos más, mija." Raising her chin, she studied her face as she filled the remaining space in each cup. "Now, what do I do con éste pedazo de mierda?" She said pointing her chin towards her own reflection.

"Leave it to me, Mamá." Lety rummaged through the dresser drawer, extracting a tube of liquid makeup, Dusky Peach, it promised. She squeezed a pool of it into her palm and began applying it gently to her mother's cheeks, forehead and temples, throat. Lety stepped back and took a look. More like a dusty lemon, she thought and began to apply a second coat. With careful, feathery strokes, she outlined her mother's brows in Revlon's Raven, then drew delicate wings across the eyelids. With great concentration, she stroked the sparse lashes of each eye again and again with the mascara wand, coaxing them toward the brows. Lety stepped back and appraised her work. "What color shadow, Mamá?"

"You get the dress from Alma?"

"Si, Mamá." She held up the dress she had borrowed from her friend who was almost as skinny as her mother had become.

"Then put me eyeshadow to match." She looked at the dress, a sapphire blue silk. "Alma always had good taste. How's her boy?"

"Billy? The same, maybe a little more twisted to the left."

"And what is it she does for a living?"

"Alma? She works in the radiation lab at St. Mary's Hospital."

"Is the pay good?"

"I guess."

"Then she should take her son to Lourdes and put him in the water."

"She talks about it. Maybe someday. Hold still." Lety dusted each lid with powdery azure. Next, she patted her mother's lips with a tissue then painted them with Firecracker Red. This she did slowly and carefully, so that the color did not bleed into the soft crenellations above and below each lip. She fanned rough across the cheeks and chin, softening the sharpness that was new to her mother's face. Finally, she patted a film of powder to keep everything in place and stepped back so her mother could see.

Zulema took a long look. It was some moments before the tear cut its path down her cheek.

"Don't, Mamá."

"Don't what, Leticia? Where's the dress?"

"Raise up your arms." Her mother obeyed and Lety slipped the dress over her head. It fell easily over the bony shoulders. Lety buttoned the front of the dress and patted the wig.

"There, Mamá. You always look beautiful in blue." Lety paused and leaned close. With her tongue, she licked the streak of mascara staining her mother's cheek and rubbed it away with her thumb. "Now you're all ready to go. Jonny will be here in a few minutes. He's bringing his mother and sister."

"They're coming down from Tucson? ¡Ay, por Dios!"

"Tía says el Greco was some kind of a relative, the padrino of a nephew or something."

"Sofía claims to be related to half of Nogales and one third of Sonora. I'm dying. She just wants to wear me out with her prayers before I go. I knew she couldn't let me die in peace."

Zulema looked again in the mirror, smoothing the dress across her chest and sighed. "Gracias, mija. Gracias por todo. You tried your hardest."

Heads turned as they entered the chapel for the rosary. Tía Sofía, Jonny, Regina and the children went first to shield Lety and Zulema from the women who sucked in their breath and twisted their rosary beads.

Lety stepped aside so Jonny could help her mother kneel, supporting her beneath the arms then lifting her to her feet. If she had had any breasts, his hands would be touching them. The familiarity with which he held her mother made Lety's throat itch as if a small feather were caught there. She swallowed.

They slipped into a pew not three rows behind the widow. Lety sat between Araceli and tía Sofía. Last fall, her tía had failed to plant her winter garden, the only passion, other than prayer, that held her on earth. Now, every time tía Sofía shifted in her seat, she rustled like a sack of raked leaves. That's how old and dry she was. All winter, Lety had been expecting to be called to her deathbed. How strange that it was her mother, not tía Sofía, who was dying. Who would have thought her mother's big chichis that all the men had loved so much would have turned on her?

Jonny sat next to her mother, holding her hand fast to his chest. Though he now wore it in a ponytail, his hair was as dark and thick as it had been more than fourteen years ago when he and Lety had first become lovers. He had a little belly now, but his hips were lean and his legs long. Their thighs touched, Jonny's and her mother's. Lety wondered what their thoughts might be as they clasped hands.

Next to tía Sofía, was her daughter, Regina. Though she was ten years older than Lety, with her dark head bent over her beads and her slight frame, Regina could have been mistaken for her younger sister. The Virgin shields the simpleminded, Lety thought, protecting them from the sins that turn a woman's hair gray and add fat to the hips. Above the sound of rustling leaves,

Lety could hear her mumbled words as Regina sped mechanically through Our Father, the Hail Mary and the first Mystery.

Feeling lonely, Lety took her daughter's hand. Araceli didn't have a voluptuous body like her own, but her mouth was wide, and when she smiled, her full lips stretched over perfect, white teeth. In that way, she was like her father. Lety remembered his mouth. How she used to bite his lips to make them swell and run her tongue across those white teeth. It was hard, after all these years, to remember anything else about him. Poor Chuy, he never got to see his beautiful daughter.

Jonny stood at her elbow as she heated water for coffee. "My mother tells me you got you a real good job," he said into her hair. "Now what kind of job would that be?"

Lety jabbed him with her elbow. "You're in my way, Jonny." She went to the refrigerator and took out a quart of milk. "Here, take this into the living room."

He took the milk from her hand. "She tells me you do something at a high school."

"I'm a campus monitor."

"Campus monitor?" He leaned close, his lips grazing her ear, and whispered, "Who do you have to fuck to get one of those campus monitor jobs?"

Lety pushed his smirking face away. "You know Jonny, people say your mother's a saint, and many times I have thought so myself. But what I don't get is how a saint like your mother could give birth to an hijo de cabrona like you." She took the milk carton from his hand and took it into the living room.

Tía Sofía and Regina were still droning the rosary. When Lety put the milk on the coffee table next to the roses from her aunt's garden, Sofía raised her head. "Leticia, in Jonny's truck there are sacks of clothes and blankets from Saint Margaret's. Tomorrow, Regina and I are going to the other side and distribute them in Colonia del Sol. We could use your help."

Lety smiled to herself. She remembered all too clearly the old clothes tía Sofía gave to the poor people of Colonia del Sol. "I need to stay with Mamá."

"It will only take a few hours, Leticia. You should go. It's an act of humility."

Humility, Lety thought. The thought of the countless bills – the crisp twenties, the fives, the tens, the crumpled, soiled ones. By her reckoning she had conducted a thousand humble acts. "I can't think about it now, tía." She turned toward her daughter who was watching half a dozen girls in stiletto heels prance across a silent television screen. "Araceli, get the cups and sugar."

Her mother was propped up on the couch. "Mamá, can I get you a little something to eat?"

"A little rice, maybe, with some warm milk, a little sugar and vanilla?"

Lety smiled and patted her mother's cheek. "Bueno, Mamá."

As she stepped into the kitchen she heard Jonny's familiar, mocking laughter, and looked at her daughter to see if she shared his joke. The girl's eyes were downcast and she was not smiling. "Take this coffee with you, mija. See if you can get your nana to take some with milk."

When the girl had left the room, Lety picked up a boning knife from the drawer and waved it toward Jonny. "If you ever touch her, I'll kill you. Then I'll cut off your cojones and throw them to the dogs over at El Tirabici."

Lety set the wig on the dresser and helped her mother out of the blue dress. "Lie down, Mamá, and I'll put some cream on your face." She helped her mother into bed and sat beside her. Lety scooped some cold cream from a jar. Brushing back the hair from her mother's face with the back of her hand, she applied the cream, smoothing it over her eyelids, cheeks, forehead, then gently wiped the makeup and cold cream off with a tissue.

"Are there any of those empanadas left, mija?"

"Si. Piña o calabaza?"

"Piña."

When Lety returned with the empanada, her mother was already asleep, mouth slack. She set the plate on the bedside table and watched her mother's chest rise and fall at irregular intervals. After a few moments, Leticia picked up the empanada, broke it in two and took a big bite from the middle.

"I thought you were on a diet."

"Oh!" said Lety, startled and embarrassed. "You're awake. I'll get you another."

"Don't bother, mija. I've lost my appetite for it. You go ahead."

"No. You take it. I brought it for you."

"Well then, just a taste. You know what they say. Lo que no le mata, engorda. Since I'm almost dead already, what can it hurt? Do me my feet, Leticia, will you?"

Lety extracted one foot from the blankets, rubbed a little lotion onto her hands and began to massage her mother's swollen arch.

"Ay, Leticia. You do that better than anybody," she said closing her eyes. "Listen, don't return that wig, I want it for later."

"But it's only rented for twenty-four hours."

"Let them come take it from my coffin if they got the nerve. And take twenty dollars from my coin purse. It's in the loaf of whole wheat, remember? I want you to buy the dress from Alma so I can be buried in it. And do me this makeup just like today.

I want my closed eyelids to be blue to match the dress. You understand?"

"You want your eyelids blue."

"Don't forget."

"I won't forget, Mamá." As she squeezed each joint of each toe, Lety remembered how Jonny helped her mother kneel, thought of her mother's hand and Jonny's joined. "Did you ever sleep with Jonny?"

Her mother leaned up on one elbow. "Ay, what a question!"

"Did you?"

"Go close the door."

Lety went to the door. Araceli and Eddie seemed hypnotized by MTV, but she closed it anyway. "Well?"

"That's no kind of a question to ask your mother, a dying woman. Besides, if I did, it was a long time ago and has nothing to do with you."

"It has everything to do with me." She gave her mother a hard look. "So it's true. I hate him."

"Si, pues. You hate him like I hate him. Listen mija; let it go. He's a good man."

"To me he's a cheap bastard. Besides, I don't want him anywhere near Araceli."

"Araceli?"

"Araceli!"

"That Jonny!" Her mother, chuckled dryly, coughed, chuckled again.

"How can you laugh?"

"How can I not? Tráeme una copita de tequila."

"Tequila?"

"¿Por qué no? Like they say, 'Para todo mal, tequila y para todo bien tambien.' "

"Where is it?"

"In the back of the cupboard inside the Bisquick box."

By the time she returned with the bottle and a shot glass, Lety's mother seemed to be dozing once again. "¿Mamá?"

"Ay, Leticia."

Lety handed her mother the glass half filled with clear liquid. Her mother tipped her head back and swallowed. She held the cup out. "One more. I have something to tell you."

"¿Qué?"

"Dame otra, pues."

Lety filled the glass and drank it herself, then poured her mother another half shot. "Tell me what?"

"Jonny's been giving me money for Eddie."

"Giving you money? How much? Since when?"

"One hundred a month."

"For how long?"

"Ever since Eddie and Araceli came to live with me."

"Why didn't you tell me?"

"He made me promise not to. You see? He's a good man. He's been supporting his son all along. I put half each month into the bank for Eddie, for his future, because with what you sent and with el Greco, I had more than we needed. When I die, remember there's money for your son."

Lety took her mother's other foot and pressed her thumbs lightly along the ankle, working her way slowly down to the arch before she could trust herself to speak. "If he had given that money to me, I could have kept the kids in Tucson. It would have been enough. I could have..." She could not go on.

"I guess he wanted his son close by."

"Yes, but to me and everyone else he denied Eddie was his son."

"He was protecting his wife."

"Maricela? That fat cochina?"

"She's a good woman."

"And I am not!"

"I didn't say that."

"He wanted me to stay a whore, Mamá. He could have had me for free, but he wanted to be a big man with his twenty-dollar bills. His fucking garbage money."

"He's not like that, Leticia. I swear."

Lety looked hard at her mother. And you, Mamá, she thought, what are you like? But she didn't ask. It was too late for another commotion between them. What would be the point? "So when were you going to tell me all this?" she said, massaging her mother's wasted calf.

"I put it in a note. It's with my important papers. You would have found it after. Are you mad at me for not telling you? I promised him."

Lety stared at her mother. The woman seemed brighter, rounder somehow. "I am beyond angry with you, Mamá."

"And I'm beyond tired, mija. Get into bed with me, Leticia. I'm cold."

Lety slipped off her shoes and lay down beside her mother.

The woman settled her head back against the pillow and took Lety's hand. "Just like when you were a little girl," she said closing her eyes. Soon she was lowing softly.

Lety got up from the bed and went into the living room. "Mijitos, we have to talk for a minute," she said turning off the television.

Her son shifted so he could see around her. Lety turned the set off. "Just listen for a minute." She placed her hand on Eddie's shoulder. The muscle hardened beneath her palm, and she took her hand away. "I want you to come live in Tucson with me."

Eddie dismissed her with Jonny's eyes, hooded and arrogant. It was Araceli who tried to reason. "But all our friends are here."

"I know, mija, but you can't stay here with no one to take care of you. My job is in Tucson and I have a place there. I have to go back. I want my children with me."

"I'm not going," Eddie said flatly.

"At fourteen, you need to be with me." Even as she said it, she knew it was not true. The boy did not need her.

He didn't bother to argue. He simply turned the television back on.

Lety turned the set off again. "You can't live here by yourself, mijo."

"I'll go live with Jonny."

"With Jonny?" she laughed.

"He said I could."

"I see." She should tell him right now, tell him what Jonny had done to her, to him. She should make him understand what kind of a man he was. But as she looked into her son's eyes, his father's eyes, they cut her like a knife.

"Do what you want, mijo," she said quietly. "If you stay, I'll send Jonny money to take care of you. I'm your mother, after all."

She turned to her daughter. Lety had no claim of loyalty to make, but perhaps her daughter had the ability to imagine how things might have happened in her life, to understand, if not forgive. "And you, mijita?"

The girl shrugged and looked into her lap.

Lety sighed. "Did Jonny say you could live with him too, because if he did..." She reached out and touched her daughter's hand.

The girl looked up at her mother and shook her head. "I'll go with you."

Propped on one elbow, she listened to her mother's soft moans. Lety examined the woman's face. Her brow was smooth and she did not seem to be in pain. Perhaps she moaned merely from the labor of her death. Maybe tonight she'll die, Lety thought. She could accept that, almost longed for it now, so tired she was of the old push and pull of love and betrayal.

Lety slipped her hand around her mother's. It was cool and dry. Her mother was only 48. In sixteen years, she would be 48. Lety's life seemed to run in series of 16. Sixteen years a child, sixteen years a... a what? A mother? A whore? She had never been very good at either.

Her mother stirred and Lety searched her face for any trace of need, but her sleep seemed peaceful enough. Lety thought of the men her mother always seemed to need so badly – el Greco, Jonny and Javier – just a few among many. "You're a worse whore than me, Mamá," she whispered. "I only needed men for their money. You needed men to breathe."

Was there anything to be learned from the past sixteen years, Lety wondered. Anything she might tell Araceli to spare the girl her own pain? Lety had learned you can reach out for one thing and lay your hand on something entirely different. Would it help her daughter to know that? Probably not. What her daughter needed to learn was to be as arrogant as a man. It was the only thing, it seemed, that would protect her from hurt.

And what about the next sixteen years? Lety touched her own breasts. Would there be sixteen years left to become someone different? It felt like her life was practically finished already.

For a time she lay quietly by her mother's side. The amber light from the candle spilled across the covers like honey. Gradually, she became aware of the slightest tearing away in her chest, like the loosening of a congestion, and for a moment she was convinced there would be enough time to learn arrogance for herself and to teach it to her daughter.

Lety sat up and studied her mother's face. Its worn serenity caused the familiar lump to form in her throat. She swallowed, but the lump would not go down. "You don't deserve such peace, Mamá." Lety whispered, willing her mother to open her eyes one more time. "Mamá," she said. The woman slept on. Lety bounced up and down on the bed, first gently, then with some force. "¡Mamá!"

"Leticia? For God's sake stop making the bed jump."

"Tell me one thing, Mamá."

"Ay, Dios. What now?"

"Were you sleeping with him before Eddie was born or after."

"Sleeping with who?"

"You know who! Before or after. I got to know."

"Who can remember? Before, after. I'm dying. Who cares anymore?"

"Me, mamá. Tell me. Before or after."

"Before, pues. Ay, Leticia! And after. I can't lie to you, I just made my confession and there may not be time for another. Because of you, I didn't want to, but you know how Jonny can be. So persistent."

Lety knew exactly how persistent Jonny could be. "I'm taking Araceli and going back up to Tucson, Mamá."

"When? You mean now? Before I die? You're leaving me just because I slept with Jonny a hundred years ago?"

"It's not that. It's Araceli."

"Because of Jonny? You think they're…"

"Mamá! She's only 15. To her he's just a horny old man."

"Old? He's still young, handsome, strong."

"To you, yes."

Zulema arched a faded brow. "And to you?"

"To me he's nothing. Less than nothing."

Zulema's head dropped back against the pillow. "What about the boy?"

"He wants to stay with Jonny."

"Can you blame him?"

Lety shook her head. "They are the same, those two, as you've often pointed out, and I was never much of a mother to him. Of course, now I realize you had a part in that."

"Me! What are you saying? You did what you wanted to do."

"I did what I had to do!"

Zulema propped herself up with an elbow. "So you say."

"So I say."

"Ay, Leticia. Don't do this to me."

"I'm doing this for my daughter."

"But can't you wait till I'm dead, at least?"

"No I can't." Lety stood up. "But don't worry, I'll come back to do your makeup, just like you want. In the meantime, Javier can come and take care of you for a change."

For a moment her mother's face brightened then dimmed. "He won't come."

"Yes he will. I'll make him."

"Make him? How?"

"I'll threaten to tell his wife he's been sleeping with Celina Leon."

"He's been sleeping with Celina León?" Her mother was silent for a moment. "Javier won't care."

"You're right. Javier doesn't give a damn about his wife." Lety grew thoughtful. "I know. Tomorrow I'll call Celina and threaten to tell her husband. She'll see that Javier comes."

"Hmm. That might work. But Leticia, nobody can take care of me as good as you."

Lety leaned over and kissed her mother's cheek. "I know, Mamá, but I got to take care of Araceli. I'm her mother first."

"You're her mother second. I was her mother for years."

The words scalded her cheek. "Por Dios, Mamá, are you trying to kill me before you die? Sure you've been a mother to Araceli, but don't forget you were my mother too. Look how I turned out. I don't want that for Araceli."

"I'm sorry, Leticia. I didn't mean that. We can't start fighting now. I'm dying." She reached for her hand. "Stay with me."

Lety took her mother's hand. "No puedo, Mamá."

"No matter what, I love you, mija."

Lety sat back down on the edge of the bed. "I know. And no matter what I love you, but I've got to leave. You go back to sleep now." She held her mother's hand and waited until the woman drifted into slumber. "Goodbye, Mamá," she whispered, kissing her hand. Lety rose from the bed then, leaving her mother alone at last. In her wake, the nearly gutted candle fluttered wildly, the Virgin of Guadalupe pulsing golden before its flame.

———◆———

hijo de cabrona son of a bitch
El Tirabici a massive garbarge transfer station in Nogales, Sonora

lo que no le mata, engorda that which does not kill you makes you fat

traime una copita de tequila bring me a little glass of tequila

para todo mal, tequila, y para todo bien también for every ill, tequila, and for every good as well

THE EIGHTH MORTAL SIN

———

Siempre en Mi Corazón
(Ernesto Lecuona)

...Siempre en mi corazón el recuerdo de tu amor...

Another oldie. This is a very sad song. Although it doesn't say so exactly, I think it's about a woman whose lover has died, not just gone away, and she will never forget him. Even though she can't hold him in her arms ever again, she will love him as long as she lives.

– Lety

THOUGH THE LAMP ON THE bedside table was draped with a filmy green silk scarf, bathing the room in pale, watery light, Zulema could still see the objects outlined on her dressing table: the cheap black wig on its stand, the jewelry box with a life's collection of mostly worthless adornments, the box of sterile latex gloves. The nurse, who came in three times a week to care for her now, would not so much as wrap the blood pressure cuff around her arm without first donning the gloves.

More than anything else, Zulema missed the touch of human flesh. The death of El Greco had been hard enough to bear, but then her Leticia had abandoned her, the heartless little cabrona. That's a terrible thing to call one's own daughter, but what else could be said of a woman who'd leave the side of her dying mother. Even worse, she'd somehow convinced Araceli to go with her. The girl she'd raised from the age of four was more like a daughter than a granddaughter. And now there was no one left who would touch her, rub her feet or even hold her hand. She longed for sleep, but how could she sleep when her skin ached for the press of warm flesh.

She picked up the bell that rested by her pillow, rang it once, waited, rang it again with more force until her daughter-in-law, whose already round body was further rounded out by pregnancy, appeared at the door. "At last. Why does it always take you so long, pues?"

"I was stewing the chicken for your dinner."

"Eat it yourself. I have no appetite. When is my son coming?"

"After work, I guess."

"But when will that be?"

"You know Javier. When he's good and ready. Why did you ring the bell?"

Searching the room for some distraction, Zulema's eyes fell upon the jewelry box. It was made of silver plated brass, a gift from a lover whose name she could no longer recall. "Bring me that jewelry box on the dresser."

Though she moved with calculated leisure, la nuera did as she was told. "Is this it?" she said, setting the box on the bed.

"Sit a minute, Luz, can't you? You're always in such a damn hurry."

"I've got dinner…"

"It can wait. Sit down," Zulema said softly, patting a spot beside her.

With a sigh, the woman sat.

"¡Ay, hijo de tu madre!" Zulema cried. "Can't you be more careful. Even my liver pains me."

"Lo siento, but you told me to sit."

"I told you to sit, not collapse?"

"I said I was sorry. I'll go if you want."

"No, quédate… por favor."

Luz settled her wide bottom on the bed, while Zulema dumped the contents from the box.

"All this will be yours very soon."

"What about Leticia?"

"What about her?" she said, raking her pale blue fingers through the assortment of rings, bracelets, necklaces and pins. "Ah, here they are." She plucked a pair of earrings from the pile. Each was a pendulous cluster of garnet grapes wound in tendrils of gold. She held them up to the light on the nightstand. "Pretty, eh? El Greco gave me these. He was a very good man, very generous. Put them on me," she commanded.

Luz fed the gold wires through the withered pierces in her mother-in-law's earlobes.

"These I want to take to my grave," Zulema said, touching an earring. All the rest you can have but these. Now, put me my wig so I look nice for my son."

The earrings brushing against Zulema's neck felt like the lightest of caresses. "Ah, mi Greco, how I miss you," she sighed. She patted the wig in place, then dismissed la nuera with a wave of her hand.

Zulema leaned back against her pillow, recalling how they had met. It had been after she had moved from Colonia del Sol. With the help of this and that boyfriend, and a job taking orders and washing dishes at a taquería, she had managed to rent a small apartment. But her pay never went far enough. It was January or February and cold. El Greco, the gasman, had come to her house because she had neglected to pay her bill.

She remembered standing there in the winter sun, which slipped in and out of blue-gray clouds that threatened rain. Her daughter, Leticia, little breasts already budding, stood by her side and Javier, so clingy and insecure for a boy his age, was watching from behind her. With his solid paunch and great wooly gray head, the Greek looked scary even to her. His heavily lidded eyes gave him a sleepy, indifferent appearance, as he turned the valve on the tank to the right.

"I can pay part of it today," Zulema said, searching through her handbag. "I can give you... here's seven dollars, right now. I promise the rest next week."

"No good. You got to pay at the gas company."

"But you could take the money and pay for me. It's so cold, my kids, my son," she said, pulling Javier from behind her to impress the man of her honest need.

He was shaking his head. "It's my job, little lady. Sorry. Lo siento mucho," he said, his Spanish almost unintelligible. From his pocket he took a pack of chewing gum. Offered it to the children. Leticia refused, but Javier smiled shyly and accepted a piece. Before he could put it in his mouth, Zulema slapped it from his hand. "He doesn't need, gum, señor. It's heat he needs. How am I going to cook his dinner? You can't cook beans without gas, and beans is all we got."

The Greek stared down at his shoes, then up at the clouds. The sleepy eyes looked defeated now. He shook his head again. "Tell you what. I fill the tank up. That way, once you've paid the bill, alls you got to do is turn this valve. See it, this valve right here, aquí. Alls you gotta do is turn it to the left. A la izquierda, ¿comprende? Then the padlock goes on, like this. See how it goes? You got to snap it closed for it to lock. It looks like it's locked, but it ain't, see, 'cause I didn't snap it shut." He spoke very slowly, as if speaking to a child. "Make sure you snap it shut after you pay the bill. Otherwise, anybody finds out I've been careless with the lock, it could mean my job. Understand? ¿Comprende?"

Zulema did and was grateful because he had asked for nothing in return. So many others had. For some time, she kept expecting to see him again, was disappointed even when he didn't drop by. But it would be years before Zulema and el Greco would meet again.

Zulema felt a weight on the bed. She opened her eyes. "Eduardo?"

The man took her hand. "No, Zulema, you're dreaming. It's Jonny."

"Of course, querido. But you look so much like your father. For a moment I thought…"

"Did you think you were in heaven already?"

Zulema laughed weakly, Jonny's father would be the last man she expected to see in heaven. "No, Jonny. For a moment I had forgotten, that's all. What time is it?"

Jonny shrugged. "Las seis, más o menos. I just stopped by on my way home from work. How are you feeling?"

"Like a dying woman, what do you expect? Dáme un beso, pues."

When he kissed the air by her cheek, she felt a pang of nostalgia. There was a time when he could not get enough of her lips. Ah, but that was so long ago. "Where do you suppose that son of mine is? He promised to come by and do me a rubdown this afternoon."

"I've heard he's been spending a lot of time with Celina León."

"This, while his mother is dying!"

"Pues, I'll do you a rubdown."

To feel Jonny's hands slide across her flesh once again… Zulema was tempted, but she did not want him to know with his hands what her flesh had become. Better he remember the way she used to be. "No, querido. We're beyond rubdowns, you and me."

"There was a time, Zulema… but we're older and wiser now, ¿verdad?"

"A poor tradeoff. Ay, I'm getting tired of all this."

"¿Necesitas algo?"

Do I need anything, Zulema thought. ¡Necesito todo! "Nothing you can provide, pero gracias, Jonny. You got a good heart. I've always known that."

He took her hand then, kissed it. "To me you're still the most beautiful woman in the world."

"Liar," she said, tears gathering.

"I've made you cry."

"No, amorcito, you've made me happy."

Long after he had gone, Zulema lay there smiling to herself. Jonny had always been such a nice boy. When they first met he was so young, with just the barest soft hairs on his upper lip. How he had pestered her, never giving up until she'd given in.

They met shortly after she'd come up from Imuris. She'd been so sure that in no time she'd have the money to make the trip al norte. At that time los coyotes were asking only $200 per person, and though $600 was more money than she had ever seen at one time, Zulema was young, beautiful and confident that the money would come from somewhere. What a joke! But she wasn't laughing when she moved her children into one of the plywood and tin shacks clustered on the barren hillsides of Nogales, Sonora. Living in Colonia del Sol could hardly be called living. The shack had been provided by a novio, and she was expected to show the proper gratitude. It was going to be a temporary arrangement, the shack and the novio, she had been so certain. If she had thought otherwise, she would never have been able to endure it. No water, no sewer, no heat and a novio with no teeth!

But for Zulema, the hardest to bear was the summer monsoon bringing with it the pervasive miasma steaming up from the sticky, sucking mud and over that the fruity rot of limón, mango and avocado. Every woman had her own remedio for the stench: cheap cologne, candles burning 24 hours a day beneath algo santo, a pot of marigolds in an open window. For Zulema, it was cilantro. She grew it in a cast-off tire by her front door. When the smell got too much for her, she would rub the cilantro between her palms to release the fresh, green essence of the plant.

The rich have a way of keeping los pobres pobres. As they say, "Si mierda era oro, los pobres no tendrían culos." She'd gotten a job in a box factory, but no matter how many extra hours

Zulema worked, there was never enough money. To survive... pues, there were her boyfriends, many of them, but she was no puta. She never had more than one at a time, staying faithful to this one or that until someone with more opportunities came along. A woman alone with two kids does what is necessary and love becomes a thing of the past. In her lifetime, Zulema figured she'd committed all seven of the mortal sins repeatedly. But her worst sin, the sin of poverty, was the one that sent her into hell.

But even in Colonia del Sol, Zulema had had her moments. One of those moments was Eduardo Guerrero, Jonny's father. Another was Jonny himself.

Jonny had come to her shack one afternoon with two garbage bags full of clothes his mother had collected from the church ladies. She was supposed to be grateful for this assortment of rags, but as Zulema searched through each bag, she began to laugh. Really there was no other response possible.

"Look, Jonny," she said, holding up an enormous pair of cotton underpants, the elastic stretched and worn. "I guess I could wear these to keep my ankles warm."

How they had laughed that afternoon, heads together, then lips, then hips. Of course, she had tried to discourage him. Not only were they practically familia, but at sixteen, he was eight years her junior. That afternoon, however, his youth prevailed, and after several attempts, he finally managed to enter before coming. It was sweet, in a way, his clumsy determination.

How naughty she'd been back in those days — the son's first lover and the father's last. Eduardo had been with her only moments before he'd been struck by a taxi. But it really wasn't as wicked as it sounded. She'd always had such a soft spot for both. And why not? The son was only a younger version of the father. Ay Jonny! Ay Eduardo!

Amid the jewelry that was still strewn across her bed there was an old photo. Zulema picked it up, ran her finger around the serrated edges. It was the only picture she had of Eduardo. In it, he was standing with her aunt. They were both young and dressed in their finest clothes. She turned it over, the names were faded, barely legible: Eduardo Mateo Guerrero y Concepción Balderas. Whether they had been novios, or primos or just friends, she did not know. The photo had been one of many on her aunt's dresser.

"Who's this boy?" she had asked.

Her aunt had taken the photo from her hand. "Let's see. Oh. That's me and Eduardo Guerrero. ¿Qué guapos, no? I just loved me in that white suit. That was taken at Olga Fuentes' quinceañera."

"Eduardo Guerrero. How come I never see him around?"

"Oh. He got married years ago. Then I heard he moved up to Nogales. Heard he's doing quite well."

When her aunt turned her back, Zulema slipped the photo down the front of her blouse, an impulse, nothing more, like a young girl pressing the photo of a handsome movie star to her breast. At the time, she had no idea how the photo would be of use.

Eduardo, now there was a man! And generous. It was Eduardo who got her the green card that allowed her to finally leave behind Colonia del Sol, los pobres, los indios, la basura, los borrachos, y los niños whose only comfort in life was a whiff from a glue-soaked rag. Zulema knew she'd gotten lucky.

She'd had a son by Eduardo, though she hadn't wanted to go through with the pregnancy. After all, her daughter, Lety, was already fourteen. But he had begged, "Please querida. We can't have such a sin on our souls."

He'd told her of a godson in Tucson. Told her how the boy and his wife had been praying for a baby. How they would raise the child as their own.

She'd first hidden her growing belly under her big chichis, then under sweatshirts and thick sweaters. In the seventh month, she went home to Imuris, ostensibly to nurse her ailing mother. Eduardo's wife, Sofía, la pobrecita, even took care of Leticia and Javier while she was away. Zulema could hardly keep her mouth straight when she kissed them all goodbye. "¡Qué sinvergüenza, era yo!" She said, still unable to suppress a smile.

The day after their son was born, Eduardo and the young couple came to take the baby away. At the time, Zulema had felt only relief to see him go, but since her illness he'd been on her mind. Her love child must now be only a year older than her own granddaughter! How times gets away. What did they name him? Rafael? Refugio? Rigoberto? R something.

Once again she pawed through the contents of her jewelry box. "Ah. Aquí está," she whispered, picking up a small envelope made of Chinese silk. Inside was a scrap of paper with a name. "Refugio Maldanado. How could I forget?" It was her intention to visit him some day. Oh she wouldn't have revealed herself. Would have simply said she'd been an old friend of his father's. "Ha! Too late now."

Though he'd never mentioned it, Eduardo had probably watched over their son all along. That's the kind of man he was. Since his death, she'd said a rosary for him every week.

Once in a while, she'd even say a rosary for the pobres she'd left behind in hell.

Colonia del Sol, it took her a long time to get the stink of it out of her nose. And she would never forget the miserable handouts from tía Sofía and her church ladies. Years later, when she was in a position to provide aid to the poor, Zulema always bought new, in sizes that would fit the residents of Colonia del Sol who were mostly flacos. One doesn't get fat competing with los zopilotes.

Zulema was rousted from her reverie by a familiar voice. What does that old woman want of me now, she thought, closing her eyes in the pretense of slumber.

Tía Sofía entered the room, dropping her plastic bolsa on the wood floor. "Are you sleeping?" she demanded in her shrill voice.

"Not anymore, tía."

"I didn't mean to awaken you, Zulema. Lo siento mucho. I was just over at Jonny's and he told me you needed someone to do you a back rub," she said, removing a jar of Vicks from her bolsa.

"Javier said he'd give me a back rub. He's supposed to be here any time."

Tía Sofía set the Vicks on the nightstand. "How is the pain?"

"I take the pills. They help for awhile, then it returns like una rata nerviosa gnawing at my spine. I can't rest."

"I stopped by la botánica on the way over and got you something. Señora Almeda said to boil this up and drink it when you want to sleep," she said holding up a paper packet."

"What is it?"

"Yerbas."

"What kind of herbs?"

Tía Sofía shrugged. "No sé. Señora Campos said it works very well to ease your pain so you can sleep. But if you take the tea with alcohol, it will stop your heart. So cuidado, mijita."

In all the years Zulema had known tía Sofía, she had never before used this term of endearment. Zulema didn't know whether to be pleased or suspicious. "¿Mijita?"

"Why not? Though we don't share our blood, we've shared so much else, ¿qué no?"

"Are you referring to Eduardo?"

"Who else?"

"You must hate me, pues."

"No, Zulema. Not any more."

"Why not?"

"I don't know, truly. But I think you... I think in this man's world every woman just does the best she can. Sometimes what she can do is very little, pues. Who's to judge? Now, should I do you a rubdown, or should I make you the tea?"

"You think I've been a bad mother."

"I think you spoiled Javier and nearly ruined Leticia, yes."

"Leticia. She hates me."

"No, Zulema. She loves you."

"And I love her, but sometimes...I want to tell you something so you'll understand better, but you must promise never to tell my daughter."

"Andale. Te lo prometo."

"Back in Imuris, when I was a girl, there was the big shot político. He had an estancia outside of town. You know the kind of man, el jefe, always shaking everybody's hand and giving sides of beef to the poor. The kind of man who gambles, drinks, screws all Saturday night and goes to church con toda la familia Sunday morning. The kind that don't take no for an answer."

Tía Sofía was nodding her head. "Every pueblito has one of those, pues."

"It was just before some election, so he threw a big barbocoa out at his ranch. Half of Imuris turned out for the free beer. Mi familia también. Nobody ever turned down free beer in my family."

"Everybody'd been drinking all afternoon," she continued. "Me too, I'd had me some beers. El jefe sees me. Says he's got some cigars to hand out and needs some help carrying the boxes which he's got stored in the back of the house. I didn't think anything about it, pues. I was fifteen. He was sixty if he was a day, con una panzona así," she said demonstrating with her arms rounded. "You know I wasn't willing."

Zulema considered this half-truth. In fact, she had been willing initially. It had been her mother's suggestion; she'd sent a bottle of Bacanora by way of introduction. The man was a rich man, after all, and Zulema, whose son had been born earlier that year, was clearly not a virgin, so there was nothing to lose. What neither she nor her mother had anticipated was the revulsion she would feel, how she would struggle against the thrust of the old man's tongue, his rough hands tugging at her clothes, her breasts. She remembered his smell combined of whiskey, sweat and cigar smoke, how it choked her.

Sofía touched her hand. "So this was Leticia's father?"

Zulema nodded. "Later, when my father came to him, he laughed. Called me una putita. Then he gave my dad fifty dollars, saying he'd forgotten to pay me. I didn't want his baby. I got even with him, though."

"How?"

"Several years had past. He probably didn't even remember who I was, but I never forgot how he did me. By that time I had Javier too and no future in Imuris."

"So you came up to Nogales."

"Yes, but the night before I did, I had my novio, Javier's no good flojo father, drive me out to the old man's ranch." Zulema smiled with satisfaction. "I put a block of salt in his well."

"¡Bravo, mijita! Muy bien hecho."

"It's been hard to be a good mother to Leticia. You can see why. But I don't want her to know this. I want her to believe that her birth was the result of an act of love."

"But of course her birth was the result of an act of love. You brought her into this world, not el cabrón who sired her, verdad?"

"Tienes razón."

"Of course. Now should I to do you a rubdown, or make the tea?"

"It looks like my son has forgotten the promise he made to his dying mother, so I guess the rubdown first, then the tea to make me sleep. ¡Madre de Dios! ¡Qué cansancio tengo! ¡Qué dolor!"

Zulema turned her back as she pulled her nightgown over her head. "You've been so good to me all these years, tía, and I've been nothing but ungrateful," she said, holding the nightgown over her breastless chest. "I owe you an apology for sleeping with your husband."

"You're not the only woman who owes me an apology for that one."

"And for sleeping with your son."

"You slept with Jonny?"

"I thought you knew."

"I suppose, in my heart, I did. Hijo de tigre, tigrillo."

"Too true. Anyways, lo siento mucho."

"It's easy to be sorry when you're dying, pues, but I accept your apology," tía Sofía said, rubbing the Vicks gently over Zulema's bony shoulders.

The pot of tea was cooling on Zulema's nightstand while she considered her options. Each day held nothing for her now. Her children? Pues, what could she say? Perhaps she deserved to be abandoned, left alone to face the pain and the hours – no longer for careful spending, precious like money, but merely for getting through.

There had been a time when life was so delicious. Three of the best men wanted only her, and she could choose between them. Like candy from a box, she thought with a smile. Today I'll have the caramel. Is it chocolate cream I yearn for or the nougat? Each was tan sabroso in his own way. It didn't matter that none were free to marry her. To trade freedom for marriage had always seemed a poor exchange.

But now... Pues, perhaps it was time to take her chances elsewhere. She rang her bell. After a few minutes, her daughter-in-law stood in the doorway. "¿Qué quieres, ahora?"

"I can't sleep. There's a box of Bisquick in the cupboard. Bring it and a cup."

Zulema alternated between una tacita de té y una tacita de tequila. While she was waiting for her heart to stop beating, she thought of el Greco. Of all the men in her life, he was the one she had come closest to truly loving. One afternoon he'd walked into the restaurant where she'd been working, ordered a cup of coffee and a piece of apple pie.

As she filled his coffee cup she asked, "Do you remember me?"

"How could I forget you?" he answered.

Of course he was married – the good ones always were – but that fact didn't cause her to pause for even a single moment. It was their destiny to be together, ¿qué no? They began their affair that very afternoon, and when he opened his own restaurant the following year, she was the first person he hired. The job paid very well. Very well.

In her mind, she could still see him as he was in those days. Strong as a bull, such staying power, and such ardor his wooly head sometimes left a rash on the inside of her thighs. Perhaps he was the best lover she had ever had. But God had decided to punish her, taking el Greco first, thus depriving her of his comforting presence in her final days.

She closed her eyes. Dwelling in that place which is not quite sleep or wakefulness, each memory fell upon her heart, the moments of joy and despair, the blind passions and excesses that had brought her to this exact point. There were so many sins she had failed to confess, so many secrets. She revisited each one, until she was truly repentant. Such is the awful grace of God, the language that speaks directly to the heart.

The next day Zulema opened her eyes and was mildly happy to see that she was still alive after a night of uninterrupted, dreamless sleep. What a surprise! What a hangover!

For Zulema, there would be two more weeks of dying. Javier would give her a back rub at last and provide her with another bottle of tequila. Sharing a few tacitas with his mother one evening, he would hold her hand, even shed tears, begging her to forgive him for being such a pendejo of a son.

Jonny would continue to visit each day, sometimes bringing a single rose or a fistful of daisies from his wife's garden. And daily tía Sofia would sit at the bedside praying the rosary until Zulema thought she would die a crazy woman. But Leticia? She kept her word and stayed away. Zulema could only shake her head; any sense of guilt she'd had was erased by her daughter's cruel abandonment.

Finally, one morning Luz would discover Zulema still warm, but unresponsive to little pinches and slaps in the face. Blankets tucked neatly beneath her chin, her expression was relaxed, almost blissful, as if she had not a single sin to account for.

———•———

quédate stay
necesita algo do you need anything
necesita todo I need everything
que guapos how good looking
quinceañeran the celebration of a girl's 15th birthday equivalent to a coming out party
si mierda era oro, los porbres no tienen culos if shit were gold, the poor would have no assholes
que sinvergüenza era yo how shameless I was
zopilotes vultures
tienes razón you're right
hijo de tigre, tigrillo the son of a tiger is a little tiger

The Hunchback
of Barrio Anita

———

Hey Baby Qué Pasó
(the late great Freddy Fender)

... Come on baby turn around, let me
show you how I feel, don't you know that
I love you and my corazón is real ...

I think we all know what the guy singing this song wants
to show this girl and it has nothing to do with his corazón.

– Lety

THE STAIRWAY WAS CLOGGED WITH bodies during the passing period,
and no matter which side Billy was on, he seemed to be going
against the flow. Turning his slim shoulder into the crowd, he
pressed through it like a blade. When he reached the top of the
stairs, he listed down the hall, compensating for his natural gait,
which veered to the left, by turning his head slightly to the right.

They called out to him baboso, cabrón, Quasimodo, a name he especially despised. Still, Billy knew these were words of inclusion, so, raising his chin, he responded in kind. And always there was a slight smile on his face, which was pointed and foxlike, for Billy had achieved the fame reserved for the truly beautiful, the truly bad, or in his case, the truly other. Everyone knew Billy, El Chueco.

Billy swung into his favorite class, Algebra X, for boneheads. He knew it was a bonehead class the moment he passed through the door last fall because it was filled with homeboys, flojos and clowns and the same shy girls from Barrio Anita he had watched all these years expanding silently into lushness and beauty.

His narrow chest widened with delight. In this class, not only was he king of the boneheads and clowns, but he had the additional advantage of being the smartest, an entry to the table where the most beautiful of the beautiful, lush girls sat. Her real name was Estella, but they called her La China for her Chinese eyes.

He slid into the seat next to hers and tried to think of something to make her lips, bowlike and full, lift in silent appreciation of his wit. "What's up?" he said, pretending to look inside his shorts.

She did not laugh. China rarely laughed, but a single deep dimple set at the corner of her mouth and her slant, green eyes became lively.

But making China smile was only a secondary pleasure. What pleased Billy most was lifting the shadow of uncertainty that fell across her face, watching the way it gradually lightened to concentration, then cleared at the ascent of comprehension. It was Billy who taught her in Spanish what the teacher was unable to communicate in English – a process that drew them much closer together than simply allowing her to copy the correct answers from his paper. No, instruction caused their heads and shoulders to brush, his fingers to rest for a moment on the smooth, coppery skin of her arm. A demonstration, which button on the calculator to push to achieve square root, for instance, could bring the back of his wrist in brief, but sure contact with a high, round breast. And there was always her smell, which was of coconut and sun-dried cotton.

So when the teacher announced the new seating chart, it was only reasonable that Billy would refuse to move, saying "Shit, I ain't going nowheres."

"Pardon me?" said Mr. Craig, the bald algebra teacher who was El Pelón behind his back and often to his face, not that it mattered, because in some important ways, he was a greater bonehead than many of his students. In fact, he was such a bonehead, he thought Kiko Ornales was called El Cojón because he was from a city in California with a similar sounding name.

"I said, I ain't moving. This desk es mío, ése. It even has my name on it, see?" Billy smiled and pointed to the words carved in florid cursive on the top of the desk. "El más chingón" he read in a clear voice. It didn't matter that he was El Chueco or that his good friend, Kiko Ornales, who had only one nut, a result of an unfortunate childhood accident, which was why he was known as El Cojón, had painstakingly carved those words into the desk last quarter with the point of his compass. Everybody knew this, but El Pelón.

Billy's fox face closed upon itself in concentration. Tonight, like many nights, he stood before the ironing board, his spine curving to the left beneath a shoulder blade that was round instead of sharp, as if a box turtle resided there just beneath the surface of the skin.

Headphones in place, he took up a pair of boxers and ironed, setting creases along the paisley legs, while his head bobbled to a cumbia. He folded them over a hanger, which he hooked on the door along with his freshly ironed Dickies. Next, he chose a T-shirt. After ironing out the clothesline stiffness, he folded it along the vertical axis and again set the crease, giving the T-shirt the perfect symmetry his body lacked. Billy contemplated the laundry basket. A single blouse, his mother's, lay at the bottom. She had worked a ten-hour shift in the radiation lab at St. Mary's that day and had entrusted all the ironing to him. Billy did not mind this chore. It gave him time to think and Billy had a lot to think about.

He adjusted the black nylon stocking that wrapped tight around his forehead and was knotted over the cap of his skull. It was supposed to train his black, sheenless hair back into a smooth unit of hair. But his hair, like his spine, was twisted and went where it would.

Billy took the blouse, a flowered one, from the basket and held it to his face. Breathing in its sun-dried-cotton fragrance, he closed his eyes and locked his mind on the single image of his longing, La China. Her beauty had inspired him through countless baskets of ironing. The memory of her breath against his ear as she studied his algebra paper gave him an immediate chubby. China. How he longed to do it to her, but there was no way, of course.

At that moment his mother emerged from the kitchen where she had been washing up after dinner and his near erection collapsed.

"I still don't get it, Billy," she said squinting up her eyes at him. "Why couldn't you just move like he told you."

"He had no right to make me move. I was doing good where I was. At least a B.

This was true, and if he started turning in the homework, he probably could still pull an A. He sprayed the blouse, front and back, with water from an old Windex bottle and gave it a good shake before smoothing it over the ironing board. "He shouldn't have messed with me, Ma."

"So where did it get you? Now you're kicked out for five days."

Billy shrugged, thinking of China. Five days was a long time, but it had seemed like the best course of action at the moment. He turned the blouse over and quickly pressed the sleeves and front, taking special care with the collar. His mother liked it ironed so it would lay flat and smooth on the outside of her white lab coat. "I'm finished," he said, hanging the blouse, still warm and damp, on the hanger. "I'm going out now."

"Oh no. You're kicked out of school, mijo. You can't go out."

"I'm going out. I told Kiko I'd meet him."

"Too bad. You're grounded. Besides, Kiko's a gangster."

The corners of Billy's mouth pulled down in disgust. "He's my compa."

"Yeah and all your so-called compas are gangsters. They're going to get you shot in some drive-by one of these days. You can't go out," she said folding her thin arms across her chest.

Billy adjusted his stocking and tugged his Dickies in place so exactly four inches of his plaid boxers showed.

Shaking her head, she reached out and held his face between her cool palms. "What is it you want, Billy? You want me to wear a T-shirt 'In Loving Memory' with your picture on it. Is that it? You hang out with gangsters, mijito, and you'll end up dead."

Actually, it was one of Billy's favorite fantasies. His homies, China, everybody crying, and wearing T-shirts with his picture above the words, "Billy Díaz, In Loving Memory."

"And that would kill me too, mijo. Don't you know that? I swear," she said, pressing Billy's face. "I'm going to send you to live in Las Cruces with your father and Nana Fufi. Don't think I won't, you keep doing what you're doing."

His mother had been making that threat for as long as Billy could remember. When he was little, he used to spend all his holidays at his nana's. But now it was only for one week in summer when his father took him fishing, and again each fall when his father and his tío took him deer hunting. His cell phone vibrated in his pocket. Billy jerked his face from his mother's grasp. "Okay, Ma, chill." He started for his room.

"Deep down, you're a good boy. And thank you for ironing. It's perfect, like always." She said to his back and then positioned herself on the couch so she could watch both the front and back doors at once.

"I'm going to take a shower, well."

His mother clicked the television remote, then blew him a kiss. "Okay, I love you, mijo. You're everything to me. Never forget."

Billy closed the door to his bedroom and quickly dialed Joker's number. His friend picked up the phone after the first ring.

"What's up?" Billy asked.

"Where the hell you been, man? I've been waiting for the longest."

Billy shrugged. "I had some things to do, ése."

"Things to do! Oh really? Well, tonight, dude, is going to be your lucky night, unless you got too many things to do, Man. China's been jumped into West Side, ése, and she's gotta do you."

Billy was speechless. Just the words "China" and "Do you" joined in a single thought reinstated his hard-on. Billy swallowed and rubbed his palm over the front of his Dickies.

"Well?" El Joker said. "You still too busy, or you want to meet us at Los Betos?"

"Okay, well, cool."

He soaped his armpits, asshole and crotch. Billy couldn't believe it was about to happen at last.

"Me and China!" he whispered. Billy had not asked if he was to be the only, the first or the last. He didn't want to know the answer. In fact, he didn't want China to have to do him at all. He wanted her to fall in love with him and then do him. But how likely was that? This confusion was messing with his head. It was best to ignore it.

Awhile back, Joker had told him: "If it's your first time, man, you should always jerk off at least once before, or you might come all over the chick's leg and look like a fool."

Billy imagined China's leg, round and smooth. It seemed like good advice.

The Polo he slapped on his hairless face made his pimples sting. Billy's eyes were still watering as he combed mousse through his hair. He pressed it in place with the palm of his hand, trapping it there while he counted to sixty. Finally, he brushed his large, white teeth, his best feature, and made a cheesy smile at the mirror. Satisfied that this was the best he could hope for, he adjusted the heavy gold crucifix around his neck, then inched the bathroom window open. Billy was certain his mother was asleep in front of the television by now, but wanted to avoid risking confrontation. No way was he staying home tonight, but why make the old lady all hysterical about it?

China was the first one he saw. She was surrounded by the other chicks, La Gordita, Roja Loca, Shy Girl and Lil' Chica, but she stood out as if they were moths and she the light.

After huddling with his homies, it was settled. Billy would use Joker's car, the '78 oxided blue Buick Le Sabre his friend was always getting ready to chop and fully load. Kiko offered Billy a leño. He took a single hit to calm his nervous stomach.

At his approach, the other girls fluttered apart, leaving China alone in the acid light from Los Betos Taquería. Without a word he motioned, then turned and walked away, praying China would follow.

The Buick was parked on a dark side street. Billy was grateful to Joker for this unexpected consideration. The glow from China's white, sleeveless blouse was the only light in the back seat.

"What's up?" he asked, struggling to keep his voice deep and casual.

"Just kicking it."

"Joker tells me you're down for West Side now."

"I'm down."

"You get hurt?"

"Na-ah. Just my lip."

"Let's see."

China stuck out her lower lip. Billy ran his index finger over it gently, feeling the swelling and beneath that, the slightest quiver which then traveled through his finger, magnifying in intensity as it shot up his wrist, arm, shoulder.

"Why you want to claim West Side?" he asked, forcing the casual back into his voice. "Why you want to get into all this lame mess?"

She swatted a strand of long, crinkly hair from her face. "Why did you?"

He could tell her the truth, he supposed. Could tell her how lonely he had been in his otherness, how painful it was to stand in this body, but instead, he lied. "Because I'm a stupid pendejo, pues. But you, China..."

"I guess I'm a stupid pendeja too then. Besides, I live here; like they say, it's mi familia."

"¿Tu familia? So how many of your primos did you have to do?"

China was silent for a moment, then answered head bent, barely audible, "All's I got to do is you."

Billy considered this. Tried hard to see it as his good fortune to be so ugly, so unlikely, that to prove her loyalty to West Side, China had only to do him. He should just go for it. ¿Qué no? Any fool would. After all, there should be some compensation for being El Chueco. "You ever done it before?" he asked.

There was another long silence, then a rush of pent up air. "What do you think?"

Her voice sounded different, impatient, hard. Billy felt a hole open in his chest and fill with hopelessness. "You know, you don't have to. Like, it's against my code to make a chick do me. I only do the ones who want it."

"If I don't, I'm not down," she said.

"Like, I'm going to tell." He could feel her considering.

"So you don't want me to do nothing?"

"Nothing you don't want to do," Billy said, suddenly wondering if China was any more able to claim what she wanted than to refuse what she didn't. The hole in his chest grew wider.

"Come here." He looped his arm around her and pulled her head to his chest. She did not resist, and he settled back to study his choices.

He could make her do him, then China could tell her home girls all about what it was like to hump the humpback. Would that finally make her laugh out loud? If he didn't make her do him, he might remain her friend, continue to be her teacher, might still feel her hair brush his cheek, her breast the back of his hand. Either way, there was a lot to lose. And what about China? What, if anything, did China have to lose? "It's up to you, China. Like I said, don't do nothing you don't want to."

He did not expect her to answer. For a long time they sat like that. Billy could feel her soften against him, feel her breath moisten a little circle on his T-shirt just above his heart. He breathed in the coconut scent of her hair and closed his eyes. At least, he would have this much of her.

Billy watched the moths circle and reclaim the light. Then, arranging his face into what he hoped was the satisfied expression of the freshly laid, he turned to join his homies. Joker, Kiko, Cuco and Guapo rubbed his hump for luck as they walked, hip joints loose, to the Buick. Billy started to get into the bitch seat, but Cuco, who was handsome and cool and could have any chick he wanted, took him by the elbow and shoved him into the shotgun position. Moments later, they spun onto South Sixth.

Billy stuck his head out the window. The spring air, sweetened by the smell of hot grease from Los Beto's, felt cool on his face. Tomorrow he would again sit in the bitch seat, but for tonight things were different. For tonight, he was different. Billy touched the exact spot where China's breath had made its moist O. Though his T-shirt was already dry, he could still feel her lips sending little pulses of heat to his heart.

———•———

corazón heart
chueco bent, twisted, lame
compa/compañero companion, partner
baboso stupid, fool

CUCO MALDONADO'S LAST NIGHT

Reloj
(Roberto Cantoral)

... Reloj detén tu camino
Has de esta noche perpetua Para
que nunca se vaya di mi ...

This old song is one of my favorites. The guy is saying he wants time to stop so the night will last forever and his love will never have to leave him. So beautiful.

– Lety

IT WAS EARLY MARCH AND the first Friday of Lent. The blossoms on the citrus trees in the yards of Barrio Anita were falling away, leaving the just set fruit exposed and vulnerable to killing frosts, which were known to strike as late as Easter Sunday. Just last night there had been a light, cold rain in the valley and a dusting of snow on the mountains.

Refugio "Cuco" Maldonado stood across the street from Tucson High School with its fanciful ledges and pillars that provided such excellent shelter for pigeons and killer bees. He was leaning against a chain link fence, arms folded casually over his chest, which was well muscled from evenings spent lifting weights in the garage of his compa, Kiko Ornales. A toothpick was loosely lodged between his lips. His best feature, they were full and pouty.

His Dickies hung low on slim hips, as he absently caressed his belly and dreamed of making love to his vieja, Araceli Mendoza, with her pretty little chichis, firm and round as apples. It was not easy these days for the lovers to find privacy, and even though they had been novios for a year and were about to celebrate their anniversary, Cuco and Araceli had actually only done it five times. The last was with less than satisfactory results, because Joker was in a hurry, and they were using his car, after all. And now that his mother was out of work, she was always home making the dozens of red chili tamales that she sold in front of Albertson's on Friday afternoons, and watching Channel 40, from "Despierta América" to "Noticiero Telemundo," without a break, so there was even less opportunity.

At Araceli's house it was just as bad. Every day after school she had to watch a neighbor's kids until their mother came home in the evening. The minute Cuco walked into the house, it was all, "Uppy Cuco, uppy" and "My turn now, Cuco," "Levánte me, Cuco, Cuco, me, me, me." The kids were three and four and would not leave him alone for a second so he could kiss his vieja and cup his hand over her warm breast. What he needed was a car.

"Borrow my car, mijito?" His mother had said. "No way. You gonna have to take the bus, Refugio, that or get a job and buy your own car. And what about the insurance, pues? It's not cheap."

Cuco loved his mother. After all, it was she who had given him life and provided for his every need to the best of her ability, but sometimes she could be a pain in the ass. He knew very well that her refusal to allow him to borrow the car had less to do with insurance than it did her terror that something bad might happen to him if he had the kind of freedom a car could provide. Her love and her fear were at the heart of their every disagreement.

So he had gotten a job at Los Dos Memos on South Sixth, working 30, sometimes 40 hours a week. And school? Well, let's just say, though he had not yet quit out of respect for his mother, he spent more time out than in. It simply felt better to make a little money than it did to sit in classes all day where the teachers seemed to think it was their sworn duty to make him feel like a baboso.

Cuco usually worked in the kitchen, but sometimes when Memo Junior, who was the manager and a pinche cabrón, was out putting it to one of the putitas he cheated on his vieja with, Cuco would work the register. The owner, Memo Senior, had promised a raise after three months if he did a good job. Now Cuco was working toward his second raise. Of course, with his mother out of work, he helped with the rent, paid the telephone bill and kept his younger brother and sister in tennies, so as yet there was no car.

The sun that had been warming his shoulders dipped behind one of the clouds drifting in the spring sky, causing the sparse black hairs on his arms to stand up and his nipples to stiffen. Cuco thought of his jacket lying on the back seat of Joker's car and made a mental note to retrieve it. Just last Saturday, he had wrapped that jacket around Araceli's naked shoulders to protect her from the chilly night air while he kissed her breasts.

Cuco felt the vibration of his beeper against his hipbone and checked the number — work. Junior probably wanted him to fill in tonight. "Chúpame," he said without malice. He was scheduled to work Saturday night and all day Sunday as it was. Friday night was his and nobody was going to change that now. Cuco had made plans.

Thanks to Kiko, whose family was already on their way to Nogales to attend the First Holy Communion of a niece and would not be returning until Sunday night, he and Araceli would celebrate their anniversary by doing it in a real bed for once. The house key was already in his pocket. Of course, Kiko, who had flat out refused to go with his family, had given his word to stay away all night if necessary, for that's what it meant to be compas, que no?

To mark the occasion, Cuco had bought a bottle of Cold Duck, two plastic Champagne glasses, a single rose so red it was nearly black, a heart shaped pendant with sixteen diamond chips, one for each year of Araceli's life, surrounding a ruby, his heart. He had also purchased three rubbers.

Of course, Cuco did not know that it was already too late for the rubbers. It was not that Araceli was withholding this information from Cuco. It was simply that she was as yet unaware of the minute ball of cells doubling and redoubling at that very moment within the cushion of her womb — the result of their hurried, and therefore careless, lovemaking in the back seat of Joker's car.

At last, the final bell rang, and Araceli was among the first out the door. Cuco watched as she ran down the steps in the platform shoes, which made her just tall enough to stand with her head tucked beneath his chin. Though Araceli was not beautiful by most standards, she was delicate and fastidious about her appearance, and her hair, which swayed across her back at the exact point where her perfect nalgas began their outward curve, was black and smooth. But the best part about Araceli was that she was his, only his. Unlike his former rucas, she had been with no other and loved him with a devotion that made him want to put her under a little glass dome. He would then set her on the altar that stood in the corner of their living room, right next to the statue of la Virgen de Guadalupe, where she would always be safe from harm.

And then she was there, her head against his chest, slim arms tight around his middle. He breathed deeply, filling his nostrils with her fruity scent, which was exactly like strawberry Kool-Aid, and made him think of warm summer evenings. "El Joker tells me I'm pussy whupped," he said kissing the top of her head and smiling.

Araceli stepped back for a moment and scowled. "And when he tells you that, qué dices?"

"Nothing. I don't say nothing at all because it's true. You've got me pussy whupped." A playful smile rippled across his beautiful lips.

Araceli hugged him to her again, standing on her toes to press her pelvis against his, as if his words were the most poetic declaration of love.

As one, they turned and walked hand and hand in the slant, bespangled light toward the Dairy Queen, where each afternoon, rain or shine, he bought his love an Oreo Blizzard.

Cuco's mother placed a bean burro and three tacos on his plate, the dark smudge still on her forehead where the priest had made the sign of the cross in ash. His mother never washed her ashes off, and if she were really careful, sleeping only on her back, and pulling the shower cap low on her forehead when she washed, she could make them last an entire week. Her record was nine days. Cuco peeked inside a taco. As he suspected, it was filled with potatoes. There would be no meat for a month. His mother was devout and a traditionalist.

She set plates before her other children, a boy of ten and a girl of twelve. Before serving herself, she stepped back a moment to watch them eat. "So you going out tonight, mijito?"

Cuco nodded, his mouth full of burro, a drizzle of salsa running down his chin.

"With Araceli?"

Cuco shrugged. He considered any conversation related to Araceli off limits, and his plans were always privileged information. The less his mother knew, the less his mother needed to know, was how he figured it.

"Refugio?"

"Ay, Mamá!" pleaded his sister, who loved and respected her big brother more than anyone else in her narrow world and would do anything in her power to make his life even more perfect that it already seemed to her to be. "You bother him too much."

"Eat your dinner, mijita," la mamá ordered. "Refugio?"

"I'm just going out."

"With who?"

"The usual."

"The usual who?"

"Ay Mamá," he said. Irritation squeezed his throat, making it hard to swallow the burro, which was a little dry to begin with. He made himself very busy spooning additional salsa inside the tightly folded tortilla, but his mother only stood there, staring down at him, arms folded over her chest.

"Joker's picking me up," he said at last, knowing how it was useless to try to evade his mother once she became determined.

"You mean Alfonso?"

"You know who I mean."

"Mire, Refugio. I've known that chamaco since before he was making pee pee standing up, and his given name is not Joker!

"Take it easy, Mamá. It's just a name."

"Alfonso is a name. This Joker is the name of some vándalo, a ganster, a hood and a good for nothing, mijito, and I won't have none of that in my house. And do you know why that is?"

"Because you love me."

"Are you being smart with me, Refugio? Don't get smart, mijo. You're not a man yet to be getting smart with your mother. No, Refugio, it's because I love you. I love you and your brother and sister." She opened her arms wide to include everyone seated at the table, then nailed each with a glare, one brow raised in determination. "You, your brother and sister, son mi vida. Without you, I... would... die. ¿Me entiendes?"

"Yeah, Ma."

"Yeah, Ma?"

"Si, Mamá," he answered, eyes cast down on his plate. His mother's furious love felt like a punishment. It always left him deflated.

El Joker tossed the jacket at Cuco as he slid into the front seat. Kiko and Guapo were already in the back, with El Chueco between them in the bitch seat. This was always the seating arrangement when Cuco and his hommies cruised, something he was doing less and less these days because of his other responsibilities, not that he was no longer down for West Side. It was just that real life, which is how he thought of his mother, brother and sister, and his need to provide for them, was a higher priority. And then, of course, there was Araceli. She was not a thug. Had nothing to do with West Side, and that's the way he wanted it to stay.

Everybody seemed to think that was cool but Joker, who punched Cuco hard on the arm, before starting the engine. "S'up, pussy?" he said, smiling broadly, big yellow teeth making his long face resemble a mule's.

"Hey bitch, who you calling pussy?" Cuco answered, returning the punch and the smile. Then they were off, the Buick laying rubber as Joker popped the clutch and slipped from first into third.

"I need to stop by work and pick up my pay," Cuco said, adjusting the bass on the speakers until every loose screw on the car buzzed and rattled to the beat.

"That's cool."

"I told Araceli we'd pick her up at 9:15."

El Chueco, who was much more of a joker than El Joker, poked Cuco in the head with his index finger. "You supposed to pick her up at 9:15? You sure it ain't 9:14, or maybe 9:13? Don't be late, now, Refugia," he said, slapping the beak of Cuco's cap from back to front. "You are whupped, for reals, fool."

Cuco ignored him because Chueco, who was basically a harmless, easygoing pendejo, could be ignored. He readjusted his cap, head working with the beat as he scanned the passing cars.

Joker pulled up to the stoplight at 22nd, his chin pointing toward a black '82 Impala in the opposite turn lane. "See them Slobs?"

Cuco recognized the driver of the Impala, a Blood from South Park. Damn, he thought, inching down in his seat almost involuntarily. He knew if they got caught up in some shit with that hood, he'd never make it to Araceli's.

When the Impala pulled into the intersection, Joker ran through the red, turning left across a lane of traffic onto 22nd. Cuco prayed a cop had seen that action and would pull Joker over. Better Joker get a ticket than mess up my plans, he thought, checking things out in the rearview mirror. He was disappointed to see no spinning red light.

Joker accelerated until he was alongside the Impala. Guapo stuck his arm out the back window and threw up the West, middle fingers crossed, thumb tucked against his palm. Scowling, the dude riding shotgun in the Impala, threw up the South.

Cuco ground his teeth and stared straight ahead. Sure he was down, but tonight he had other plans. He turned to Joker, willing him to back off, but Joker, the crazy shit, just grinned and threw up a sign, expecting Cuco to issue the first challenge. He could feel the pressure building in the car as everyone, Kiko, Guapo, Chueco and Joker waited for him to do something provocative.

"I got plans, Joker, remember?"

"Puta madre! You want me to back off?"

"I said I got plans, ése."

Joker looked at him hard, then took his foot off the gas, pushed into second gear and turned onto 10th, tires squealing. He pulled over to the curb and slammed on the brakes. While the Buick lurched from front to back to front, Joker reached across Cuco and opened the door. "Go take care of your plans."

"What? You just going to leave me here?"

"Fuck you, pussy."

Cuco watched Joker execute a U-turn and lay rubber. He looked at his watch, a Rolex knock off, and started walking. What he needed was a car.

As he walked up his driveway, Cuco figured he had two options: He could sneak in, steal the keys out of her purse, roll the car out of the carport and be off before she noticed, or he could simply tell her the truth and beg her to lend him the car. Both options were risky.

The aroma of cumino and cilantro still hung in the air as he stepped lightly through the back door into the kitchen. From the living room came the familiar voices of his mother's favorite telenovela, "Las Tres Mujeres." Usually, she kept her purse on top of the refrigerator, an old habit left over from the days when she needed to keep it out of his reach, because he would think nothing of emptying her coin purse to buy a pocketful of the Mexican candy made of tamarindo, chili, sugar, and lime that he still loved. He ran his hand over the warm surface, but it was not there. With the skill of a cat burglar, Cuco crept back across the kitchen, out the door and around to the front yard.

"It's only me," he called out as he turned his key in the lock. His mother was on the couch, bare feet propped up on the coffee table.

"You're home early, mijo. That's nice," she said without looking away from the television screen. "Did you get your pay?"

Leaning over, Cuco kissed his mother's cheek. "No, Mamá. Alfonso's car broke down so I figured it'd be better if I came on home. Thought I could just borrow your car for a minute and go pick it up. That way, tomorrow you could get your groceries or whatever."

"You got no insurance. I told you. No car, mijito. Would you like me to drive you over? I could, right after my soap."

"But Ma, I'd stick to the back streets all the way. It would only take a minute."

"Lo siento, Refugio; the answer is no."

"You got to let me use the car!" Cuco said, his eyes burning with tears of frustration.

"I don't got to let you use the car!" she said, giving him her full attention at last. "What is it, mijo? This is not about your pay. Tell me what's going on?" she said, reaching for his hand.

Cuco looked at his watch. It was already past nine. Time was running out, and so it was that Cuco had no choice but to tell his mother almost everything. Tell her how he had refused to get involved in a fight with some Bloods from South Park, how Alfonso, este hijo de puta, sorry Mamá, but that's what he is, kicked him out of the car, how he had to walk all the way home, and how he was supposed to be over Araceli's to help her babysit, and that he had a rose and a heart-shaped pendant with 16 diamond chips to give her because it was the anniversary of their first date — though date did not quite describe that first time he had seen her at Los Betos Taquería, that cool Saturday night, how she had been standing among a group of laughing girls, her eyes cutting shyly his way, how they had made out in the back seat of Joker's car, how she had demanded that he respect her when he tried to stick his hand into her stretch jeans that were so tight they looked like black paint.

"Ay Refugio," his mother said, pulling herself up to her feet. "I shouldn't be doing this, but I've been in love too. I know how it is, mijo, and I feel sorry for you."

To his ears, her words were like a beautiful melody.

Cuco found a parking spot half a block from Los Dos Memos. Inside the restaurant was his pay and the cooler with the single red rose and the Cold Duck.

"S'up?" he said to Junior who was slouching behind the register.

"How come you didn't answer my call?"

"You called me?"

"Sure as hell did."

Cuco shrugged. "Got my pay?"

Junior reached under the cash drawer and removed an envelope with Cuco's name written on it, but as he reached for it, Junior pulled it back, the way he might pull a dog biscuit from under the nose of a dog. "¿Vas a chingar a tu ruca?" he asked, now holding the envelope behind his back.

Cuco was not amused by Junior's antics. In fact, given the frustrations of the evening, he had an urge to bust him in the mouth for disrespecting his woman, but of course, that was out of the question. Instead, Cuco laughed and feigned disinterest, sauntering into the kitchen, instead, to pay his respects to Memo Sr., who was standing over a great pot of menudo, which he always prepared personally every Friday night.

"¿Quiúbole, Cuco?" the old man said, pulling his face above the steam from the pot and smiling. "How about a bowl of menudo, mijo? It's good for whatevers," he said with a smirk.

"No, gracias. I just come over to pick up my pay and my ice chest," Cuco said, lifting his chin towards the back of the kitchen where he had stowed the Styrofoam chest.

"The big aniversario, que no? I guess you ain't got time for a bowl of menudo, pues."

"No señor, not tonight."

Memo Sr. clapped his big hand on Cuco's shoulder and guided him out front. "Junior," he said, snapping his fingers at his son. "He needs his pay. And reach me an extra veinte." Junior sucked his teeth and handed the envelope and a twenty-dollar bill to his father.

"Your share of yesterday's tip, plus a little extra," the old man said, handing the twenty to Cuco.

Cuco just stood by the car, savoring the moment as he inhaled the fragrance of carne asada from Dos Memos. A nearly full moon rose and rose again out of the clouds. In minutes, he and Araceli would be alone together, a real bed close at hand to fall into after their toast, after he offered his heart, after he told her how he loved her, after he kissed her and ran his hand over her smooth, warm skin, removing each article of clothing, piece by piece. For the first time he would see her body, every part of it naked all at once. Closing his eyes, he shuddered slightly.

He felt the vibration of the bass before he saw the car. Forcing his eyes not to stray from the moon, he waited until the black Impala slowed and finally stopped in front of him.

"Estoy chingado," he whispered. If it occurred to him to run, it was only a fleeting thought. Taking a deep breath, he tucked the fine gold chain Araceli had given him last Christmas into his T-shirt and put his hand into the deep pocket of his Dickies where it touched the key to Kiko's front door, then came to rest on the set of brass knuckles he kept there just in case.

"Hey punk?"

"What the fuck?" Cuco responded, trying to keep his voice in neutral.

"Weren't you the Crab throwing up that weak-ass shit?"

"That was my homie," he said, thinking there might still be a way to avoid getting the shit beat out of him. "What you wanna get at?"

"Punk, this is straight up South Park Blood."

Cuco nodded. Took a deep breath. Unavoidable. "What you wanna do with it, fool?"

"Fuck this. I ain't got time to scrap."

The click as the clip slipped into the chamber swelled within Cuco's brain, and he knew it was over even before the trigger was pulled.

Within the hour, the police would be knocking on his mother's door. Of course, she would not make it to the hospital in time. Araceli wouldn't hear of his death until the next day. Though they would never speak of it, both women knew that the great rush of their love had had a hand in it. Kiko, Chueco and Guapo – all would agree that Cuco should not have been out on the streets alone that night. Only Joker would say it was fate, Cuco's, and unavoidable.

And Cuco, what did he feel in those last moments, fingers pressed against his throat just beneath the jaw as he lay there bleeding, heart defeating itself with each beat?

———◆———

pinche mean, punk, hoodlum
chupame, suck me
nalgas, butt
ruca, girlfriend
quiúbole, what's happening

LOS PECADOS DE LOS PADRES
(The Sins of the Parents)

———◆———

Piensa en Mí
(Traditional)

*Si tienes un hondo penar, piensa en mí. Si
tienes ganes de llorar, piensa en mí ...
Piensa en mí, cuando beses, cuando llores, tambien
piensa en mí cuando quieras quitarme la vida ...*

The song says that if you are suffering, think of me. If
you want to cry, think of me. Think of me when you kiss,
when you cry, think of me when you want to leave life behind. A beautiful song, that always brings on tears.

– Lety

THE MOUNTAINS SURROUNDING TUCSON WERE dusted with snow, which
was quickly dissolving like the sugar on a plate of warm churros.
On the ledge outside a classroom window, a pigeon struggled to

keep her two half-grown chicks pressed beneath her wing. First, each downy head poked out of this confinement, then the barely feathered wings and last, the pink, naked legs. They were now quite free, free to fall off the ledge, but of course, they could not know this.

Inside the classroom, Araceli rubbed away the last of the Lenten ashes from her forehead, as she watched the minute hand sweep around the clock above the chalkboard. In less than fifteen minutes she would be free. She closed her book and watched the pigeons test their wings against the chilly March breeze. The classroom was warm. Araceli lifted the hair off her neck, then twisted it around her fist, securing it at the back of her head with a pencil. This hair, thick and glossy, was Araceli's single vanity. Refugio, her novio, loved its aroma of strawberries, loved to press his face in her hair, rub it against his cheek, like a baby might the silken edge of his blanket.

The teacher was talking now, very slowly in English, pausing at the end of each phrase to lift her eyebrows and search the faces for comprehension. This was a class for students up from Mexico as well as other recent arrivals to the United States. Araceli had been in the country for just over a year, and though her English was still halting, imperfect, her comprehension was good enough that she often whispered translations to the girl in the next desk. She had Refugio to thank for this. This and the blossom of anticipation that glowed on her smooth cheeks.

Soon after she had moved from Nogales to be with her mother, Araceli had become aware that Refugio was watching her. In the morning he watched as she climbed the steps in front of the school, books clutched to her chest. He watched as she passed the stairwell where he and his compas gathered between classes. And after school, he watched as she sat among her girlfriends at Los Betos, laughing at nothing, while trying not to feel the thrill of his eyes on her skin. But she had not known him. Because of his reputation as a player and gangster, she had not even wanted to know him, until one year ago to the day, when he tried to crawl into her grocery cart in the produce department at Food City, saying, "Take me home with you; I think I'm in love."

"¡Quítate!" she said, trying not to smile or look at his lips, which were full and beautiful. "You're squeezing my tomatillos."

"Squishing," he corrected.

"Whatevers," she said. "Get out of my cart baboso." He had gotten out, but not before making her promise to meet him at Los Betos that very evening.

Everyone thought they had started doing it that first night in the back of Alfonso Chacon's old hoopty, but that was not the case. No. Theirs had been a true romance, one demanding great patience and finesse on the part of Refugio, because as it turned out, Araceli was una virgin de primero grado. This was a great surprise to Refugio, because it was a fact, well known to everyone but Araceli, that while she was being raised by her nana in Nogales, her mother made a living in Tucson sobre la espalda, as they say. Had he known of Araceli's purity, Refugio would never have gotten into her shopping cart that afternoon. Who has the time? However, from that first night, it was true love, so what could he do but respect her while slowly chipping away the layers of propriety, modesty and fear that encased her luscious innocence.

As for Araceli, who had been slapping off hands since she was twelve, including those of her own cousin, who was more than twice her age and the reason she came to live with her mother in

Tucson, she was won over by this very respect, this patience, this painstaking finesse that made the heat rise from her body like the steam from a bowl of menudo. How she loved Refugio! Even so, it had not been until recently that she had overcome her fear and inhibition, and surrendered at last to her pleasure and his.

And tonight they would celebrate their primer aniversario. Instead of the back seat of Alfonso's old Buick, where there lingered a vapor combined of the juices and after-shave of countless young vatos who rode their rucas upon its vinyl surface and steamy windows provided the only privacy, there would be a real bed. To this anniversary celebration, Araceli would bring her very own gold medalla de San Cristóbal to place around Refugio's neck and an aqua-blue nightie with an inch of creamy lace at the thigh.

She closed her eyes now and saw clearly how it would be, her skin glowing in the light of a single candle, Refugio's hand trembling at the edge of that lace.

As Araceli walked in the front door, she was greeted by the nearly twin voices of her mother and her closest friend, Alma. Every Friday they met to share exactly two beers before starting dinner in their respective kitchens, one door apart.

Alma, still wearing her flowered scrubs, the uniform of the radiology technician, rose to embrace her. Not only was this woman Araceli's madrina, but her role model. She too would train to be a radiology technician or maybe even a nurse practitioner. Araceli could see herself in her colorful scrubs reassuring a child with a broken leg or delivering a baby, which she would do in either Spanish or English, because by then she would be perfectly fluent in both. She would make good money, and she and Refugio would buy a two-story house in the foothills where their children, twin boys and a girl, would each have their own bedroom and a backyard to play in. Summer nights they would sit outside and watch the city lights twinkle below and leave the windows wide open because there would be no crime in that particular neighborhood. They would go to their children's soccer and baseball games and never miss an open house at school.

This was Araceli's dream. It would come true only in part. Instead of three children, she would have only one, a son. He would always be small for his age, and nearly blind, he would never play soccer or baseball. Araceli would have her house in the foothills and go to all the open house meetings, but the man by her side would not be Refugio.

But at the moment, she was embracing her madrina with the impatience of one so stricken with longing that her only wish was for the next few hours to dissolve so she could be with her love.

"Mijita," Alma said. "¿Como estás?"

Araceli's mother answered for her. "She still thinks she's in love con esé Refugio."

"Thinks? I remember when you were Araceli's age, so crazy in love, there was no thinks about it. How furious you'd get at your poor mother because she didn't like Chuy! How the two of you would scream at each other every time you went out with him. ¿Recuerdas, Lety?"

"How could I forget. And my mother was right. Do you remember how he left me?" she said, rolling her eyes towards Araceli.

"Si, pues. But I've known Refugio since he and my Billy were little boys in cowboy boots, and he isn't a borracho cabrón como Chuy. Besides, Araceli's got her head on her shoulders. Right mijita? This girl's in l-o-v-e, Lety. You remember how that is, or have you forgot?"

"I haven't forgot nothing worth remembering. That's the point. Love. Pfft! No me hables de amor."

"You can fight it, Lety, pero te vale nada. You might as well let her enjoy it, pues."

Araceli often wished she were Alma's daughter, for it was Alma, not her mother, who truly understood her. And unlike her mother, a hall monitor who had to struggle to get passing grades in the introductory computer class she was taking at the community college, Alma was a professional, a home owner, una mujer del mundo, pues. She gave her madrina another hug and escaped to her bedroom.

The next hours Araceli spent in luxurious preparation. She had bathed in strawberry scented bubble bath, smoothed strawberry scented lotion over every inch of her body, polished her fingernails with coats of magenta until each finger tip looked like a petal from a small rose. With great care and subtlety, she applied the sable pencil to her arching brows, lined and shadowed her eyes, curled and coated her lashes, painted and repainted her lips in the same magenta as her nails, then dressed in her tightest black lycra and highest platform shoes. Just as she was taking the hot rollers from her sleek hair, her mother opened the bedroom door. She did not knock. She never knocked, and the pleasure Araceli was experiencing in these painstaking preparations, was replaced by a stab of resentment.

Without a word, her mother began to unwind the remaining rollers from Araceli's hair, gently brushing each curl as she went. "Qué bonito tu pelo, mijita. Qué guapa eres. So tonight is something special, all this trouble you're taking," she said, picking up the bottle of nail polish from the dresser. "Nice color. It suits you."

"Refugio is taking me to a party." The lie didn't trouble Araceli in the least. Though she owed her mother respect because she'd given birth to her and provided her with food and shelter, she did not owe her the truth.

"A party?" Lety said and continued stroking Araceli's hair. When at last, it fell down her back, a dark liquid with only the very tips curling like an ocean wave in moonlight, Lety opened the bottom drawer of her daughter's dresser. From beneath the layers of panties, tee shirts and gym socks, she pulled the aqua-blue nightie. "Do you plan to wear this at the party, mijita?"

"You've been going though my drawers?" Araceli said, snatching at the night- gown.

"Just to borrow a pair of clean socks, mijita. Mira, Araceli, I don't want to fight you. I've had all the fights I can stomach with your nana, rest her soul," she said crossing herself. "I always swore I'd never do you like she did me. All the yelling and screaming. And for what? It didn't stop me, and I know it won't stop you. You think you're in love."

"I am in love."

"Okay, so you're in love. Believe me, I remember what it's like. I was IN LOVE with your father, and all that fighting, all those ugly words between your nana and me solamente agitaron el fuego. Only made me more determined to prove that I was right and she was wrong."

"You heard what Alma said. Refugio is not like my father."

Lety shrugged, "If he is, he's a fool, mijita, and you don't deserve no fool. You deserve a real man, one who will be forever with you. I don't want you to go through what I did, is all."

"It won't be like that."

"Maybe not. I'm not going to ask you if you are sleeping with him. If you were, you'd only lie to me anyway," she said, her eyes shiny with emotion. "I understand that, pues. I understand that I was never the mother you deserved, but it was me who put the food on your nana's table for you to eat. Me, Araceli! And it was me who sent you to school with the nuns, me who made sure you got good clothes, and never had to be ashamed of your shoes. Entonces, listen to me!" Lety paused to wipe her eyes. From her pocket, she produced a little packet. "Here," she said, forcing it into her daughter's hand. "Give this to Refugio. If he's really a man and not some little pinche pendejo son of a bitch, he'll want to protect you."

Araceli looked at the packet as if it were a tarantula spider resting in the palm of her hand instead of a condom. Her shock, which made her feel light-headed and slightly sick to her stomach, was not because of the terror of rubbers the good sisters at La Purísima Concepción back in Nogales had for years tried to instill in her, but because her own mother was suggesting she use one.

"¡Me prometes, mijita, that you'll use it!"

"No lo necesito." She handed the condom back to her mother, determined to deny her this intimacy between them.

"Pues," Lety said, shrugging her shoulders, then placing the packet on the dresser. "Lovers come and go, but mothers are forever. Te amo, mija. Nunca olvides."

It occurred to Araceli to tell her mother that she loved her too. Instead she turned back to the mirror, not yet ready to forgive her for being right. After all, this was not just about love. It was about impatience, and Araceli was impatient to begin what she thought would be her real life, which did not include a mother butting into her private business.

Of course, it was already too late for condoms, but neither woman knew that yet. Neither did they know that Araceli had already seen the last of her lover.

Much later, she would recall her mother's words, her own stubborn refusal to accept her love, and a flush of embarrassment tinged with remorse would rise to her cheeks. And in years to come, she would think of Refugio, often during odd, quiet moments, washing the dishes say, or driving to work in the blue morning light. Her hand would stray to her lips then, and she would remember the fullness of his mouth, recall his shoulders, smooth and cool beneath her palms, his gentle urging, the heat of his breath on her skin. Always such thoughts would fill her with warmth and something, not quite grief, pero algo como una dulce herida. Yes. It was like a sweet wound that never quite healed. Now and then it would break open in her chest. Isn't that always how it is for the one who must go on living?

But now, as Araceli sat at her dressing table making adjustments to her makeup while she waited for her lover's knock, she regretted nothing, felt nothing but the thrill and beat of anticipation.

———•———

> **sobre la espalda** on the back
> **madrina** godmother
> **no me hables de amor** don't talk to me of love
> **pero te vale nada** it won't do you any good
> **solamenete agitaron el fuego** only stirred up the fire
> **pero algo como una dulce herida** but something like a sweet wound

BEAST AND THE BEAUTY

—◆—

Baby Heaven Sent Me You
(Huey P. Meaux, Spanish lyrics, Freddy Fender)

He buscado en todo el mundo, he buscado por ti y el
Dios cielito me ha mandado una ángel para mí.

I've been looking, seeking, searching for somebody like
you and my prayers were answered, baby heaven sent me
you. What more do I need to say? Even my tía Sofia knows
this one by heart.

– Lety

ALL DAY THE GUY ON Radio Fiesta had been advertising the car
wash. They had a good corner, South Sixth and 22nd, and the
line of lowriders, 4x4s and assorted hoopties, each vibrating to
the combined bass of cumbia, rap and oldies, extended beyond
the parking lot of Ricky's Shell and down the block. The air was
party, as people, mostly la gente de Barrio Anita, waited in the

dazzling spring sunlight to have their cars washed by Cuco's primos, tíos, padrinos and, of course, his many compas from Westside Anita.

The cost of a wash was five bucks, but if you bought a Cuco Maldonado memorial T-shirt for twenty, the wash was thrown in free of charge, though many who bought the T-shirt pressed an extra bill into the hands of El Joker who was collecting. After all, they'd expect the same if the loss were theirs, qué no?

Billy, or El Chueco as he was known to his compas, was wearing the black T-shirt with Cuco's picture on the back. Beneath the picture the words *In Loving Memory* were written in large, ornate script. It was too bad there wasn't a recent photo of Cuco. The last time he was in school on picture day had been in the eighth grade. But this was a nice picture. In it, eyes moist with possibility, he was a softer, rounder Cuco than the taut young man he had become by the time of his death. Still, his mouth, full lips caught in a shy smile, was unchanged by the three short years since the photo had been taken.

Terry rags in hand, Billy and Kiko Ornales waited as a new Chevy Blazer pulled up, its chrome already bright as the driver's silver-capped teeth. Mario Fuentes, an old G from the barrio, extended a bill through the window. Each knuckle of his left hand was tattooed with a blurry cross. Billy nudged Kiko who nudged Joker who took the money, a crisp one-hundred-dollar bill, then fumbled in his pocket for change.

"Give me a T-shirt, doble X, and keep the change, mijo."

"Gracias, Jefe," Joker managed and passed the note to Billy who shoved it into his pocket. With the casual gait he had mastered to compensate for his tendency to veer off in the same direction that his humpback twisted, Billy crossed the parking lot. La China, who was guarding the cash box and a card table covered with T-shirts, watched his every step.

"Dáme una doble X," he said, handing her the money. "No necesito feria."

"No change? Who's this from?" China asked, straightening the bill and slipping it carefully beneath the cash drawer.

"Mario Fuentes," he said, pointing to the truck with the barest pursing of his lips.

"It's a hundred dollar bill, dude," China said, clearly impressed. When Billy didn't respond, she added. "Come on, ese. Cuco's mom needs the money. Besides, he made his own choices just like the rest of us."

But it was exactly this question of choice Billy had been struggling with. It was the old G's like Fuentes who made it hard to turn your back on the life. Did anybody have a choice about hooking up with West Side or any gang, with chingones like Fuentes ready, willing and able to bust up your ribs, or worse, if you didn't? "Yeah, well."

"You live next door. Have you seen Araceli?"

Billy shook his head. Yesterday his mother had taken over a box of churros, pan de huevos and empanadas from La Estrella Bakery because she didn't know how to cook anything that would be better than that, but she had not seen Araceli. "Maybe she's sitting with Cuco's mom."

"Que triste. Araceli and Cuco were like casaditos, and now…"

"I know."

China only nodded, laying her warm, smooth hand on Billy's arm. The familiar pulse of heat from her touch shot up his arm and slammed into his chest. He tried to ignore the sensation. Didn't want to feel it, especially now. All he wanted to feel was his anger and his grief. With uncharacteristic self-discipline contrary to every nerve ending in his body, he moved his arm, just the barest twitch, and China's hand fell away. Billy owed Cuco that much respect, ¿qué no? After all, his compa would never again feel the warmth of such a touch.

"Dime, Billy. What are you thinking?"

As he looked into China's golden, slant eyes, Billy was tempted to tell her. He wanted to tell someone. What would she think if he told her how scared he'd become deep in his bones? He didn't want to end up like Cuco, shot and left to drown in his own blood by some vato loco who had nothing to lose but his bad-ass reputation. And how could he explain that part of him wanted exactly that – would gladly change places with Cuco just to have the whole mess over with. Terminado. Nothing more to prove.

"Nada, China," he said at last, picking up a T-shirt from a pile on the table. "Nothing you would understand."

"Oh yeah? How would you know what I understand and what I don't understand? You think I'm just a dumb piece of ass," she said, eyes shining. "But you don't know ass from a hole in the ground, bro, so get offa that."

Billy winced at this last. Had she guessed his secret? Not only was he a coward, but he'd never been laid either. To conceal his shame, he threw the T-shirt back on the table and walked away. Halfway across the parking lot he felt her presence at his side.

"Don't get all pissed, dude." China said, plucking at the sleeve of his T-shirt. "Hey. It wasn't your fault you know."

"He was alone. He shouldn't have been alone."

"But it was Joker who kicked him out of the car."

The back of her hand brushed his as if she were making an offering of her touch. If only he had the courage to reach out and take it, but certain people were undoubtedly watching. What would they think if he took her hand? Pussy whoop. That's what they'd call him. But that wasn't the real problem. The real problem was that he still gave a damn what his so-called compas thought and his inability to reach for China's hand was just another example of his basic lack of cojones.

But Cuco'd had cojones. That night El Joker had tried to make Cuco take on those Bloods from South Park, calling him pussy and acting all hard. But he wasn't taking any bullshit from Joker, not Cuco. He was going to spend the night with his vieja, and nothing Joker could say or do was going to change that. Now THAT took cojones. After all, Joker was the only one among them who had wheels.

When Joker kicked Cuco out of the car, Billy should have said something, made a joke, stood on his head, jumped out of the car. In his heart, Billy knew even the smallest act on his part might have changed the outcome of that night. But he'd been too afraid of the consequences. As it was, he sat in the bitch seat. Now Cuco was dead and it was too late for Billy to stand up for him.

Without speaking, Billy and China continued walking, hands and shoulders grazing. At the stoplight China broke the silence. "What about the car wash, dude? Cuco was your homie; you're supposed to be helping."

Billy continued to ignore her even though it pained him to do so. China was not the one who deserved to be dissed. But he couldn't confront El Joker and the likes of Mario Fuentes with his hundred-dollar blood money. Billy had to get out of there, he knew that much, or his heart would bust open from the sheer pressure of his rage and shame.

"Where you going, Billy?" she called, but Billy didn't dare answer. Tears threatened his vision, and China's concern was only making matters worse. He didn't wait for the green light before crossing the street.

"That's weak, dude," China shouted, but he just kept veering steadily through the oncoming traffic.

The living room was shrouded in pale, amber light, shades pulled down to the windowsills – something his mother now insisted on. It wasn't the sunlight she was trying to shut out, but a clear shot into the room by some gangbanger who wanted to score a drive-by. Billy yanked on the bottom of the shade and it rolled up with a snap. For a moment he stood looking out at the empty street.

"Billy?" His mother called.

"What's up?" he answered.

His mother emerged from the kitchen, wiping her hands on a paper towel. Without a word, she pulled the shade back down. "You're home early, mijo. Did they make a lot of money at the car wash?"

He shrugged and raised the shade, but only halfway this time.

"I feel so sorry for his mother," she said. "If it was me, I'd tell 'em to keep their damn money. What's money when you've lost your son?"

"It'll pay for the funeral."

"Better to bury Cuco in a cardboard box than accept money from gangsters. When you're dead you don't know the difference between cardboard and brass. What do you think his mother's going to say? 'So much money, que bueno. We can get the really nice coffin, the one with the pretty handles. Now I can dry my eyes.' Madre de Dios, a million dollars won't dry that woman's tears."

Billy didn't want to hear it. Didn't want to think that there was nothing anybody could do to make Cuco's death easier. If his mother didn't shut up about it, he was afraid of what he might say, might do.

"I spoke to your father this morning."

Billy turned away from the window and for the first time, looked at his mother, noticed she seemed more tired than usual. Her hair, with its artful auburn streaks, was uncombed, and she had yet to apply the dark pencil that made each brow a perfect, graceful wing. If she had spoken to his father, that could not be good news. "What's up?" he repeated.

"For once he agrees with me."

"Let's get a pizza and celebrate."

"Don't get smart with me, Billy. I'm too tired."

"Well?"

"Your father's coming to get you tonight or maybe tomorrow morning."

"Coming to get me for what?"

"You're going to Las Cruces to live with your father and nana Fufi."

"I ain't going to no Las Cruces."

"Stop talking like a gangster."

"I ain't going to no Las Cruces."

"Mira, Billy. Do you think I like sending you to your nanna? She's been trying to get her hands on you since the day your father left. And wouldn't it have been easier for me if she had? But you're my son. The thought of sending you to her is killing me, Billy, but better me than you. I've made up my mind."

"What about school? I got only a couple of months left in the semester."

"Oh, now you're worried about school. That's a first."

"This is stupid. You think they don't got gangs in Las Cruces?"

"Maybe this time you won't let yourself be sucked into one. Maybe since Cuco... Your dad says he can get you a job bagging at the Fry's. You could save up some money. Maybe buy a car to drive to school next fall. Your dad says..."

"School next fall, where? Las Cruces? ¡Ni modo!"

"I've made up my mind, mijo," she said, talking hold of his chin until Billy was forced to look into her eyes. What he saw there was a dark determination.

Twisting his face free, he recognized that there were only two choices left to him. He could do as she said or he could run away.

"Well, mijo?"

"I ain't going to no fucking Las Cruces." Before she could say another word, he slammed out of the house.

It was a long walk back to the car wash so Billy had plenty of time to review his options. He couldn't move in with Guapo because the house was already full of his primos. There was room at Joker's, but the way he felt right now about that asshole, no way could he do that. Kiko might be willing to share his room with him. But Kiko's parents hated Billy for the same reason Billy's mother hated Kiko. Bad influence. He could get a job. Maybe he could have Cuco's old job at Los Dos Memos. Maybe he could even stay with Cuco's mother, pay rent, help her get by like Cuco always did. For a moment the thought lightened the weight pressing on his chest. Then the absurdity of it struck. Cuco was perfect, his body straight, his face handsome, and he was... well, he was Cuco. Billy was his exact opposite – twisted, ugly, a coward. No way could Cuco's mother look at him and not be reminded of the magnitude of her loss.

Of course, there was Mario Fuentes. Mario could put him to work – make a reality of his mother's worst fears. Billy always had assured her that she was crazy to think he would get involved with that heavy shit. Still, if he started dealing, not just the occasional leño, but big-time, Billy could afford a place of his own, a car. With plenty of spending money, maybe then he'd even be worthy of La China.

By the time Billy got back to Ricky's Shell there wasn't much left to be done. All of the spectators were gone and most of the crew had taken their rags and buckets home. La China had abandoned her post at the cash box and was washing a '60 Jimmy. It had once been in the service of roofers and was stained with ropes of tar. Its owner, a young national wearing a straw cowboy hat, was leaning against the side of the building studying China as she worked, brown thighs splashed with suds, black T-shirt sopping. Kiko, Guapo and, of course, El Joker were just standing around. Why wasn't anybody helping her? Billy felt the heat of his rage return.

"Hey Chueco, where you been, ese? Your piece of ass is still here, so I know you ain't been with her," Joker said rubbing Billy's hump for luck as he did every day, a dozen times a day.

Billy grabbed Joker's arm and closed his hand around it. Despite his small stature, Billy's arms were long, his hands big and strong. He squeezed hard. Satisfied that he'd made his point, Billy let go. For one thing, China was not his piece of ass. For another, if she were, Joker would have even less right to disrespect her.

"What's up with that?" El Joker said, examining the reddened fingerprints left on his wrists.

Billy picked up a bucket of soapy water and sauntered over to the truck. Without a word, he climbed on the hood and started washing the windshield.

Ignoring him, China got into the cab and began wiping the dash. Billy pressed his face against the soapy windshield, making a smear of his nose and mouth. When she still ignored him, he flattened his tongue against the glass and crossed his eyes. Though she pretended not to notice, Billy could see the dimple deepen at the corner of her mouth. Rag in hand, China started to wash the inside of the window. Billy matched his strokes to hers until they were both making mirrored, languid circles across the windshield, graceful as a swan on the mirror surface of a lake, or so it seemed to Billy.

When the window was cleaner than it had been since its manufacture, China jumped out of the cab. Billy followed her to the rear of the truck.

"You got soap on your nose," China said, flicking it off with a perfect, midnight- blue sculpted fingernail.

"You've got soap on your everywhere," Billy said, his fox-face bright. China's laugh washed over him like filtered sunlight, golden and warm.

"So why'd you come back?" she asked. "I thought you were all pissed."

Billy shrugged. "No place else to go."

"Oh," she said. "I thought maybe…"

"Maybe what?" Billy was hopeful.

"Maybe nothing," she said and Billy's hope dissolved.

"Hey, Quasimodo," Joker yelled. "Finish up that truck so we can get the hell out of here." Joker was smiling broadly, making his face appear more mule-like than ever. Billy wanted to take that face and turn it inside out.

"Fuck you," Billy said. "If you're in such a fucking hurry, esé, why don't you get over here and wipe the truck with your ass." He shot a look at China and was surprised to see that not only was she not smiling at his clever insult, the tell-tale dimple at the corner of her mouth had disappeared.

"Careful, Billy," she whispered. "You're gonna get your ass kicked."

Just then, it occurred to Billy that, not only was he willing to get his ass kicked, he wanted to kick ass, something he usually tried to avoid. Throwing his rag in the bucket, he stood facing Joker as square and erect as possible. Guapo and Kiko stepped back as Joker stepped forward. "What's this about?"

"Cuco."

"Look, ese. What happened to Cuco was what happened. It ain't my fault…"

"You kicked him out of the car."

"He wasn't down, man. You want to ride in my car, you gotta be down for Westside."

Billy considered this. It wasn't about loyalty among compas, it wasn't about watching each other's back, hanging out with your homies or any kind of love or trust among friends. It was about being down for Westside. What the fuck does that mean to anybody, he thought, and it became clear what he had to do. "I ain't down no more, Joker."

After the first punch, Billy was still standing. He didn't fall until the third or fourth, hardly felt it when Joker kicked him in the ribs. By the time the cop arrived, Billy was out cold.

His mother was waiting for him when he came out of emergency; but the cop was the first to speak. "You want to press charges, or what?" he asked.

"Nah," Billy said, trying not to breathe too deeply. "I was the one who started it."

The cop looked skeptical, a look he shared with Billy's mother. He started to protest, but only raised his eyebrows. "Have it your way," he said. It was obvious to Billy that the cop and his mother had been reviewing options, and had come to an understanding.

"He's all yours," he said.

Billy's mother sighed deeply as though accepting a great burden. "Thank you, officer."

On the way to the car, his mother was silent. She was still silent as she slipped behind the wheel, rolling up all the windows against the chill that had set in as soon the sun dipped behind the mountains. Billy turned the radio on. His mother snapped it off. It wasn't until they were belted in and headed down St. Mary's that she spoke.

"You were lucky this time, mijo. A cracked rib, a mild concussion, two black eyes, a broken nose – lucky."

"You should have let me take those tae kwon do lessons when I was ten."

"This is not a joke, Billy."

"Who's joking?" In fact, Billy truly wished he were proficient in tae kwon do, or karate or that one where you wave the sticks around. He'd have split Joker's mule face with its heehaw smile in two. Would have punched his head around so hard, he'd spend the rest of his life looking down at his own ass. Would have kicked his cojones so high, Joker'd have two sets of tonsils. As it was, Billy was unsure whether any of his punches had actually connected. His knuckles were scraped, but that could have happened when he was flailing on the ground.

Billy wondered briefly what people were saying. Were they laughing? Were they saying Quasimodo es loco? Was Joker telling everybody how he'd jumped the hump? He was surprised to find he really didn't care one way or another. Closing his eyes, he felt a strange satisfaction.

When Billy opened them, he saw his mother flick at her cheek as though a fly or a particle of ash had landed there. One of Billy's eyes was nearly swollen shut; still he couldn't help but notice with the other that his mother was flicking away one tear after another as she pulled over to the curb so she could cry without concern for the rush hour traffic. And cry she did, in loud, ripping sobs, shoulders shaking.

Billy's satisfaction drained away. His mother didn't cry often, hardly ever. In fact, he could not recall ever seeing his mother cry. "Ma, I'm okay. Really, Ma."

"Shut up," she sobbed.

Billy hung his head, but the position made his nose throb. "Lo siento, Mamá."

She faced him then. "Oh really? Dime pues, Billy, cause I really want to know. What exactly are you sorry about?"

Billy thought about this for some time. Considered the many ways, starting with his birth, that he had been a disappointment to his mother. Having been born ugly, he could have been an "A" student. That would be something, at least, to compensate for his being such a pinche baboso. "I'm sorry I make you sad," he said at last.

"Is that it? How little you understand, mijo," she said wiping her tears with the edge of her blouse. "I'm not crying because I'm sad. One emotion you've never made me feel is sadness, Billy. ¡Nunca! I'm crying because I just had my hair tinted and I don't want to pull out the black roots. I'm crying because I'm so angry I could slap your face and crying keeps me from doing it! I'm crying because tomorrow your father is coming and he's going to take you with him."

"Let me stay then."

"No, mijo. Once again you've made it clear that I've failed as a mother. I must be a terrible mother for you to go out and get the shit beat out of you like that. You never listen, do you Billy? I warned you about your compas. Thugs, gangsters, good for nothing pedazos de mierda, every one. But no, Billy, you're too smart to listen to me. Or maybe it's that I'm too stupid. You're better off with nana Fufi. You deserve each other."

Billy didn't know what to say. Although he wasn't always as respectful as his mother deserved, and he didn't do what he was told half the time, he loved her, knew her to be the best mother of all the mothers he knew. It was his turn to cry. Tears started slowly, like rain, one drop at a time.

For what seemed like a very long time they sat in silence. Billy could feel his mother's eyes drilling him, hot where her glare touched his skin. Finally, she pulled him to her, none too gently, bumping his swollen nose against her shoulder where he cried to prove his love for her, cried for his dead homie, cried for China, whom he'd surely lost, cried because he was such a weak-assed fuckup, and it was nobody's fault but his own. They both cried.

Though he'd taken another Percocet before sneaking out of the house, his body ached and his nose howled. Despite the pain, Billy had to see China one more time before his father came to take him away probably forever or until he turned eighteen, whichever came first.

China, who was the last of four girls, had warned him about her father, a tall, muscular Cubano. According to China, boys were against his religion or something and weren't even allowed in the house. No way could he simply knock on her door. So he had stood across the street, the cold making his nose swell like a ripe mango, until he saw her enter her bedroom and pull the shades down. He waited until the last light in the house went out, waited some more for her father to fall asleep, then waited for another eternity just to be sure. At last, his heart pounding painfully against his cracked rib, he crept onto the porch beneath her window. Scratching on the screen, he whispered her name.

The shade flapped up. "What took you so long?" she hissed. "I've been waiting."

"You were waiting for me?"

"You've been standing across the street forevers, well."

"You were watching me?"

"Wait a sec."

When she returned to the window she shone a flashlight over Billy's face. "Chingado," she whispered softly. "Oh Billy, he really did you a number. You okay?"

Billy shrugged. "Okay, just uglier than usual."

"Usual's not ugly, not really, Billy, not to me. So what you did today, why did you?"

Billy shrugged again, feeling his throat swell. Had China actually just told him that usually he wasn't ugly, or what? At that moment, Billy's mind was such a chaos of longing and confusion, he could hardly think. "Cuco," he said at last. It was all he could manage.

"Yeah, Cuco," she said, and Billy could tell from her voice, which was warm and soothing as a bowl of sopa de arroz con pollo, that she understood everything.

"Can I come in? It's cold out here."

"My old man nailed the screen shut after he caught my sister, Vela, climbing in the window at 4 a.m. That was three years ago. He's crazy, my old man."

"That's okay. I just came to say goodbye."

"Goodbye? Where are you going?"

"I've decided to go live with my old man in Las Cruces."

"Las Cruces? I hear Las Cruces is pretty cool."

"Not really."

"Why you going then?"

"Cause I don't want to have to see that mule face Joker or hear his heehaw ever again. Cause every time I do, I'll think of Cuco and the way he kicked him out of the car that night. Every time I see that puto, I'll want to beat the shit out of him. For the rest of my life, I'll want to beat the shit out of him, and every time he'll beat the shit out of me instead. Basically, I guess you could say that I don't want to go though life getting the shit beat out of me; it kind of hurts." Billy tried to laugh like it was all a big joke, but the sound that came out was more like somebody had their hands around his throat, squeezing.

"I'm going to miss you, pues," China said without a trace of a smile in her voice. "I respect you, man. You're the only dude who's never like, tried to exploit my pussy, you know what I mean?"

Sadly he did. "It's a matter of respect. You respect me. I respect you," he said, conscious of the half-lie. Right now, Billy could use less respect and more love in his life. "Dáme un beso, pues. You know, out of respect and all."

"Through the screen?"

"Why not?" China laughed out loud and Billy wished he could see her dimple. "Shine the light so I can see your face," he said. When she did, the sight of her caused an ache in his testicles equal to the ache of his cracked rib. She was still wearing the T-shirt from the car wash, her hair falling about her shoulders like a dark cloud, and there was the dimple, deep and sweet. "You're so beautiful, China, but not that kind of beautiful, although you are that kind of beautiful too, but what I mean is that you're not just that kind of beautiful..."

"What are you trying to say?"

"Just that you're the kind of beautiful that can look at me and see not just my outside, which is ugly as sin, but my inside too, which is … not so ugly.

"Don't say that. You're beautiful too that way, Billy."

"Yeah, we're just like Beauty and the Beast. Pues, dame un beso, and we'll see what happens. Maybe I'll turn into a handsome prince."

She pressed her lips against the screen then and he strummed them softly with the back of his finger before placing his mouth against hers. Mixed with the flavors of dust and rust was the minty tang of her tongue, the coconut scent of her hair. With his eyes closed, he could still see her hair, her eyes, her breasts rising beneath the black T-shirt, and his whole being throbbed. So great was the throbbing in his nose and his balls that he felt all three might explode. Still he could not take his lips away from hers.

At last, as tears of pain sprang from his eyes, China withdrew her lips from the screen.

"Just like in Beauty and the Beast," he said.

"Nah ah, ese. Just like China and Billy."

It was then she did something so amazing, so totally wonderful and unexpected it would fill his dreams for the rest of his life. She yanked the Cuco Maldonodo Memorial T-shirt over her head then flashed the light across her torso. And there they were, just as Billy had always imagined them – her golden chichis, high and round, nipples like Hershey's Kisses.

"Para ti," she whispered. "So you won't forget me, pues."

"Never, China. Nunca te olvidaré."

Billy took his time walking home. With every step, the thought of China stabbed him in the chest, or perhaps that was just the

Percocet wearing off. Whatever the cause, his pain was real, but so was his joy. It was a new sensation this pain, this joy, mixed up like it was, and he wondered if this was how life would always be.

Then he remembered how his compa died all alone, his life pooling around him. What was he thinking in those last moments, Cuco? Did he feel only pain? Could he find comfort in thoughts of Araceli? Did he long for her hand to hold or was it his mother he wanted?

No one would ever know. Billy only hoped that somehow Cuco would know – in heaven or in limbo or wherever Cuco was now – he'd hoped Cuco would understand how sorry he was about letting him down that night. More than that, he hoped Cuco would understand how changed he was, not only by loss, but by love. If anybody could understand, it would be Cuco.

As he approached the house, Billy saw his father's car in the drive. The lights were out, and he knew his mother's bedroom door would be closed. He pictured them in each other's arms. Why they could love but not live together, Billy didn't know. Tomorrow his father would take him to Las Cruces, but tonight, they were sharing a moment of joy. He understood now how sweet this could be. Wondered if the moments of joy were enough to balance all the rest. They would have to be, qué no, or why would anyone bother to go on living?

Quietly he entered the darkened house, determined to think only of China, so for this one night he could forget all the rest.

———•———

casaditos little married couple
vieja old woman, wife, girlfriend
pedazos de mierda pieces of shit

HABÍA UNA VEZ
(There Was a Time)

———◆———

Dos Arbolitos
(Chuco Martinez Gil)

Han nacido en mi rancho dos arbolitos, dos arbolitos
que parecen gemelos, y desde mi casita los veo
solitos bajo el amparo santo y la luz del cielo.
Nunca están separados uno del otro porque
así quiso Dios que los dos nacieran

This is a sad, sweet song. Like twins, the woman sings, two little trees were born on my ranch, and from my little house I could see them standing alone beneath the holy light from heaven, and so on and so on. I think the trees stand for babies who have died and the mother must leave them behind when she has to goes north.

– Lety

TÍA SOFÍA LET HERSELF IN through the back door. The house was quiet even though the sun was streaming through the window above the kitchen sink. The old woman filled the teakettle then set out coffee cups, sugar and spoons. From her bolsa of woven plastic, she extracted a box of cream-filled bizcochitos, a can of sweetened condensed milk, and one dozen of the three dozen tortillas she had made just that morning. There was a bakery box on the counter. She extracted a day old churro from the box and broke it in half. While she waited for the water to boil, she sucked on the sugary baton until it was soft enough to chew. The kettle began to scream. With care, she arranged each cookie on a plate, then opened the can of milk and sat down to wait.

When, at last, Lety came into the kitchen, eyes squinting against the sunlight, Sofía removed the kettle from the heat. "I hope I didn't wake you, mija. ¿Cómo amanecistes?"

"Ay, tía. What time is it?"

"No sé. The sun is up, pues. The water's ready. Shall I make us coffee?"

"What a night!"

"¿Dónde está la niña?"

"In bed, where I should be, of course."

"But shouldn't she be getting ready?"

"The funeral isn't until 10 o'clock. Besides, I don't think she's going."

"Not going? But she must."

"Six hours at the visitation. You saw her. She couldn't even make herself look at poor Refugio. It's a shame, he was lying there so pretty, so peaceful with the rosary tucked in his hand, la medalla de San Cristobal around his neck, it would have done her some good. Instead, she just sat there like a little rag doll. Why should she have to go through that again this morning?"

"Out of respect for Refugio's memory, out of respect for his mother... out of respect for herself."

"People will understand."

"No, mija. People will talk, and what they will say won't be pretty. Besides the boy's dead, and Araceli has yet to shed a single tear. She must face it. She must sit through the funeral, then stand by the grave until they throw the last shovel of dirt over his coffin. She must cry her eyes out, cry until she thinks there are no more tears left inside her and then she must cry some more. Until she does, she will hold him in her heart like a cold stone and will never be able to love again. I know something about letting go of the dead, mija, and what happens when you don't."

"You go talk to her, pues. I don't know how to talk so she'll listen."

"Coffee first, Leticia, por favor."

Lety put a rounded spoonful of instant in each cup, then filled them with boiling water.

Sofía poured a thick stream of condensed milk into her coffee until it was the same shade of brown as her own skin. "She's your daughter, not Isabela queen of Spain. Just talk to her."

"I can't."

"I've never known you to be shy about expressing yourself, Leticia. Why is it you have so much trouble talking to Araceli?"

"Because I'm afraid her eyes will get stuck in the top of her head, and she'll have to go through life como una ciega con los ojos siempre mirando al cielo," Lety said, demonstrating for her aunt the expression combining contempt, boredom and disbelief that all children master by age twelve. "Maybe it was wrong for her to come live with me after all these years."

"It was what God wanted." Sofia said, twisting a cookie apart to expose the filling.

"How do you know God wanted it?"

"She's here living with you, ¿qué no?" Sofía licked the filling from the cookie, then softened the rest in her coffee before placing it in her toothless mouth."

"Pues, God must want you to talk to her then, because you're here."

"Ay, Leticia," the old woman sighed and rose from her chair. "Do her a cup of coffee with plenty of milk and sugar. I'll take it to her. Si Dios le quiere, she'll listen to me."

Tía Sofía knocked on the door, but didn't wait for permission to enter. "Mijita, I brought you coffee." The girl did not stir.

"Araceli. Wake up now. You must get ready for the funeral. It's getting late and we have to be there at least a half hour ahead." Slowly the girl opened her eyes.

"Sit up now and take your coffee."

Without a word, Araceli did as she was told.

"Your mother tells me you're not going to the funeral, but that is impossible. Everyone will be there and they'll expect to see you. Refugio's poor mother will expect to see you. His friends and relatives will expect to see you. Refugio from heaven, if that's where he is, will expect to see you. You cannot let them all down."

Araceli, staring into middle space, simply shook her head.

Tía Sofía patted her cheek gently. "I know," she whispered. "I know too well."

After a few minutes she began spooning the sweet, thick liquid into Araceli's mouth, holding a napkin beneath the girl's chin to catch spills as she would for a small child.

"Había una vez, mijita, when I was young like you, I lost my son. My first. Did you know that? No. How could you know, pues? It was many years ago, but I will never forget that one, even though I never saw him with his eyes open or heard him cry. We were living, Eduardo and I, en un ranchito, way out in el campo, a day's drive by wagon from Imuris, half a day if we could get a ride in the back of a truck. There was no priest, so Eduardo gave our son his first and last blessing himself, using my tears instead of holy water."

Tía Sofía let her mind wander back to that time more than fifty years ago. She and Eduardo had nothing but each other, yet they were tan felices, tan enamorados. And the passion! They were at it so much that first year, she happily giving in to Eduardo's every whim, it's surprising any work got done on the little ranch. Even now, sitting by this poor, grief-stricken girl, she felt her cheeks glow at the memory of their lovemaking. When their son was stillborn, she knew he'd been strangled in the womb by her lust. Never again did she put the love of her husband's body before the love of God.

What was left of the coffee was cold when she again turned her attention to the girl. "I'm getting old, mijita. Look, I've let this coffee get cold."

"It's all right, tía. I've had enough."

"Get up, pues, and I'll comb your hair."

"I need to wash it."

"No. At a time like this, you should never look too good. People will talk. I'll put it simple. A braid, maybe, or a knot. Which one?"

Araceli shrugged her shoulders.

Sofía considered the options – a tight braid versus a loose knot at the back of the head. What would be the effect? A braid would stay neat, whereas a knot could be loosened by grief. She imagined the girl's beautiful hair, streaming over her trembling shoulders like a dark river. "The knot, pues," she announced.

"But first, what are you going to wear? You go make pipi and brush your teeth, while I pick something out for you."

As Sofía stood in front of the closet, it was as if a hand were pressing on her shoulder, directing her back to her last day on the ranch. There had been a drought. How many seasons had they gone without rain? Too many. What cattle hadn't died of hunger and thirst, had been slaughtered for their hides. Only a few chickens remained, and these too old and thin to lay. Eduardo and Teodoro, their oldest boy, had taken the journey al norte, to find work and a place for them all to live. It had been months since she'd had any word. The corn was nearly gone and they were down to the last of the beans. Every week she would kill another chicken, always choosing the scrawniest, the one most likely to be caught by a coyote or simply die of natural causes. To this she would add a few beans, chiles and the tender young pads cut from the enormous nopal that grew in her front yard and make a thin soup. In this way, she was able to provide for herself and her daughter, Regina, who at age four did not yet speak in sentences and displayed a passivity that was at once a worry and a blessing, for the child seldom complained of hunger or boredom.

Every day Sofía anticipated Eduardo's return. Nevertheless, she was oddly unprepared when, at last, a plume of dust appeared on the horizon. Eventually, the truck, a battered Chevy faded by years of desert sun, pulled into the dirt yard where the last two chickens scratched for bugs at the base of the nopal. Despite the drought, the prickly pear was covered with an extravagance of waxy, yellow blossoms, which in time would swell into dozens of sweet, seed-laden fruit.

Eduardo took his time getting out of the truck. When he did, Sofía greeted him almost shyly, so long had they been apart. "I expected you sooner," she said, though this was not what she felt in her heart.

"Ay vieja, what did you expect?" he said, gruffly. "I work every day. To miss a day's work is to be fired. At any rate, I am here now, and this is how I'm welcomed?"

Sofia reached up and caressed his unshaven cheek with her rough, dry palm. Eduardo snatched her wrist and brought it to his lips. Sofía smiled at last. "Are you hungry? There's sopa de pollo."

"I promised I'd have the truck back before dark. Are you ready? Where are your things?"

In truth there wasn't much, but it was not easy to decide what should go and what should be left behind. She gave Regina a string bag and allowed her to choose for herself, as she gathered up certificates of baptism and marriage, her wedding portrait. From the trunk, she took the coverlet she had crocheted as a girl for the cama matrimonial. Because of the yellow dust that defied her vigilant efforts, her one beautiful possession had only been used that first night. She looked around the little adobe. What else of value was there but a few articles of clothing for each of them, her brush, her comb? After fifteen years, except for the children, casi nada. Still, leaving would be difficult. There was so much happiness, so much sadness captured within those four walls.

Sofía's thoughts turned to her firstborn resting in the mesquite bosque next to his sister who died before her third birthday. Though their graves were surrounded by a white picket fence, left untended, the wild grasses would soon overtake them, would obscure the fence even, if the rains returned.

She lifted Regina into the truck. "What about the chickens?" Sofía asked.

"Leave them. There are lots of fat chickens en el norte," Eduardo said, tossing the bundles into the back of the truck. "¿Estás lista?"

"Momentito." Taking the machete from its hook on the side of the house, she hacked two fat pads from the nopal, each crowned with blossoms. "I'll be right back."

She hurried to the mezquite bosque, entered the little white gate. With the machete she scooped out a shallow basin for the prickly pear pad at the head of each little grave. The prickly pear would root. Come Los Días de los Muertos, her babies would not go hungry. Eduardo was suddenly at her side then. "Regresaremos, amor, when the drought it's over."

Sofía wanted to believe this, but once people left for el norte, they rarely returned. When she closed the gate securely behind her, she knew it was for the last time.

Was that the hardest thing she had ever done, leaving her dead babies behind? Sofía thought that perhaps it was.

Lety was standing over the sink eating a buttered tortilla. "Well?"

"She's getting dressed. Would you like me to fix you some huevos revueltos to eat with that tortilla?"

"No gracias, tía. I have no appitite. But you go ahead."

"No gracias, mija. Maybe just another bizcochito. I just have to put my dientes," Sofía said, withdrawing Kleenex wrapped dentures and a tube of Polygrip from her bag. When the teeth were in place, she snapped at the air, then gingerly nibbled on the corner of a cookie. "Estos traviesos, como me duelen."

"I'm worried about her."

"She'll survive. What other choice does she have? Besides, God does not give us burdens that are too heavy to bear, though it may seem that way. Tú verás."

Lety sat to the right of her daughter, but it was tía Sofía who held the girl's limp hand in her own while Araceli stared blindly ahead. Regina was reciting the rosary with her usual fervor, seemingly oblivious to the young man whose beautiful head rested on a satin pillow. Only Lety was crying. But it was not for Refugio that she shed those hot tears. They were not even for her grieving daughter. Lety was crying over her own losses, the fathers of her children, one dead, the other all too alive and well. And she cried for her mother. Gone just over a year – long enough for her to forget the woman's true nature – Lety was now able to mourn for the mother she had wanted, rather than the one she had gotten. Such is the purpose of funerals.

As for Araceli, too numb to understand the meaning of death, her mind was as blank as her face. If she felt anything, it was a longing for the day to end so she could sleep and dream of nothing and sleep again. Perhaps it was best that her lover be put to rest before she came to her senses. Who is to say?

And tía Sofía? She was drifting here and there among the pooling light and dark that was her past. Certainly, she was reminded of the deaths of her babies, and that of Teodoro. He had grown to beautiful manhood only to die in a war over a country she'd never heard of. Unlike Germany, England or Africa, which she could easily locate on a world map, this country was so small she couldn't find it even when she put on the anteojos she bought at the Walgreens. With those glasses, she could easily

thread a needle or pluck a spine out of a finger, but she could not
find the place where her son had died.

And of course, there was always Eduardo, long departed from
this earth. They were still living in Nogales, back then. Teodoro
and Regina were already grown, though Regina remained at
home. And Jonny, born to her late in life, had to be sixteen. He
was eight years younger than Zulema. That would mean she was
twenty-four when they had first met. How beautiful Zulema had
been then, like Leticia, pero más güera, más gordita. Sofía had
taken an instant dislike to the woman as she stood on the threshold, two children in tow, a skinny girl of six or seven, and a husky
boy a bit older with ruddy cheeks and a snotty nose.

"Buenas tardes, señora," said the woman. "You don't know
me, but I'm the daughter of your husband's first wife's sister."

"You must be mistaken, señora. I am my husband's first wife."

"Is your husband Eduardo Mateo Guerrero?"

"Si pues, pero…"

"Here, my aunt gave me this picture."

In the picture, Eduardo, slick and handsome as the devil,
was arm and arm with a girl. A large corsage of roses was pinned
to the lapel of her white suit; her eyes shone with joy. "Come in.
What did you say your name was?"

"Zulema Mendoza, and this is my son, Javier." She pushed the
boy forward. "And esta morenita is Leticia," she said pointing to
the girl with her thumb.

Before the woman left, Sofía gave her five dollars for rice
and beans. Around the little dark one's shoulders she wrapped
her warmest sweater, for Nogales in the winter was harsher than
a newcomer would expect. This was especially true in las colonias, hovels without water or electricity that teetered along the
windy arroyos y cerros del otro lado, where Zulema and her

children had taken residence among the thousands of other failed pilgrims.

Sofía promised to bring food, blankets, shoes and clothing. With the help of Regina and Jonny she did again and again, not for Zulema's sake, of course, but for the sake of her fatherless children. It was her duty as a Christian woman, just as it was her duty to forsake her husband's bed. Certainly she knew there had been other women. Sofía was not blind, nor was she a fool. But this business of a first wife – no matter how much he denied it – was another matter. If there is a first wife, then there cannot be a second. Though they continued to live in the same house, it was no longer as man and wife. And that's the way it remained between them until Eduardo was sent to the next world by taxi.

Ah, Eduardo, she thought. Where does your soul rest?

How angry she had been at the time of his death, so angry she could not shed a single tear even for the sake of propriety. But at Eduardo's funeral, Zulema had cried too many tears for an uncle she hardly knew. Heads had turned.

Barely two weeks after the funeral, Zulema came by the house with a few day old buñuelos, and complained. "Ay tía, I feel so fat. I was wondering, maybe you know of something that will bring my regla. I'm past due."

She studied the woman's smooth face. "How much past due?"

"Not much," Zulema answered, turning away from Sofia's gaze.

She hesitated, weighing her Christian values against the tears Zulema shed at Eduardo's funeral. At the time of his death, Eduardo was still tan robusto, with a head of blue-black hair and strong white teeth. Her own hair and teeth began to fall out shortly after Jonny's birth. So long and hard that one had sucked at the breast, he had drawn the very marrow from her bones. She was worn out, but not her husband. Eduardo had gotten a green card for Zulema. What had he gotten in return?

"I'll make you some té de ruda y epazote," she said, putting the kettle on the stove. "That's the best I can do."

"Make it strong, pues,"

"If God wants this baby to be born, Zulema, there is nothing you or I can do."

"Who said anything about a baby? She said, dropping into a chair. "Besides, this has nothing to do with God, tía. It's my stupidity."

"Don't you think God has a hand in your stupidity?"

Zulema made no response, and the women waited in silence as the tea steeped. "Take this now," Sofía finally directed. "And don't leave your house for 24 hours."

"Twenty-four hours? What about my job?"

"Tell them you have the flu. If the tea works, you'll wish you had."

Two days later Zulema came to her again complaining, "Do you have anything for cramps?"

"No, Zulema," she had told her, not without a certain degree of satisfaction. "I am all out of remedios."

But this was not true. She had provided her with one final remedy. Years later she had given Zulema another herb to ease the pain from a cancer that was eating at her from the inside out. One night, Zulema had taken too much of the herb and too much tequila.

Sofía made her confession to the priest. Had she acted out of compassion or had there been only the guise of compassion masking a darker purpose? Certainly she had once hated Zulema, but passions fade, ¿qué no? And both love and hate become something else, a reluctant companionship, perhaps, when memories are shared.

But if Sofía had provided a means to hasten death, it had been Zulema who had provided the will do to so. At any rate, Father Tom had absolved her of guilt.

Pues, Zulema, no doubt about the resting place of your soul. So many years ago and I'm the only one left alive to remember. I'm an old woman, she told herself.

And it was a good thing too. Sofía now had a freedom she'd never enjoyed in her youth. Hiding behind the veil of age, she could say or do whatever she pleased and she was as content in old age as she'd ever been. So why should it still matter? It shouldn't, but apparently it still mattered very much.

A clot of doubt lingered in Sofía's heart over the purity of her motives that day. This intensified her rancor for the woman, leaving Sofía without the peace of mind that was otherwise her due.

She patted a tear from her eye with a crumpled tissue. Ay, Zulema, she thought. You plagued my life and now you throw a roadblock across my path to heaven. Where is the fairness in that?

At the gravesite, the bright sun drained the grass and trees of color. Though Araceli did not cry, she did collapse to her knees at one point, causing the knot at the back of her neck to unravel just as Sofía had envisioned, thus satisfying the old woman that those present would be impressed by the girl's deep and lasting grief.

Sofía put the kettle on the stove while Leticia helped her daughter into bed. From her bolsa, she withdrew a bottle of tequila and poured a generous amount into three teacups, to which she added azúcar y limón. When the water boiled, she added a little of that too, then placed the cups and bottle on a tray.

When Sofía entered the room, the shades were drawn and the two were sitting on the edge of the bed, Leticia brushing the girl's hair in the yellow light.

"Take this, mijitas," Sofía said, selecting a cup for herself.

"What is it?" Leticia asked, sniffing the fumes rising from the cup. "Tequila?"

"Si, pues. For the nerves." She handed a cup to Araceli. "It's good for you. Drink it and you'll feel better."

For a few moments, the three women sipped in silence. "Había una vez, I was young and in love like you, mijita. Only love can bring tanta alegría, tanto dolor. All other joy, all other sorrow is dull by comparison, verás. But that's the way God wants it to be."

"Do you really believe that's what God wants, tía?" Araceli asked, an edge in in her voice. For the first time in days, the girl seemed fully awake.

"Sí, pues, because that's the way it is."

"That's wrong. It's wrong that Refugio should be dead. It's wrong that my father should be dead, your husband. All dead too soon. It's wrong."

"No, mija, la muerte is like joy and sorrow. Without death, there is no reason to love life."

"I don't understand."

"Habra una vez, Araceli," Sofía said, lacing each cup again. "When you're an old woman like me, you will understand. It takes awhile, but the time will come. Now take your tequilita. As they say, toma cerveza to bring down milk. Toma tequila to bring down tears."

———◆———

como amanecistes literally, how did you meet the dawn/how did you sleep

como una ciega con los ojos siempre mirango al cielo like a blind woman always looking at the sky

los días de los muertos the days of the dead, November 1st and 2nd

regresaremos we will return

estos traviesos, como me duelen these trouble-makers, how they hurt me

tu veras you'll see

más guera, más gordita lighter skinned, plumper

arroyos y cerros del otro lado the gullies and hills on the other side

La Secreto de Lluvia
(The Secret of Rain)

La Reina del Sur
(Teodoro Bello Jamies)

Voy a cantar un corrido escuchen muy bien mis compas
Para la reina del sur traficante muy famosa
Nacida allá en Sinaloa, La Tía Teresa Mendoza...
una mujer muy valiente, que no la van a olvidar

This is a ballad about Teresa Mendoza, a famous drug dealer with bigger huevos than most men. It's a true story. She disappeared a long time ago and nobody knows if she's dead or alive.

– Lety

CHINA WAS LYING ON HER bed, golden belly protruding slightly between hip hugging Spandex and cropped top. As she listened to Radio Caliente, she contemplated the strange twists and turns fate, or God, or whatever, imposes. It was the capricious nature of these impositions that bothered her, though China wouldn't use the word capricious, had never even heard the word. She would simply say that la vida es una chingada.

Conceived during one of Tucson's kick-ass summer storms that knock out electricity and leave la gente to huddle in the warm dark while water the color and consistency of chocolate milk laps at the foundation, she was named Lluvia, rain, though nobody called her that but her sister, Vela, and her father. Since sixth grade, everybody that mattered called her La China, for her slant eyes and golden skin.

Bored and vaguely pissed, she readjusted the pillow. Los Tigres del Norte were singing "La Reina del Sur," a corrido about Teresa Mendoza, una mujer con muchos huevos, who ran drugs all over the world. In most Mexican songs, women are only loved for their bodies, but this song tells how Teresa is admired not for her looks, but her intelligence and bravery.

Usually the song energized her, but this afternoon, she wasn't even motivated enough to call one of her home-girls so they could go to the mall, at least. Since her novio, if that's what Billy was, left town, China had lost her ambition. She missed Billy, missed his sweet, jokable ways. She also missed her sister, Vela, who ran away from home last month to escape their father's rules. For now, Vela was cleaning rooms at a Ramada Inn in La Mesa, but pretty soon, she'd find a real job, one worthy of her, perhaps something like a dentist's receptionist. But China wasn't allowed to even mention Vela in her father's presence, much less discuss job prospects, pues, though sometimes when he wasn't home, she'd call Vela's cell and they'd talk for hours. If her papa noticed the charge on the phone bill, he never said nada.

And she missed her mother, or at least the idea of her mother. China had been only four when her mother's Ford Escort was run over by a monster truck with outsized wheels. According to Vela, they had used the Jaws of Life to extract her from the wreckage, but in her mother's case they'd been the Jaws of Death.

She'd been one of those white Mexicans, her mother, with hair the color of autumn leaves, green eyes and a dusting of freckles across her nose and shoulders. Delicate and beautiful, she'd been the exact opposite of her father, who was a tall Cubano from Miami with lustrous dark skin and a deep, resonant voice.

When he first moved to Tucson to begin training for airport security, he thought it would be temporary, but then he met her mother at a party and it had been love at first sight and for reals, or so Vela tells it.

Suddenly, China had such a longing for her mother. She felt as if her chest had been opened, and instead of a heart, there was a stone that bled. Only a mother would have the words to explain such a feeling.

The only photo of her mother was in a silver frame on the shrine in the corner of her father's bedroom. China needed to look into her mother's eyes, needed to behold the lips that still might open to whisper the words that could alter her life. She rolled off the bed. On the way to her father's room, she passed the kitchen where she grabbed an apple from a basket on the counter.

Standing before the shrine, China absently gnawed the fruit. Illuminated by small votive candles – there were always seven – and the weak, sulfur light that sifted through the drawn blinds, the photo stood before a statue of la Virgen de Guadalupe. China picked it up, stroking the wings of the doves that lit on each corner of the frame as she gazed at her mother's face. The lips held a faint smile, and the eyes seemed to caress China's face. Her mother had loved her very much. Many times Vela had told her so.

She wiped a slick of apple drool from her chin then kissed her mother's picture before replacing it exactly as she had found it. Her father didn't like her to touch the shrine and its mysterious articles of devotion. In addition to the seven candles, there were seven blue plastic carnations in a white vase, seven polished stones, smooth and dark as her father's skin, a glass with a bouquet of watercress, pale roots feathering the green stems. All was arrayed on a tablecloth of starched white crochet, beautiful and, at the moment, serene.

It was getting late. Soon her father would be home and she needed to start dinner. China wandered back into the kitchen, still dissatisfied with life in general and her own in particular. Some days she wanted to run away like Vela, but that would leave her father alone. Sure, he was one crazy-assed nigger, especially when it came to boys. He kept chickens out back like some damn hick and had a pet turtle named Orfeo that he'd bring in the house every so often to chase out los espíritus malos, pues. But she couldn't hurt him like that. No, for better or for worse, she loved her father. Often he told her how much she reminded him of her mother, so China knew he loved her too. That's why, no matter how crazy he might get, pues, with his voodoo shit and duendes, she'd never tell another soul, not even Billy, that it was her father who killed Alfonso Longoria, the one everybody called El Joker.

It all came down not long after Billy left town. China and her homies, Li'l Chica, Roja Loca and La Gordita, had been kicking it at Los Betos when El Joker drove up in the old Buick he thought was so fine he even polished the rust. Guapo was riding shotgun and Kiko, looking sorry, was in the bitch seat. El Joker jerked his chin at her and smiled his big yellow-toothed smile.

In China's mind, El Joker was at the heart of her pain. Because of him, Billy had left town, left her. Did Joker actually think he could put the moves on her? Ni modo, she thought, turning her back.

"I don't want nothing to do with that pinche mule-face ca-brón," she said to her home girls.

Joker laid rubber pulling into a parking spot. Before getting out of the car, he untied the sharply pressed blue bracero scarf that he wore around his head, Apache style. This he hung from the rearview mirror then smoothed back his black, well-oiled hair with his palms. Flanked by his homies, Joker ambled over, legs splayed as if to make room for a pair of enormous cojones between them.

"Here he comes," Gordita whispered.

China rolled her eyes and twisted her plump lips, exposing the deep dimple at the side of her mouth. When she felt the hot weight of his hand on her shoulder, she shrugged it off, saying to no one in particular, "Do you smell something feo? Something kinda like a steaming pile of dog shit?"

Her home girls, especially La Gordita, really thought that was funny. They laughed like crazy, slapping each other on the backs. China turned then, took El Joker in from the top of his seal-slick head to the bottom of the oversized jeans that covered his shoes and said, "Oh. It's only Joker." Again a roar of approval from the home girls. China had a hard time keeping her mouth straight.

"Who you dissing, bitch?" he said, grabbing China by the arm.

China held him with her slant eyes. "Nadie," she said, digging her lavender acrylic nails into his wrist. "Cus, you ain't nobody, pendejo."

That's when he hit her, a quick jab to the mouth.

She fought the urge to bring her hand to her lip. "Is that all you got, Joker?" She said to his back, as he swaggered to his car, a study in indifference.

That was only the second time in her life anybody had dared hit her in the face. The first was when she got jumped into Westside, but that was with her permission, more or less, so it was okay. This time it was definitely not okay. "Damn," she whispered, as tears threatened to shame her in front of her friends. "I'm going to kill his sorry ass."

When she got home she'd put ice on her mouth but it hadn't done much to dull the pain or lessen the humiliation. She winced as she applied another coat of Black Cherry to her lips. But even Black Cherry couldn't hide the swelling and the angry split. Man, she thought, examining her lip in the mirror. How am I going to explain this? Part of her wanted her father to know nothing about her life outside the house they shared. Part of her wanted to tell him everything so he could take care of it for her, just as he had always taken care of her, matter of factly, without an excess of emotion.

He didn't notice it right away. Just came in the house, dropped onto the couch with no more than a glance in her direction. "Bring your papá a glass of iced tea," he said, clicking on the evening news.

When China set the glass on the coffee table, he asked about school. "You stay out of trouble?" When she didn't respond immediately, his eyes snapped from the television screen to her face, where he expected to see the answer.

Before she could turn away, he grabbed her tightly by the wrist. "Sit down, mijita," he said quietly, putting the television on mute. "I thought I told you not to get into any more fights. Thought I said one more fight and I would take your cell away, ground your little yellow ass for the rest of the year. Did you think I was joking, mijita?"

"I wasn't in a fight."

"¿No? Entonces, ¿que le pasó a tu boca?" He said, reaching out to touch her bottom lip.

"Nada," she lied, jerking her head away. "I just... bumped it on... a door."

"On the door? Either you're telling your papá a lie, Lluvia, or you've become very clumsy. Since I've never known you to be clumsy, you better bring me that cell phone you love so much that it seems like it's growing out your ear."

"It wasn't like that," China said. The tears she'd been trying not to spill suddenly slipped from her eyes in ones and twos at first, like the start of a summer rain. Soon there was a flood of tears, and she could not speak. Her father sat quietly at her side, waiting out the storm.

Several minutes passed before the clenching in her throat eased enough for her to tell him how it had happened. China opened her heart to her father then, as she hadn't since leaving childhood behind. She told him how her friend, Cuco, had been killed, and how Joker had beaten Billy up, the one with the twisted spine, pobrecito, and how everything that was making her life a chingada was Joker's fault.

"No uses palabras tan groseras, mijita," was her father's only response to this outpour, so China told him how Joker had laid his hand on her shoulder as if he owned her. Of course, she edited her response to this advance, saying only that she had told him not to touch her.

"Y por eso, Papá, he hit me in the mouth," she said, watching her father's skin grow a shade darker as she waited for him to speak.

For a long time he merely sipped his tea while gazing at the muted television. At last he said, "You bring me... let me think." He sat there another long minute, lips pursed, patting his fingertips together. "Bring me a piece of his clothing – a cap, a handkerchief. Any little thing will do."

"What are you going to do?" She asked, picturing the blue bandana hanging from Joker's review mirror.

Her father shrugged. "You are the blood that runs through my veins, mijita, entonces... I'm going to make him regret."

The four girls met in the bathroom at the appointed time. La Gordita wanted to comb her hair first, but China grabbed her hand and pulled her into the hallway. Since it was only midway into third period, the halls were empty. Quietly, they descended via the northwest staircase of the second floor. It was farther from the exit to the parking lot, but they were less likely to run into the hall monitors who usually hung out in the southeast stairwell, gossiping and complaining instead of canvassing the second and third floors. The detour necessitated that they pass the big window in front of the counselors' office. They did this one at a time, each girl striding along purposefully, a slip of white paper held aloft to simulate a hall pass. Once outside, they scanned the parking lot for the faded Buick. It was not there.

"Now what?" Li'l Chica wanted to know.

China shrugged, tonguing the split in her bottom lip. "Damn."

"Why don't you just touch his arm and say you're sorry," Roja Loca suggested. "You don't have to mean it, pues. Then he'd let you have anything you want, the fucking engine from his fucking car even."

"Say I'm sorry? Nunca, girl. Let me think."

La Gordita took her compact from her purse. Smiling into the reflection, she pulled a coil of stiffly moussed hair from behind her ear and let it dangle along side her round face. After a moment, she slipped it behind her ear again and closed her compact. "Hurry up and make up your mind, well. I've got to get back to class before El Pelón sees me gone."

"So go, bitch. No one's holding you back."

"Don't get all hard, girl," La Gordita said, refusing to take offense. "It's just that if I get another cut… My dad will kill my ass if I get suspended one more time. Besides, I still don't get why you want to steal Joker's stupid bandana. What kind of revenge is that? If it was me, I'd just key his car and be done with it."

"I'm going to his house," China said with finality.

"Shit," Li'l Chica whispered. "Now?"

"¿Cómo no? He's probably home right now, just sitting around getting high with his compas."

"You're crazier than I am," Roja Loca said, arching one slim red brow. "I'm going back to class."

"Me too," Li'l Chica said.

Only La Gordita hesitated. "If I get another cut…"

"Go on, pues," China said, clearly disgusted. "I'll do it by my own damn self." She regretted the words as soon as they were out of her mouth. The idea of going to Joker's house alone made her stomach roil. Then she thought of La Reina del Sur. La Reina didn't need nobody but La Reina, andlLa China didn't need no-body but La China. Gordita, Chica or Roja, pues, they had their own fucked-up lives to live, ¿qué no?

Though it was only April, the sun was hot, and by the time China arrived on Joker's block, perspiration was making her scalp itch. She stood in the shade of a mesquite to cool off while she stud-ied his house. Though she'd driven by it once or twice, she'd never really noticed what a dump it was. The torn screen door and weeds poking through the chain link fence gave it a lonely, hopeless feeling. Why didn't somebody fix the place up – a little paint, a new screen door – she wondered. At least Joker, that lazy cabrón, could pull a few weeds.

The old Buick was parked in the shade of the house, the blue bandana hanging from the rearview as usual. China was about to make her move when the front door opened and a woman with a face to match the house came out the front door clutching a large black purse. China stepped deeper into the shade.

"Apúrate, mijo," the woman called, turning back towards the dark opening. "We're going to be late for your sister's doctor's appointment. After a moment, El Joker stood in the doorway carrying what at first appeared to be a heap of clothes. When he adjusted the load, China realized that the heap had arms and legs and a head larger than one would expect from so small a bundle. The child was smiling broadly. She screeched unintel-ligibly, but with obvious delight, as Joker bounced her playfully in his arms. Joker was smiling too, a smile with light in it. China had never seen such a smile on his face before. The woman got into the back seat of the car, and Joker laid the child across her lap as if she were some delicate and valued cargo, a dozen long-stemmed roses perhaps.

From her hiding place beneath the mesquite, China watched until the car was out of sight.

On the way home, she couldn't escape the image of a bundle with arms, legs and a head, and how tenderly Joker had carried it to the car. And the mom, pues. She looked like her sorry life had beaten a path across her face.

How does that happen to people, she wondered, and vowed it would never happen to her. From now on, she'd only smoke dope on special occasions. And she would never get pregnant until she was old, twenty-five or even thirty, when she could afford a good house. Maybe she'd even start doing her homework. After all, she wouldn't be young forever. She had to start preparing for real life, pues, whatever her real life might turn out to be.

Lo que pasa es lo que Dios desea, a voice whispered in her ear. Part of China believed that God had a hand in all things. The other part, La Reina del Sur part, figured you get what you go after. All a person needed to do was figure out what she truly wanted, then go for it.

They never caught her, La Reina del Sur. One day she just disappeared. People say she's dead or maybe hiding out in Spain or Italy, but China liked to think of her in some tropical place in Mexico, mangos and plátanos hanging from the trees free for the taking, where she would live the life of una reina verdad, dispensing food, clothing and medicine to the poor indios. She would have started an orphanage and built everybody a new house, because China had decided long ago that for La Reina, drug running had never been about money. No, it was about survival against all odds, it was about fighting injustice, it was for the love of life and adventure.

Once home, China stood before her own house, really seeing it as others might. In the yard, the oleander bushes were covered with red and pink flowers; her mother's irises bloomed along the walkway. Her father had repainted the house just last fall, pale pink on the walls and bright blue around the windows and on the door. Here, it seemed, a hopeful family lived.

By the time China walked through the front door, all thoughts of revenge were gone. But what would she say to her father? Although Joker had no right to hit her, she had misled her father, lied actually, about her part in it. China went into her bedroom and stood before a closet so crammed with clothing that she had trouble choosing. Finally, she selected a blouse at random and tore off a button.

"Is this all you could get, a button?" he asked, an edge of impatience in his voice.

"But you said any little thing would work okay."

"Did I? Then this will have to do, pues." Getting up from the couch, he added, "Don't you have some homework to do?"

"Not tonight," she lied, and followed him into his bedroom where he dropped the button on the crochet-covered table before the statue of Virgen de Guadalupe.

"Go to your room, mijita, and do the homework you say you don't have," her father directed quietly.

"You can't ask la Virgincita for revenge, papá. She won't do it."

He simply shrugged. "Before she was known as la Virgincita, Lluvia, she was Yemayá, so it depends on who's doing the asking and how. Andale, pues. I'll call you when it's time for dinner."

Reluctantly, China left him contemplating the photo of her mother. Not ten minutes after she closed her bedroom door, a single strangled squawk lifted the fine hairs on the back of her neck and along her arms. It grew dark and she grew hungry but China knew better than to leave her room before her father called. When he did, she smelled the stewing chicken and her appetite left her.

"Heat up the beans and rice, Lluvia, and set the table. This stew is almost ready."

"Why did you kill her? There's chicken in the freezer."

"She was old. Hasn't laid an egg in months, pues."

When China still hesitated, he added, "Las orejas no pasan la cabeza." It was a phrase she heard often and hated. The ears never get ahead of the head. What the hell did that mean anyways. Rolling her eyes, she did as she was told.

While her father took his usual nap during the ten o'clock news, China crept back into the bedroom to see for herself what her father had been up to. Everything seemed to be in its place, the picture of her mother, the Virgincita, the blue plastic flowers. But as she turned to go, she saw in the flickering candlelight that the once beautiful, smooth stones were now covered with the tarry blood of the old hen.

For awhile, China waited for some disaster to befall Joker or herself, since it had been her button. But weeks passed and nothing out of the ordinary occurred. Once in a while, China would think of Joker's mother and her own promise to change her ways, but mostly she ignored such thoughts. Figuring there was still plenty of time to grow up, homework assignments were left untouched, and she looked forward to each weekend when she and her friends would score a couple of leños and get high.

Then one morning before class, China was in the girl's bathroom applying another layer of midnight blue mascara, when La Gordita came running in, eyes as round as her face. "Did you hear what happened to Joker?" She said, nearly panting.

"No! ¿Qué pasó?" China asked, the mascara wand already trembling in her hand.

"Está muerto."

"¡Muerto! ¿Cómo?"

"They say his car hit a telephone pole. They say he was doing ninety, al menos. They say he was tripping or drunk or something."

China let these words sink in for a moment. "Drunk?"

"That's what they say."

All day she had tried to convince herself that Joker's death was not a direct result of her father's voodoo shit. After all, Joker had been drunk. Whose fault was that? Still, her father always did what he said he would do. If he said he'd make Joker regret hitting her, then he would do everything in his power to make that happen. Like a hen that refused to leave her clutch of eggs, China sat on her bed, brooding over her clutch of guilt.

"¿Por qué yo?" She asked the air.

"¿Por qué no?" The air answered.

When the front door opened, she hurried into the living room to tell her father the news, hoping he would assure her that his little brujería would have caused nothing more than a flat tire, say, or at most a broken arm.

"Papá…" she started to say, but fell silent when she saw him standing in the doorway sniffing the air suspiciously. "¿Papá, qué pasá?"

"You don't smell it?"

China sniffed. There was something. It wasn't a smell exactly, but rather a density to the air, a feeling of closeness as if she were standing inside her closet, rather than her living room. She shrugged.

"Bring Orfeo," he said. China felt the flesh beneath her skin ripple.

China and her father followed the turtle from room to room as it crept along the baseboards. Though their house was small, it was dark before Orfeo finally came to rest with his head in the last corner of China's bedroom. Her father took a deep breath. "That's better," he said, leaning over to retrieve the turtle.

China sniffed, noting a subtle, but definite difference in the quality of the air, as if a breeze were blowing through the open windows, except that there was no breeze and the windows were closed. "Is he gone?" she asked.

"He's gone," her father said, stroking the leathery folds along the turtle's neck.

"El Joker?"

He shrugged. "Some lost spirit."

"There was a car accident. He's dead."

Again he shrugged. "People have accidents all the time, pues." He put the turtle down and stood, slowing stretching his spine until he reached his full height. "Let me tell you something, mijita. When I was fifteen, I came over to this country with my uncle, un santero muy famoso en Cuba. We were piled into a rickety old boat with a bunch of jotos, criminals and locos. The boat might have sank, but it didn't; I might have been shipped back to Cuba, but I wasn't; I might not have met your mother, but I did; she might have lived, but she died. There are many things that happen in this life, and what's the explanation? The one thing I know for certain is that the only thing that stays the same is that nothing stays the same. Even you. You used to be so much like your mother, but as you grow you become more and more like yourself."

China wondered if this meant as she grew up, he would love her less and less. But then he opened his arms and drew her to his chest. "Life is like a great big bowl of menudo, mija. You dip in your spoon. Sometimes you get tripa, sometimes not. But always, if you keep spooning you'll eventually get some tripas."

"But I hate tripas."

He released her then and smiled. "I know, mijita. Así es la vida."

As she got ready for bed that night, it occurred to China that in her short life, she'd eaten a lot of tripa. She'd endured loss and had been a firsthand witness to tragedy and injustice, for reals. Each loss, each tragedy and every injustice, had created a wound to her heart. But wounds, even those that are self-inflicted, heal, ¿qué no? And though China hardly noticed it, as she brushed her hair in front of the mirror, from each healing, she gathered strength like the summer monsoon gathered moisture. Some day, she would disperse her strength to others like the rain over the desert.

But right now, as she gazed at her reflection, she knew only that Joker was dead. This fact brought no satisfaction. If she could take back the ugly things she said to him, travel backwards in time to change the future, she would, for now she could imagine a time in the past when Joker was less of a pinche pendejo and more of a little boy with a mother who loved him. And she could project to a time in the future when Joker, had he lived, would be a man with a mother and the sister to take care of. In time he might have had a wife and kids of his own. ¿Cómo no? Nobody stays a pinche pendejo forever. But now because of her actions, he'd never change into the man he could have been. It was a secret burden she'd always bear, one even her father couldn't help her carry.

Still, and beyond all reason, China expected that the future would be an improvement on the past. ¿Quién sabe? Maybe Billy would return, his spine miraculously straight, or if not his spine, then his outlook would straighten, as hers had when she realized that every life, no matter how ugly or cruel, had some value to someone, somewhere. ¿Qué no?

———◆———

huevos eggs, but also testicles
la vida es chingada life's a bitch
la gente people
una mujuer con muchos huevos, a woman with balls
brujería witchcraft
duendes spirits
ni modo no way
entonces que le pasó a tu boca then what happened to your mouth
santero voodoo priest
jotos queers
tripas tripe

Dentro de una Luz Azul
(Inside a Blue Light)

———————

Cuando Mas Tranquila
(Traditional)

Cuando mas tranquila te halles en ese sueño
hermoso oye los ruegos del quien deveras te ama.
Pa' que sepas que te quiero, te dara una
prueba, amada que en el mundo no hay
otra quien te quiera mas que yo...

This song says that when you find yourself in a beautiful, calm dream, listen to the prayers of the one who loves you – your mother in other words.

– Lety

ARACELI SAT ON THE SIDE of her bed. She was not thinking any particular thought, not focusing on any particular object in the room, not the filmy flowered curtains her mother had put up to hide the tattered shade filtering the hot September sunlight, not the photograph of her nana, dead nearly two years, not the large mirror standing in its brass frame in the corner, not the leather jewelry box sitting on the maple dresser. Inside the box was an assortment of bracelets, earrings, hair clips – nothing of value. The only piece of jewelry Araceli valued was around her neck, a heart-shaped pendant with sixteen tiny diamonds, one for each year of her life, and a single ruby – the heart of the boy she loved.

After some minutes, the girl gathered her heavy black hair, twisted it tightly around her fist, then let it fall. She sighed, rose from the bed and studied her slightly protruding belly in the mirror. She lifted her T-shirt. A vertical stripe, one degree darker than the rest of her stomach divided it down the middle and disappeared into the stretch jeans, which she could now only zip halfway. She lifted the T-shirt further then, placing her palms beneath each breast as if weighing them. They were beautiful, full breasts, with large areolas, the mellow brown of a peach beneath its stone.

Stroking her belly, she whispered to it now, "Mi corazón, mi vida, mi amor."

When she heard her mother's knock, Araceli pulled her T-shirt back in place, and though she was in her sixth month, there was nothing about her to give this fact away except a certain lushness. After all, young bodies are tight, the muscles resistant to roundness. For a long while, even Araceli had been unaware that she was pregnant, attributing all the changes in her body and mood to the absence of her lover.

Another rap and Araceli flopped down on the bed. Turning her face, to the wall she wrapped herself in the pink satin spread in a single, fluid motion.

"Araceli?"

"What do you want?"

"I want to know why you didn't go to school again today?" Lety asked, not unkindly, as she stepped into the room.

When Araceli didn't answer, Lety sat down on the bed and swept a strand of hair from her daughter's face. "¿Mijita? Sleeping again? You're sleeping your life away. It's not healthy. You don't eat. You don't go anywhere. Enough is enough. Look at you; you're like a ghost," Lety said, not noticing that, in fact, her daughter was looking uncharacteristically plump for a girl who had to be urged to eat at every meal.

"Come on. Get up now. Tía Sofía is here. At least come out and dale un beso." She steadily pulled the unresisting girl by the arm until Araceli had no choice but to stand. Once standing, Araceli jerked her arm from her mother's grasp, drilling her with a look that could not be confused with any emotion other than fury.

In the kitchen, tía Sofía was pouring condensed milk into this morning's reheated coffee. "Mijita," she said, covering her toothless smile with a hand mapped by thick blue veins. "Let me look at you. ¡Ay, que bonita!"

Araceli kissed the old woman on the cheek before collapsing onto a chair.

"What's this your mother's been telling me?" Said the old woman. "You sleep all the time and you don't go to school any more? ¿Qué tienes?"

Araceli shrugged, unwinding and rewinding her hair.

"Well, you're young. Whether you know it or not, your whole life is still before you. Sometime you're going to have to start living it again. Refugio wouldn't want to see you this way, so sad. And when was the last time you took a bath, mijita?"

"I just was about to get into the shower when you got here, tía."

Lety shook her head so tía Sofía would know this was untrue.

"Ven" the old woman commanded. Araceli bent to receive a kiss and a blessing. Tía Sofía made the sign of the cross in the air above her head. "Pues, ándale."

She studied the girl's backside until she was out of sight, then turned her attention to the café con leche, which she slurped with an air of contemplation. After several minutes she announced, "Embarazada."

"Who me? Don't be ridiculous!"

"Qué tontería," tía Sofía spat. "Not you, Leticia – your daughter."

"That's impossible. She's hardly left the house since..."

"Refugio got killed?" She thought for a moment. "That would make her five, six months at least.

"But she's flat as a pancake."

"Ella es rodonda como una guitarra. You see her everyday, but you don't see her the way I do. Why don't you go ask her?"

Lety sighed deeply. Talking to her daughter had become painful. In the past months, each time she had tried, she was met with a solid wall of indifference, much harder to bear than curses and blows.

"¿Pues?"

"Entonces, I will," Lety said, stomping off down the hallway.

"Araceli, open the door," Lety demanded, then added more softly. "Please, mija. We need to talk."

The door opened and Lety entered the steam. "Tía Sofía thinks you're pregnant."

"Está loca," Araceli said, holding the towel in front of her.

Lety looked at her daughter carefully then, noticing for the first time how full her face had become, womanly now, rather than girlish. "You're sure?"

Araceli turned to her mother then, staring, almost daring her to say one more word. "¡Pues sí, estoy segura!"

"Pues," Lety said, gently closing the door behind her.

At the sink, tía Sofía was rinsing her cup and saucer. "¿Pues?"

"She says she's not."

"She's lying."

"You go ask her then."

"You're the mother."

Yes, I am the mother, Lety thought, the mother who is afraid of her own daughter. "What should I do?"

"Ay, mija. Do something. Do nothing. Either way you're going to be a grandmother. ¡Felicidades!"

In her room, Araceli was caressing a T-shirt. On the back was a picture of Rufugio taken at age twelve, and beneath that the words, *In Loving Memory*. It was the only picture she had of him. She placed her lips on his, wishing she had not lied to her mother, so alone she felt.

And why had she? Any daughter would know the answer to that one, ¿qué no? It was simply because her mother had been right, right about so much.

Desperate in her isolation, Araceli promised herself the next time her mother asked, she would stop punishing her, punishing them both, by keeping the baby a secret.

But there would not be time, for Lety did not ask again and the very next week, Araceli awoke in the night to a tug, deep inside, and a slight wrenching. She lay still, afraid to turn on the light, afraid to move a single muscle. After what seemed to her an eternity, she felt a warm release. Whatever this was, it was too soon. She was not certain when her baby was due, but this was too soon, she was thinking, when the sharp pinching inside her widened to a pain, not unfamiliar in kind but totally unfamiliar in degree. "Mamá," she cried. "Mamá ven. ¡Mamá!"

Then there was light and her mother. "¿Qué tienes, mija? Are you sick?"

"Mamá," Araceli cried, now from fear, because in the light, she saw her nightgown and sheets stained in a pink wash. "What's happening?"

"Ay Madre de Dios, mijita," she cried, and she ran to dial 911.

But before the ambulance arrived, Araceli felt the hard clamp on her womb spring open and the baby slipped from her body like a small blue seal right into the hands of her mother.

The two women stood beneath the florescent lights, which cast the neonatal intensive care nursery in a diffuse pale blue. Half a dozen transparent incubators, each with its own complication of wires and plastic tubing, held the premature infants. Some were sleeping, legs sprawled, chests heaving. Others were crying in pain and anger. Every so often, Araceli or Lety would extend a hand though the round portal to stroke a tiny red limb.

"We should ask the priest to come baptize him," Lety whispered.

"No. I want him baptized in a church, enfrente de toda la familia."

"But…"

"You think he's going to die," Araceli whispered harshly.

"No, mija," Lety lied. Still, she didn't believe that God would turn away a baby, even an unbaptized one, from heaven's gate. "I guess there's no harm in waiting." She reached for her daughter's hand and was sure she had said the right thing when she felt the return of her steady grip. "This baby's strong like his mother."

"Refugio, Mamá. Call him by his name."

"Such a big name." And he was so tiny, like a baby bird. Under three pounds at birth, he was barely over three now after how many weeks? Two yet or was it three now? It was hard to remember when every hour seemed endless and the same, while whole days slipped by without notice. And still the doctors and nurses would not promise. Five pounds, they kept saying. Five pounds was such a long way away.

Lety, who had spent the night at the hospital while her daughter rested, was suddenly sick to her stomach with coffee and fatigue. "I'm going to go home for awhile, Araceli. Just a few hours. Will you be alright alone?"

"Si, pues. I'm not alone," she said, turning to her sleeping son.

"Pues." Lety kissed the back of her daughter's head and was surprised when the girl turned and fell into her arms. "He's not going to die."

"No, mijita. La Virgen, no lo permita."

When Lety reached the parking lot, the air, cool and filmy with the promise of early morning rain, eased her weariness. Instead of going home, she took the road skirting the desert, its giant saguaro cacti and ocotillos darkly silhouetted against the predawn sky.

By the time she pulled into the parking lot fronting San Xavier, large raindrops were pocking the dirt. The wind picked up a plastic grocery sack, sent it sailing through the air until it became impaled on a prickly pear where it fluttered there like a frantic little ghost.

Inside the church the air was warm, comforting, close with the familiar aroma of melting candle wax. Lety proceeded down the side aisle past the reclining statue of St. Frances, his satin drape covered with hastily written prayers, photos, milagros, hospital bracelets – articles of hope and gratitude. But Lety could never rely on a man, not even a saint, to whisper her prayer into the ear of God. In one of the corner niches stood la Virgen de Guadalupe, the only one she could trust with such a desperate petition. And it was in this corner she knelt within the flickering blue of the Virgin's shadow.

"Are you mad at me?" she asked, pressing her palms together. "I don't blame you. But if I haven't been a good mother, if I've been a bad one, it wasn't because I don't love my children. Many of the bad things I did, I did out of love for them. But now Araceli has to suffer because I wasn't a good mother? Is that fair? Yo te pregunto."

The cold tiles sent sharp pains though Lety's knees, pains she welcomed as penance. "You know why I'm here. You know everything about me. The baby, Refugio Maldonado Jr. The tiny baby with the big name, you know the one. My daughter has already lost the father. If she loses the son? No sé. I don't want to get all hysterical with you, Madre, but if the baby dies... pues. All I can say is that I will fear for my daughter's soul. That from a woman who has jeopardized her soul many times, como tu sabes. If the baby lives, I promise you, I will help her raise him, not like my own mother, may her soul rest in peace, who couldn't care less if to keep food on the table I had to sell my ass – perdóname, Madre, but how else can I put it. My daughter will not end up like me. Araceli, what she did with that boy, she did out of love. Pues, when we act out of love, how big a sin can it be?"

When Lety stepped out of the church, the clouds were beginning to unknot and the color on the mountains was changing from blue to rose. There is a peace that descends when you know you have done everything in your power to bring about a longed for outcome. And so it was with Lety. Slipping behind the wheel of her car, she was suddenly overwhelmed with an irresistible fatigue. She rested her head against the seat and was immediately drawn into the blissful oblivion usually granted only to the innocent.

In the nursery, amid the white noise of machines, Araceli fought to keep her vigil, but her eyes became heavy, her head bobbing to one side, once, twice, until it hung limp. Soon she was dreaming. In this dream, as in all dreams since his death, she and Rufugio were reunited. They walked hand and hand, as always, heads together. There was no baby so frail she could not bring him to her aching breast, no broken heart, no despair, just the two of them in bright afternoon, stepping into the unencumbered future.

When she awoke, happy tears slipping down her cheeks, it took only a moment to recover the reality of the present. All that remained of her lover lay within the pale blue of the incubator. Dipping her hand into that blue, she caressed fingers, each no wider than a matchstick. The round swell of his eyes rolled beneath lashless lids. Was he dreaming? What could he be dreaming of? Not his mother's breast, she thought, and her throat felt raw. She ran her finger down the velvet of his arms and over each bowed leg, as a single impression – thought and instinct coalescing – penetrated her grief. This tiny being would consume her. Whoever she had been or thought she might become would be consumed in the solid fact of her love, as certainly as a piece of wood is forever altered when it is consumed by fire.

---

dale un beso give her a kiss
qué tienes what's wrong with you
embarazada pregnant
qué tonteria how ridiculous, what nonsense
felicidades congratulations
milagros miracles, also little nickel silver objects
depicting an afflicted body part, a heart, a lung,
an arm, for which a cure is requested
yo te pregunto I ask you

ACKNOWLEDGEMENTS

———◆———

WITH EVERY BOOK, THE LIST of people who have helped me through
the long process grows. As always, my husband, Fritz, tops the list.
He untangles my Spanish, laughs and cries in the right spots, and
exhibits great patience and forbearance. For her early encouragement, critiquing, and further correction of my Spanish I am most
grateful to my dear friend Mary Goethals. I thank Amy Rusk who
applied her considerable editing skill in both English and Spanish.
George Apodaca lent his teenage ear to the manuscript and I thank
him. I am grateful to John Ridland, professor Emeritus of English,
University of California at Santa Barbara for his kind words and
helpful critique. I thank Boom Goddess, Barbara Peters, for her
sharp eye and discerning ear. Many thanks to Diane Cheshire,
constant friend and sounding board, who is always there to offer
her thoughts and reassurance. Artist and longtime friend Junardi
Armstrong created the beautiful collage that graces the cover of
Tortilla Moon and other Tales of Love. I cannot thank her enough. I
am also grateful to Roger McKasson for his emergency technical
assistance. I am ever grateful for the loving support of friends,
Caren Smith, Ginia Desmond, Jennie Vemich and Sue Ward. For
her thoroughness and patience I thank Gabriela E. Morales who
went over the entire manuscript, rewrote awkward translations

and made sure every accent, tilde and umlaut was in place. Finally, Bonnie Lemons, encouraging and talented editor and friend, ferreted out remaining typos, misspellings and brain farts. I will love you forever, Bonnie, for your enduring willingness and good cheer in the face of my many really dumb mistakes. Cariños y muchisimas gracias a todos.

GLFM